ARMAGEDDON CONSPIRACY

ARMAGEDDON CONSPIRACY

JOHN THOMPSON

HH
HARBOR HOUSE

AUGUSTA, GEORGIA

To Sarah —
With many thanks for
all the Spinning Instruction
Best Wishes!
Enjoy!
John Thompson

Armageddon Conspiracy
By John Thompson
A Harbor House Book/2008

For information address:
HARBOR HOUSE
111 TENTH STREET
AUGUSTA, GA 30901

Book design by Nathan Elliott
ISBN: 978-1-891799-38-9

Library of Congress Cataloging-in-Publication Data

Thompson, John.
Armageddon conspiracy / by John Thompson.
p. cm.
ISBN 978-1-891799-38-9
1. Investment advisors--Fiction. 2. Conspiracies--Fiction. 3. Terrorists--Fiction. I. Title.
PS3620.H6828A89 2008
813'.6--dc22
2008037718

Printed in the United States of America
10 9 8 7 6 5 4 3 2 1

For Julia,
With love and gratitude

ACKNOWLEDGEMENTS

I have more friends than I can list by name whose support has been incredibly gratifying and to whom I owe a great debt of thanks. That being said, a small group needs to be acknowledged by name. For encouragement from early in the process, I thank Peter Bloom, Carolyn Downey, Tim Fisher, Mike Dawes, Malcolm McAlpin, Maudie Shanley, and my children, Jay, Mat, Amanda and Liza. For help and inspiration along the way, Anna Cottle and Mary Alice Kier. For a light in the dark when the obstacles seemed insurmountable, Juli Huss. For guidance and encouragement, Marjory Wentworth, South Carolina's outstanding Poet Laureate. And of course, for unfailing support, friendship and love, my wife, Julia.

PROLOGUE

NEW YORK, FEBRUARY 21

STEVE ALBERS HAD no idea it was his day to die. He simply knew his sales meeting had run late, and he needed to run like hell to catch the five-ten train. Another train left at five forty-five, but that wasn't an option. Today was his daughter's birthday, her sixteenth, and in addition to having planned a family celebration, Steve had an almost-new bright yellow Volkswagen Beetle hidden in his neighbor's garage.

He generally disapproved of sixteen year olds having cars, but Kate was different–honor roll every semester of her life, state champion gymnast in her age group and class president. She deserved something special, he thought, as he rushed from the elevator and trotted toward the revolving doors. Out on the crowded sidewalk, he broke into an awkward run.

The sun had set, the cold wind was slicing through his muffler and gloves, and slicks of ice glinted from the sidewalk. He stepped around mobs of fellow commuters bundled in heavy coats, steaming warm breath into the air. After a block, his heart pounded, and he slowed to a fast walk, vowing to lose some weight. After another block he came to the throng of people moving down the escalators into the underground warren of Penn Station and began to burrow his way through.

The air grew warmer as he descended, and the smells of car and bus exhaust and metallic tang of cold air quickly morphed to the stale, slightly urine smell of the station. The jostling worsened in the long corridors that led to the commuter trains, and Steve shifted his focus, looking down for a dropped briefcase or some homeless person's outstretched leg.

The stacked cases of Coke nearly tripped him. Someone had left them carelessly placed outside a pizza kiosk, but he saw them at the last moment. He glanced up at the overhead clock. Four minutes after five. He started to relax. He was going to make it, just barely.

Exactly seventeen minutes earlier, in the drop-off area outside Penn Station's other entrance, Yusuf ben Abu Sayeed had checked his watch then had stepped out of the taxi line, where he had been standing for the past five minutes. He had tightened his muffler, raised the collar of his cashmere overcoat and walked away. Such a departure was unremarkable because cab waits often became infuriating, and the line had simply shifted forward. No one had given him a second glance.

Abu Sayeed's exit had nothing to do with impatience but with the two men in Coca-Cola delivery uniforms who had just ascended the escalator and wheeled their empty hand truck around the corner of the building. He'd been waiting to spot them, and now he crossed Eighth Avenue, walked eastward, then entered the revolving doors of a large office tower. He unbuttoned his coat and loosened his muffler, entered an elevator and rode to the thirtieth floor. There, like a man who had simply chosen the wrong floor, he stepped onto the next down elevator. Seconds later he exited the opposite side of the building where his rented limousine had been waiting at the curb for almost forty minutes.

As the driver hurried around the car and held the door, Abu Sayeed gave a weary sigh, as though exhausted from the last meeting of a long day. He slid onto his seat and checked that the glass privacy partition was up. His mind whirled with almost unbelievable possibilities as he glanced at the other passenger who had waited there the entire time. They were almost strangers, having met several months earlier in London, when the man had managed to contact him through an endless chain of intermediaries and make his extraordinary offer.

"Well?" the passenger asked, as the limo pulled into traffic. He had sandy hair going gray at the temples and blue eyes with a dangerous innocence.

"Your associates made their delivery," Abu Sayeed answered.

The man removed a cell phone from the pocket of his suit coat. He held it for several thoughtful moments as their limo snaked its way through the uptown traffic. Finally, he dialed a number then held the phone out to Abu Sayeed. "You have the honors."

Abu Sayeed pushed the phone gently away. "I insist."

The other's mouth tightened. He gazed down for a time at the backlit screen and the waiting number. Finally he pushed the send button.

Instantaneously, another cell phone rang, this one buried in the three soda cases Steve Albers had just avoided. The ring triggered an electric charge to a small detonator, which in turn set off three pounds of embedded Semtex. The soda cans were packed with bolts and steel balls, and the explosion hurled them outward. The blast shattered bodies in an immediate radius. The shrapnel cut a much larger swath.

Over a mile away, the faint boom didn't penetrate the limo's soundproofing, but seconds later the first sirens sounded. Abu Sayeed closed his eyes, amazed at Allah's beneficence. This act of retribution on American soil was excellent, but not the real reason for their meeting. His associate had arranged today's explosion only to establish the seriousness of his intent.

"Well?" the man asked, as the sirens quickly grew to a massive din. "What do you think?"

Abu Sayeed looked at this freshly scrubbed American who had just killed a number of his own countrymen. "You have impressed me." He closed his eyes and nestled into the leather seat. There would be a flight to Paris and then several days of deliberation to make a final assessment about going forward. However, he was already sure. Allah had placed this extraordinary opportunity in his lap. It would be a sin against God not to make use of it.

In the smoke and wreckage of Penn Station, scores of bleeding, blast-shocked people staggered through the rubble. Others lay unmoving. Steve Albers was facedown, his back covered by a few ceiling tiles, but otherwise he appeared miraculously unhurt, as if any second he might clamber to his feet. Sirens blared in the distance, and people screamed for help. Yet Steve did not stir. The long needle-shaped sliver that had penetrated the base of his skull had caused almost no bleeding. His last thought before the blackness washed over him had been of Kate.

Hours later the man who had met with Abu Sayeed knelt

in his private sanctum in the basement of his waterfront mansion. The room was kept locked at all times, and he had the only key. Its walls were painted bright white, and a special air system hissed softly as it removed the smell of the room's other occupants.

A table along one wall held a glass-fronted mouse cage where perhaps ten or twelve white mice scurried through a bed of cedar chips. On the opposite wall a second glass container was much larger. Inside, coiled and quiet and digesting its most recent mouse, a timber rattlesnake as thick as a beer can lay with its large triangular head pointing outward.

The man wore a white shirt and khaki trousers and sat in the middle of the room on a hard-backed chair. He had been praying hard for the past forty-five minutes, and now the feeling he'd been seeking finally came upon him. He began to twitch and jerk as the spirit of the Lord began to pour into him, lighting him with a heat and power that made his scalp tingle and shot all the way to the ends of his fingers.

As he'd done alone and in private for years—ever since he'd left his old Tennessee mountain church—he stood and went over to the terrarium where he gathered himself for a moment, his eyes shut tight. He prayed to God to witness this proof of his faith then reached down with both hands and scooped up the rattlesnake.

As always the weight surprised him—probably twelve pounds—and the coolness of the smooth skin. He held the twisting body in both hands and heard the warning buzz of rattles. Had he been in his old congregation he would have passed the snake to another worshipper, but he was alone. If he were bitten, the Lord would protect him, as He had the three times he'd been bitten previously.

"Let the blood I have shed not be in vain," the man prayed. "Let it be that any deed done to bring about Your Son's return is a blessing."

He raised the snake over his head and continued to pray until his muscles ached from the awkward weight. Gradually, he lost awareness of everything until the universe consisted only of himself, the serpent and God, the three of them bound in a strange trinity. When his prayer finally ended, he lowered the snake and replaced it in the terrarium. As he withdrew his hands it happened, a blur of movement.

He jerked away, seeing the red punctures in the thin web of skin between his thumb and forefinger. The fangs had gone right through the narrow band of flesh, which meant the amount of venom in his system would be slight. However, fire already consumed his entire hand. The throbbing pain rocketed up his arm and threatened to drag him to his knees.

He staggered to the chair and sat, willing himself to perfect stillness. He began to pray, knowing he had to embrace his pain, show God his absolute faith. This was a test, he knew, a demand for him to prove his fortitude. Only the strongest and most devout would be allowed to light the fires of Armageddon.

ONE

NEW YORK, JUNE 6

THE OLD GRANITE mansion just off Fifth Avenue in the high Sixties lorded austerely over its more mundane neighbors. Brent Lucas gazed at the brass plaque beside the polished front doors, thinking it was no accident that the name "Genesis Advisors" was barely visible from the sidewalk. GA, as it was known in the financial community, understood that its very wealthy clients appreciated understatement.

Brent took a deep breath and started up the steps. At the top he re-centered his tie and rang the white buzzer. Almost as an afterthought he pushed the record button on the tape recorder hidden in his pocket.

After several moments the door swung back, and a plump woman with a helmet of dyed black hair held out her hand. "Brent! Let me welcome you to Genesis Advisors," she said.

He recognized Betty Dowager, Executive Assistant to the firm's chairman, Prescott Biddle. "Mr. Biddle is traveling," she said. "If you'll come with me, Mr. Wofford is going to handle your orientation."

He followed her thick calves up the carpeted staircase. It was still early, the building hushed, the air smelling of oiled wood and leather. The firm was only a dozen years old, but the historic mansion provided an aura of prestige and stability. An atmosphere of blue blood and Old Money oozed from its mahogany paneled walls and from the impressive paintings and antiques.

They went down a hallway to a pair of tall doors. After several years in a Boston skyscraper, Brent thought it felt more like some exclusive private club than an office, as if any second he might stumble upon a game of heavy stakes backgammon.

Betty opened the doors to an anteroom where a secretary worked at an antique desk with an inlaid leather surface, then led him through another door into an ornately furnished office with heavy brocade drapes over tall windows. The firm's number two partner rose from his chair and strode around the desk to shake hands.

"Welcome, Brent," Fred Wofford rumbled in his slightly nasal twang. He was a bear of a man in his early sixties, with stooped shoulders, a heavy gut and a halo of perspiration atop his mostly bald scalp, an utter contrast to the athletic chairman, Prescott Biddle. "Come on in and sit down," he said, offering a damp handshake.

He waddled around the desk and crashed in his swivel chair, looked at Brent and let out a chuckle. "Yale, Stanford MBA, All-American football player," he said. "You're smart and competitive and analytical. Just the kind of man we're looking for."

Wofford went on in a similar vein for several more minutes, then folded his meaty hands on the desktop. "We covered most of it in the interviews," he said, his smile fading. "But there are a few details we didn't get to–mainly about communications. Knowledge is power, Brent. All we've got to sell here is our performance."

Brent nodded, knowing what was coming next. Everyone on the street and for that matter most investors in America knew about Prescott Biddle's legendary track record. Biddle had been among the first public investors in Microsoft, Cisco, and AOL. He'd ridden WorldCom up, then shorted it within ten percent of the top, even shorted the whole market the summer before 9/11. More recently he'd been early in Research In Motion, Google, and Intuitive Surgical. He'd in and out of real estate, commodities and high flying stocks like a man with a crystal ball.

Prescott Biddle's results had been nothing short of phenomenal. In the eyes of the Justice Department they'd been too amazing, and that was the real reason Brent was here. He pretended to scratch himself as he dropped a hand to his jacket and felt the slight vibration of the recorder, making sure it was turned on.

"People follow us on the street," Wofford continued. "They hang on our conversations in restaurants; they search our trash to find out what we're doing. My point is that we are very careful, and we don't allow leaks–ever. I can't overstate the importance of confidentiality."

Brent nodded.

Wofford glanced down at his interlaced his fingers then

gave Brent an embarrassed smile. "I assure you I'm not bringing this up because of that little . . . incident in Boston."

Brent's gaze faltered momentarily. "I disclosed all that in the interviews," he said.

Wofford held up a hand to stop him. "We know why you blew the whistle," he said quickly.

He was referring to how some of Brent's fellow portfolio managers had been making millions in their personal accounts by trading fund shares after the close of the market, at times when major news announcements would make stocks open sharply up or down the next day. It was done quietly and privately, but it happened to be highly illegal.

"In fact, your commitment to doing the right thing is one of the reasons we picked you," Wofford said.

Brent nodded, feeling a twinge of guilt at the tape recorder running in his pocket.

Wofford waved a hand. "I only mention this because we are a Christian firm. We wouldn't turn a blind eye. If you see anything improper here, you bring it to Prescott or myself. Have faith that we will correct our mistakes."

Brent was about to reply when Wofford's gaze left his face and drifted to something over his shoulder. He glanced back, thinking someone had come into the office, but saw only a large portrait on the wall that he had missed when he walked in. It was savage and violent, a depiction of Jesus on the cross, hands pierced with heavy spikes, cheeks concave and inked with shadow, eyes haunted with unspeakable pain.

Brent turned back and waited. Wofford slowly tore his eyes from the painting.

"Welcome to the firm," he said at last.

TWO

NEW YORK, JUNE 8

"HERE'S TO PROGRESS," Uncle Fred said, raising his wine glass in a toast. "It was a long slog, but you got there."

Brent smiled and raised his own glass. "Thanks."

"But you're in the same shitty industry," Fred said, shaking his head. "After all that crap in Boston, you should've wised up."

Brent would have resented the comment coming from anyone else, but Fred had raised him from the time his mother died, so he shoveled a forkful of pasta bolognaise into his mouth and took it. They were at a restaurant in Little Italy, Brent's treat on his uncle's first foray into Manhattan in probably ten years.

Fred hacked off a hunk of veal chop, shoved it into his mouth and kept talking as he chewed. "I mean, you got a degree from that fancy-ass college in New Haven and an MBA from Stanford, and these Wall Street scumbags won't hire you for six months cause you turned in a couple of crooks at your old firm." Fred waved his fork in disgust. "Guy as smart as you can't get a job cause he's too honest. Jesus H. Christ!"

"Can we talk about something else?" Brent suggested, seeing the way heads were starting to turn in their direction as Fred warmed to his topic.

"Why? Cause you don't want me to remind you that you always said you were going to teach?"

Brent leaned forward, lowering his voice, hoping Fred would take the hint. "How could I? After growing up in your house, they wouldn't allow me around children."

"Lemme tell you, buddy, you were raised in the lap of normal," Fred growled. "When people stop paying you ten times what you're worth, you'll understand what I'm talking about." Fred took a gulp of red wine and wiped his mouth with a napkin. "Boil this Wall Street stuff down, and it's all about giving the big shot assholes blowjobs in the washroom."

A well-dressed couple at the next table turned and stared

with outraged expressions. Fred fluttered his eyes at them. "What?" he asked. "I can't say washroom?"

"Forgive my uncle," Brent said. "He's suffering from Tourette's Syndrome."

The man threw a careful glance at Fred, whose pugnacious blue eyes held none of the confused vacancy of an Alzheimer's victim. A second later he looked away.

"Nice job," Brent said quietly.

Fred raised his eyebrows. "I raised you to be something better that a money vulture."

"Like maybe a dirt-mouth who can clear out a restaurant."

Fred jerked his head at the couple and scowled. "Pussies! This whole city's full of 'em."

"But you have to admit the food is good," Brent said, forking up the last of his pasta and trying again to change the subject.

"Not good enough to make a person live here," Fred replied sourly. "Nothing is."

When they left the restaurant, the evening was pleasantly warm, and they walked rather than take a cab. Neither of them spoke as they wandered up Mott Street then over to Lafayette, continuing to Great Jones. Brent went slowly to allow for Fred's bum knee. At Great Jones they turned east and, as if by some unspoken agreement, came to a stop opposite the fire station that held Engine 33 and Ladder 9. They stared at the building.

"First time here?" Fred finally asked.

"Yeah," Brent replied. He studied the dark brick façade and the Maltese Cross on the glass of the garage doors as if the structure contained some indecipherable secret message.

"You gone down to the site?"

"Nope," Brent said, thinking he never would because the emptiness was too painful. That day was branded in his memory, sitting helpless in front of his office television as the Trade Towers burned, knowing his older brother had to be inside because nothing ever kept Harry back. He'd pictured Harry charging up the fire stairs, floor after floor, past the streams of fleeing office workers, Harry always in the best shape, the one who'd get him to the top first. Get out of there, you stupid sonofabitch!

he'd shouted over and over at the TV.

When the collapse came he knew Harry had been all the way up, right where spilled jet fuel would have been melting girders, the roar of flames drowning the cries of trapped victims. Even if Harry had sensed the building coming apart, he wouldn't have budged.

Harry and his father, both firemen, both killed in the line of duty. His mother, too, killed in her own fire. Brent still awakened sometimes at night from his old familiar nightmare, the one where he and Harry were trapped in the flames. "God, I wish he'd been somewhere else that day," he said.

"Harry made his own choices."

"Shitty choices," Brent said, and resumed walking. He heard Fred limping behind him.

"He did what he wanted to do," Fred said. "So did your dad. So did I. Let's talk about your choices. You work with slime bags and then you go back for more?"

Brent spun around. "Harry made what . . . maybe sixty grand, and he went in and rescued guys making a hundred times that much. You and Dad did the same thing, and you're the only one who's still around, with a bum knee and hardly enough money to hang onto to your house! And you tell me I'm the idiot!"

"We did what we wanted," Fred said, his tone remarkably calm given his usual quick temper. "I just hope you're doing the same thing."

"I am," Brent said, the words tripping out too quickly. He felt a white-hot anger but at the same time the sharp point of a knife in his heart.

Twenty minutes later they reached Penn Station where Fred would board a PATH train to Hoboken and then catch the Morristown Line to his home. Brent was feeling calmer, having walked off the helpless rage that had seized him when he thought about Harry's death, but that was only until he saw the plywood barricades where reconstruction work was still going on from February's bombing.

Over a hundred people killed, he thought, as he was seized all over again by the familiar mix of anger and terrible loss.

Fred stopped at the bottom of the escalator and clasped Brent's arm. "Harry did good," he said in a somber voice. "All of us have to die sometime. We just want to make sure it counts for something when it happens."

Brent nodded. He was trying to count for something, too. He just wished he could explain.

Two blocks from his newly rented apartment, he turned into a nondescript bar that looked like a hangout for the over-fifty crowd. It was dimly lit, mostly empty, and he took a table near the front window. A moment later, a woman with gray hair, her plump thighs filling out a navy blue pantsuit, walked through the front door, glanced around then sat at Brent's table.

"Well?" Ruth Simmons demanded.

"It's only been two days. I hardly know where the men's room is."

Simmons', lips turned down. "I thought you were a quick study."

She was a lawyer at the Department of Justice, running a special task force that focused on the financial industry. She was also a first-class bitch, Brent thought, but she was the reason he had his job at Genesis Advisors.

She had first contacted him several months earlier, claiming they'd met sometime after he'd blown the whistle about illegal trading practices at his old firm. Brent had taken her at her word because there had been so many lawyers that the names and faces were a blur. She'd taken him to dinner and asked if he'd be willing to do something else to help the government. She'd told him the new situation involved illegal use of inside information and was much bigger than the Boston case. His country needed his help, she'd said.

At that point, frustrated from months of fruitless job searches, in arrears on his bank loans and maxed on his credit cards, Brent had signed a heavy-handed confidentiality agreement and agreed to help go after Genesis Advisors.

Now, groping for something to report, he repeated what a young partner named Owen Smythe had revealed that day at lunch—that the firm managed over a billion dollars of Prescott Biddle's personal money and that while the firm was a partnership in name, Biddle often ruled over his fellow partners like a dictator.

Simmons shrugged. "That's not evidence."

"No, but it's unusual." Brent tried to recall Owen Smythe's exact words. "Smythe said that Biddle takes control when he gets 'messages.' I tried to ask more questions, but he clammed up and wouldn't say any more."

Simmons' harsh expression softened a little. "I know I tend to get impatient. Don't push too hard. Give it time." A sardonic smile flickered across her lips. "After all, you are being paid quite well for your patriotic duty," she said, referring to Brent's three million dollar a year salary, paid bi-weekly in installments of a hundred fifteen thousand dollars before withholding. It was a staggering sum that was going to allow him to pay off his mountains of debt in only a few months. "Or maybe you'd prefer to trade that for a government paycheck."

"Unlikely," Brent said, wondering if bitterness over his salary was what made her seem so contradictory.

Simmons interrupted his thoughts by holding out her hand. "By the way, give me your cell phone."

Brent blinked in surprise but did as she asked. She put his phone in the pocket of her jacket then pulled another phone out of the opposite pocket and handed it across. "Use this one from now on. The first memory number will reach me twenty-four hours a day," she said. "If you ever feel threatened or in danger, call me."

"In danger?" Brent smiled.

Simmons leaned forward, her voice dropping to a whisper. "You're going to take their business down."

"These guys are money managers, not drug dealers. They're not going to pull something stupid."

"If your cover gets blown, I wouldn't assume anything."

Brent thought her warning was melodramatic. Everything he'd seen so far told him the Justice Department had the situation wired, starting with how easily they'd maneuvered him into the firm. Even though his resume was rock-solid, there had to have been other strong candidates. But then Simmons had sent a twenty-five thousand dollar donation in his name to Prescott Biddle's church, some kind of evangelical denomination called the New Jerusalem Fellowship. They believed in the literal interpretation of the Bible, but apparently they also believed in money because once the check had been cashed, he'd been the only candidate that mattered.

Minutes later as he walked the remaining blocks to his apartment, he glanced over and imagined his brother walking beside him, Harry's cheeks permanently chapped from flames and heat, the sleeves of his T-shirt rolled up to display the NYFD tattoo on his thick bicep.

Harry had his head thrown back. He was laughing. My little brother, the secret good guy!

Brent scowled.

So, what's your beef?

"Even if these are bad guys, I feel like a traitor."

You just hate taking crap from Uncle Fred.

Brent nodded. "I almost told him."

About working undercover? Good call that you didn't. Fred hasn't kept a secret in his life.

"I know."

Just remember, where there's smoke there's fire, little bro.

"What's that supposed to mean?"

We're the guys who put out the fires.

"That was your life, not mine."

You sure about that?

"I'm not too sure about anything."

If Harry were still alive, he would have responded by slapping the back of Brent's head or popping his shoulder with an elbow. Of course, nothing came. There was only the noise of the city all around and the echo of Brent's footsteps as he walked the avenue alone.

THREE

GREENWICH, CT, JUNE 9

FRED WOFFORD'S PHONE jerked him from a deep sleep. He felt his wife shift beside him as he opened his eyes in the darkened bedroom, checked the bedside clock then fumbled for the receiver. It was nearly five-thirty, time to be getting up anyway.

He put the phone to his ear, hearing a disembodied voice in the background announce a train, the sound echoing off a cavernous ceiling. He knew it was the sound of Union Station in Washington, D.C.

"Up two hundred thousand," the caller said.

"Two hundred thousand," Wofford repeated. "Go with God."

"Go with God," the man said.

FOUR

NEW YORK, JUNE 9

IN CENTRAL PARK before sunrise, Brent practiced his taekwondo katas in the East Meadow. As a third-degree black belt, he took well over an hour to run through all of them. The air was cool and the mist rose off the wet grass like smoke. Slick with sweat when he finished, he ran hard around the reservoir as the apartments on the West Side began to glow with the dawn light, imprinted on a pale sky. Through it all he tried to keep his mind blank and surrender to the joy of physical exertion, to the insistent beating of his heart, the in/out of his respirations.

He had planned his workout in the hope that it would help him burn off some of his confusion about his current assignment. Only the moment he finished and started walking home, it came racing back.

If the GA partners were using inside information, he was doing the right thing if he helped bust them. He thought about the firm's client list, the eleven billion dollars they managed. It seemed preposterous, maybe even impossible, that the firm's senior partners would break the law. They were making tens of millions of dollars, so why risk it?

Even if Biddle occasionally overruled the rest of his partners, it was probably because he was an egomaniac. Nothing illegal about that—egomania was as common as pigeons on Wall Street. Brent shook his head, unable to stave off his doubts. What if the Justice Department was wrong and overzealous? It wouldn't be the first time. Maybe rather than doing a good thing, Brent was about to ruin the reputation of a brilliant man.

An hour later in the morning meeting, his uncertainty continued to nag him as he looked around at the other members of the firm. It was a boys' club for sure. The partners were all Caucasian, and other than Owen Smythe, who appeared to be in his mid-thirties, they were all late forties to early sixties. Their hair was uniformly short, their shirts white. They looked as similar as members of some WASP fraternity, and he wondered how their investment style could be so much more aggressive and edgy than their appearance.

He heard little that appeared noteworthy, and it seemed like the meeting was starting to wrap up. Brent pushed away from the table and was halfway out of his chair when the room fell silent. At the head of the table, Wofford had folded his hands. "Let us give thanks," he said.

The others were still seated. They all bowed their heads, and Brent felt a wave of hungry expectation wash over the room. Instinctively, he put his hand in his pocket, found the recorder and pressed the on button.

"Lord Jesus," Wofford intoned, "we give You thanks for making our minds keen so we may build wealth for our clients and Your church. Make our hearts true as we prepare the world for Your return. In Your name we offer our obedience, Amen."

Brent glanced around. The prayer was over, but no one moved. Wofford let the silence build. "Biddle called early this morning from Europe," he said suddenly. "The Lord spoke to him last night. He is blessing us with prosperity, and the economy is strong. So speaketh the Lord."

The others began to stir. They exchanged knowing looks and brief nods as if important information had just been communicated. Several mumbled, "Amen." As they filed out of the room, Brent remained frozen, wondering whether to risk a question. "Excuse me," he said.

Wofford raised his eyebrows. "Yes?"

"The unemployment report is supposed to be announced at ten this morning." Brent noticed that several of the portfolio managers had stopped and turned. "The market expects employment to be down by maybe a hundred thousand."

Wofford nodded.

"Are you saying it's going to go the other way?"

"I think God is saying it's going to go the other way," Wofford corrected.

Brent looked at him for a moment. "Okay," he said.

From the hallway outside his office, Brent looked through Smythe's open door and saw him hunched over his computer keyboard. "Got a second?" he said.

Smythe glanced up then pushed his glasses up the bridge of his nose. He was probably six-five, maybe an inch taller than Brent, but he had narrow shoulders, bad posture and the tallowy skin of a non-athlete. "Just checking my cash position."

"Was Wofford's announcement supposed to be a buy signal?" If the employment report was up sharply, the market would explode to the upside.

Smythe nodded. He had a slight double chin and receding brown hair. "Better believe it."

"Sounds like God tells Biddle what the market's going to do?"

Smythe shrugged. "Whatever works."

Back in his own office, Brent turned off the recorder. What he had on tape wouldn't constitute evidence, but he understood its importance. Several large "short funds" as well as a number of hedge funds had made recent, highly publicized bets against cyclical stocks. The sudden perception of a strengthening economy would cause those stocks to shoot up, forcing the funds to cover their positions at significant losses, and that would push prices even higher.

Suddenly, his phone rang and he answered. It was Joe Steward, the head trader. "I'm waiting for your buy orders," he said.

"I'll get right back."

Brent quickly scanned the cash balances in the accounts he'd been assigned, checked his buy list against current positions, then called the trading desk. He invested fifty million dollars before the Commerce Department announced the much stronger than expected employment number, then he sat back and watched the market soar nearly two hundred points.

FIVE

NEW YORK, JUNE 14

THE FOLLOWING WEEK, the market rally seemed to be holding and even extending, and the firm buzzed with the kind of confidence people show when they know they've got things figured out. A few minutes before eight on Tuesday night, Owen Smythe breezed into Brent's office with a bulging accordion file. "Fred asked me to bring this," he said.

Brent raised his eyebrows toward the phone-book sized thickness. "Another account?"

Smythe winked as he dropped the file on Brent's desk. "Don't screw it up."

Smythe turned to leave, but Brent flicked on his tape recorder and said, "I have a question."

Smythe was almost out the door, but he stopped. "About?" he asked.

"The unemployment number."

Smythe studied Brent a few seconds.

"It seems like somebody's got a crystal ball."

Smythe raised his eyebrows. "I assume you belong to the same church as all these other guys. Maybe you ought to ask one of them."

"I'm a new member."

"Yeah, right." Smythe closed Brent's door and leaned against it. "Just between us girls, I think you're full of shit."

Brent sat perfectly still, but his pulse began to kick. "I beg your pardon?"

"I'm probably the only guy in this firm who's not a member of the New Jerusalem Fellowship, but they keep me around because I'm smart. I don't know how the hell Biddle and Wofford get their information, whether it's God or something else–but I don't stick my nose in it."

"You're telling me this for a reason."

Smythe nodded. "I checked you out with a couple buddies in Boston, and I know what you did at your old firm. Wofford and Biddle certainly ought to know if they did their homework, but they don't seem to give a crap. I don't know why you're really here, but whatever's going on, you stay out of my backyard, cause I'm clean." He nodded once then turned and walked out.

Brent waited a few seconds then he picked up his cell phone and called Simmons in Boston. Without preamble he reported the conversation.

"What do you want to do about it?" she asked.

"Nothing. He's not one of the insiders. Now that he's said his piece and covered his ass, I think he'll keep quiet. Still, the fact that he came in and said something suggests that we're on the right track."

Simmons was quiet for another few seconds. Finally, she said, "Just keep that cell phone with you."

Brent hung up then sat for a few seconds trying to shake off his feeling that Simmons wasn't telling him the whole story. Did she really believe these guys might come after him? He thought about Wofford, a fat lumbering guy. Biddle was too much like a professor, and Smythe was just trying to keep himself out of it. Very unlikely, he decided.

He reached for the folder Smythe had brought and read the name on the cover: Dr. Khaled Faisal. His eyes widened in recognition. Dr. Faisal was an Egyptian billionaire, famous for having spent millions in efforts to promote peace in the Mideast.

Brent opened the file and let out a low whistle. His other accounts were between five and fifteen million—average-sized for the firm—but this one was huge. Suspecting a mistake, he pulled it up on the computer, seeing that indeed it was one of the largest accounts in the entire firm, some seven hundred fifty million dollars. His name appeared beside it as the manager of record.

The correspondence folder accounted for much of the file's thickness. In testimony to Faisal's philanthropy, there were perhaps a hundred letters directing the firm to send money to various universities, hospitals and health care organizations. Brent shook his head as he read. It didn't make sense to assign such an enormous account to a "new guy."

He sat back, checked his watch. It was getting late. Deciding not to waste time on an account somebody would undoubtedly take away first thing tomorrow, he tossed some research into his briefcase and walked into the hall. A light glimmered under Owen Smythe's door, and on a whim he knocked and stuck his head inside.

Fred Wofford was leaning on one of the visitor's chairs talking with Smythe. "Sorry," Brent said, as both men looked in his direction.

"No problem," Wofford said, as he turned and came to the door, almost rushing. "We were just killing time." He pulled Brent inside and went out. "You fellows chat or go out for a beer," he said. "Don't let me keep you."

Brent listened as Wofford's heavy footsteps faded down the hall. Then he turned and studied Smythe.

"Don't worry," Smythe said after several seconds. "We weren't talking about you."

Brent looked down at his hands a moment then looked up. "You know, being a whistle-blower one place doesn't mean you make it a habit."

"Whatever you say. Just as long as you know where I'm coming from."

"It sounds like you think there's something going on."

"I don't see; I don't know; I don't ask. We straight on that?"

"Tell me something. How is it that I'm being given Dr. Faisal's account?"

"You joined the right church," Smythe said with a cynical smirk. "Biddle wanted you to have it."

"I thought it had to be a mistake."

"Nope."

Brent nodded, started to leave, then change his mind. "Feel like grabbing a beer?"

"You serious?"

Brent smiled.

Smythe gave a self-deprecating laugh. "My bark's worse than my bite." He glanced at his watch. "Give me a rain check. I told my wife I was leaving thirty minutes ago."

Brent waited while Smythe swept some papers into his briefcase. Then they went downstairs and outside into a cool evening drizzle and air that smelled of humidity and car exhaust. Overhead low clouds cut off the top floors of taller buildings and made the evening unnaturally dark. Three or four streetlights were burned out along Fifth Avenue, leaving the sidewalk deeply shadowed. Smythe stepped toward the corner to flag a taxi on Fifth, so Brent said goodnight and started walking east.

He had gone about fifty yards when he heard an alarmed shout and looked back to see two men in hooded sweatshirts standing beside Smythe, who was bent over as if he'd just been slugged.

Brent started toward them, breaking quickly into a sprint, running on the balls of his feet to cut the noise. The nearest mugger sensed motion and looked around, his eyes registering surprise and shock, but too late. Brent's shoulder slammed the guy's chest just below the armpit, lifting him off his feet and into the crosswalk light. The guy bounced off the post and collapsed, while Brent kept moving, spinning leftward around Smythe, letting his heavy briefcase swing wide and catching the second mugger in the hip. The man grunted and splayed on the sidewalk. He came back up in a low crouch, holding his side, and Brent saw the glint of bare steel.

He dropped his briefcase, deciding it was too unwieldy against the knife. The first mugger was still on his hands and knees, stunned but trying to stand. Before he could, Brent grabbed him by his pants and the neck of his sweatshirt, jerked him off the ground, and hurled him into his partner. Both muggers went down in a tangle. Brent rushed over, pinned the second man's wrist with one foot and stomped on his hand with the other until he heard bones crack.

He kicked the loose knife into the gutter as sirens sounded in the distance. When he looked around he spotted Smythe with his cell phone to his ear.

"I already called 911," Smythe said breathlessly.

Brent glanced back at the two men, both getting to their feet, one cradling his wrist. Heedless of horns and screeching brakes ,they scuttled across Fifth Avenue and disappeared over the park wall.

"Come on," Brent said, as he bent over and picked up his briefcase. "Let's get out of here."

"We have to wait for the police," Smythe said.

"You'll be looking at mug shots all night. Your wife will be pissed."

Smythe gave him an amazed look. "You're a damn kamikaze!" Still, he started walking. Halfway down the block, he turned. "You do stuff like that all the time?"

Brent winked. "Every chance I get."

"I owe you," Smythe said. He shook his head as he continued to look at Brent. "Thanks."

On the second floor of the Genesis Advisors building, Fred Wofford stood in the window of his darkened office. He had witnessed the entire confrontation–in fact he had arranged it. Even though he hadn't intended for Smythe to be involved, it had worked even better. He nodded to himself. The kid with the injured arm would have a fat wad of cash to compensate him for his discomfort, but more important, Wofford had seen what he needed about how Brent Lucas would respond.

SIX

NEW YORK, JUNE 14

HALF HOUR LATER, Brent perched atop an unpacked moving box as he sipped a cold beer and gazed out his apartment window at the shrouding yellow mist. One hand was bruised and his shoulder ached, yet he felt pleased. He'd reacted purely on instinct, just like a Lucas, like his father or Harry or his Uncle Fred, having no thought for self-preservation.

The building across the street had large picture windows, and there was a dinner party under way. In other apartments couples watched television; a man read to his daughter on a couch. He watched them, thinking that these were normal people, not those who would risk everything on a random confrontation. He sipped his beer, thought about how unlike them he was, and his mood darkened.

He'd been brought up to think he was different from the others in his family. He was smart—in school they'd called him "gifted." At Yale, as an All-Ivy football star, he'd been swept into a different world. Courted by wealthy alums, he'd gone on to become an analyst with a prestigious investment bank. Two years later he'd entered business school, then joined a fund manager in Boston. His rise had been meteoric until it all changed.

The greed of his co-workers had been a slap in the face and had brought the values of his family rushing back. He'd blown the whistle without a thought of what it would do to his career. Now here he was at GA, still making great money but an outsider and a short-termer. Where was he headed from here, he wondered?

He took a sip of beer and shook his head because his career was only part of the problem. The bigger piece was Maggie. He closed his eyes and pictured her. Lush black hair, worn short but always sexy. Serious face that could thaw in a heartbeat into a teasing smile. Dark eyes full of cool intelligence one minute and fiery passion the next. Maggie defied labels, a wild combination of lush and spare, serious and funny, sensual and tough. Her contrasts worked perfectly for him.

He'd never opened up to people easily, but with her—especially after Harry's death—it had been different. Even though they hadn't spoken in months, he imagined her walking through the door right now. Lithe and athletic, her movements quick and sure. Even in her absence she remained a part of him.

He took out his cell phone, dialed her number, but hesitated. What would he say—confess to being lonely and confused? They'd broken up because she had wanted a bigger commitment, one that he still wasn't ready to make.

For him two other things had always had to come before marriage, namely his debts to Fred and Harry. His older brother had dragged him from the fire that had destroyed their house and killed their mother, then protected and guided him for years afterward. Fred had taken in the two orphans and become the family they had lost.

For Christmas 1999, Brent had given Harry a brand new twenty-eight foot Mako because his brother loved saltwater fishing. Borrowing a hundred thousand dollars on top of tens of thousands of dollars in education debt was something most people would never understand, but Brent knew Harry could never afford that boat on a fireman's salary. In hindsight, it was the best decision he'd ever made. He and Harry had spent irreplaceable weekends fishing during the summer of 2000.

In Fred's case, Brent planned to buy him a small house in Florida. It was something Fred might have afforded on his own, only not after the expense of raising his two nephews. Brent's salary from GA would soon make the house a reality. Then, if the job even lasted that long, a few more months of scrimping and he'd finally be free of tuition debt and able to start thinking about other things.

In the building opposite, couples were still laughing, talking and sitting together in contented silence. The sight added to his hunger for the sound of Maggie's voice; however, instead of pushing the send button, he closed his phone. His regret was a cold stone in his chest. He'd never fully explained his reasons to her but held them inside the way he did so many things. Now he was paying the price.

SEVEN

PARIS, JUNE 14

AS HIS LIMO pulled up before the Hôtel de Crillon, Abu Sayeed glanced out the rain-spattered windows and thought yet again how much he detested Europe. He hated the gray skies, the springtime of constant spitting rain and the wet cold that went straight into his bones. He took his briefcase and dashed up the steps, and as he came through the front doors, his hatred bloomed to embrace all things European, from the lobby's rococo gold leaf décor, to the cigarette smoke, the ever-present wine and alcohol, even the self-satisfied smirk and chatter of the people.

Europe made him yearn for silence, for the burn of desert air in his nostrils, for sun-baked sand and the endless emptiness south of Riyadh. Unlike this northern hell, with its babble of godless infidels and honking horns, he craved his homeland, Saudi Arabia, where the aridity and bone-scorching heat reduced man to his essence.

Out of the corner of one eye, he could see his young lieutenant, Naif Abdulaziz, dressed in a dark pinstriped suit, reading *The Financial Times* in a chair where he could observe the entire lobby. Naif's hair had been styled in dreadlocks, which made him look less Muslim and more secular, like some young African businessman. His left leg was crossed over his right, the all-clear signal, so Abu Sayeed continued through the lobby to the library bar where he would meet the American.

He sat at a small table at the rear of the otherwise empty room and ordered tea. He was several minutes early, and in the brief moments before his meeting he reflected on his belief that Islam and the desert embodied the same truth. The extreme rigor of Wahaddi Islam seared impurities from a man's soul, and the desert did the same to a man's flesh. Westerners regarded both the land and the religion as inhumanly harsh, yet for Abu Sayeed truth and beauty could be accurately perceived only in utter extremes, either morally or in the physical contrast of life and death.

"Lost in thought?" a voice asked.

Abu Sayeed looked up from his tea, and from long practice his mind instantly changed gears. He searched the American's eyes for any hints of danger or betrayal. He sensed extreme nervousness, but no immediate threat. The man was clearly anxious at the risk he was taking, and he probably considered Abu Sayeed a lethal and unpredictable Arab extremist. So much the better.

"I was reflecting on the irony of your offer," Abu Sayeed countered in his flawless Oxford-accented English. He suffered a small flush of shame that he'd been caught yearning for his homeland. In the present circumstance all considerations other than the Greatness of Allah were sinful, all personal desires inconsequential. He smiled and waved at an empty chair.

The man threw an edgy glance at his two bodyguards who had positioned themselves in the entrance to the otherwise empty room, then sat. He tapped his toe against the table leg. "I see no irony," he said after a moment. "We simply believe in different versions of truth."

Abu Sayeed smoothed an invisible wrinkle from his suit. He yearned for the freedom of an abaya and thobe, but traditional Saudi garb brought unwelcome attention in the West. He was thirty-four years old, a little under six feet with a lean face and piercing eyes that people often likened to a falcon's. The eldest son of one of the richest men in Saudi Arabia, he traveled the globe managing his family's vast business interests.

The Western media fussed over his "movie star" looks, a preoccupation he despised, but he valued the accolades of its financial press regarding his brilliance. He wondered what they would say if they discovered that he also directed the terrorist group known as the Wahaddi Brotherhood.

"Clearly one of us must be misguided," he said at last. He needed what this infidel had to offer. With this man's help he would carve a wound in the American Devil that mujahideen would sing about for centuries, yet he must not appear too eager.

The American leaned forward, again betraying his intensity. "One of us is." He was a few years older than Abu Sayeed, perhaps mid-forties, also with a reputation for financial wizardry. He had the high forehead of an intellectual and the leanness of an athlete, but the odd spark in his blue eyes betrayed his barely controlled fervor.

"A belief in infallibility is a powerful weapon," Abu Sayeed agreed. "I have the same conviction about the eventual success of my jihad." He glanced at his companion's uncalloused hands, on the surface as soft as any westerner's. It was the wild passion that glowed just beneath the surface that made him formidable.

The bodyguards, too–one red-haired with freckles, the other big and square jawed, both with the rough-cut look of country policemen–had the same hot flush. All three of these men had the ardor of suicide bombers. Such emotion could make people resolute but at the same time unpredictable.

The other man nodded and raised his eyebrows. "We pursue a common course, yet I'm afraid only one of us will find Heaven."

Abu Sayeed sipped his tea. "Each of us understands why the other is here." He leaned back in his chair and smiled. "Which brings me back to irony."

The American's eyes became pinched with impatience. "Which brings me back to the package. We have demonstrated our ability to do what we promise."

Abu Sayeed knew that he was referring to the Penn Station bombing and the one hundred and twenty-five dead and wounded. He nodded in agreement.

"We will pay to acquire the items," the other man went on. "You must promise to use them as we discussed."

Abu Sayeed flicked his hand. "We have already agreed to your terms," he said.

The "items" the man referred to would be terribly costly. Over the past several years as the Wahaddi Brotherhood's bank accounts had been systematically seized or blocked by Western intelligence services, any attack like the one they were plotting had become increasingly impossible. How miraculous that the tools he needed were being laid at his feet, by a Christian no less, whose sole demand was that the Wahaddi Brotherhood use them to kill the American President!

Clearly, the Christian believed this act was going to bring

about the onset of Armageddon, which meant Allah had prepared the Christian's mind. *Thanks be to God for my enemies,* Abu Sayeed prayed in silence. "There is of course one proviso," he said.

The American raised his eyebrows, his look suggesting that beggars did not propose conditions. "What would that be?"

"That you undertake the transportation," Abu Sayeed replied. "Such a mission must not be exposed to needless risk."

The man nodded. "Of course. I will be in touch with the details."

Abu Sayeed reached into his briefcase and turned off the frequency-masking transmitter that would have prevented electronic eavesdropping on their conversation. "I look forward to our business relationship," he said as he stood. Anyone observing the two men, particularly if they recognized either one, would have found it unremarkable that Yusuf ben Abu Sayeed had hired Prescott Biddle's highly acclaimed Genesis Advisors to manage some of his family's massive fortune. It was the kind of deal done in a city like Paris every day.

EIGHT

NEW YORK, JUNE 15

PRESCOTT BIDDLE GAZED down from the mountaintop. He wore a white robe and held a scepter in his right hand. Far below, a ruined battlefield held millions of dead and dying sinners. Somewhere over his head a voice like thunder intoned, "And then the sign of the Son of Man will appear in heaven, and all the tribes of the earth will mourn, and they will see the Son of Man coming upon the clouds of heaven with power and great glory."

As the voice faded, an angel appeared bearing a golden crown. The angel placed the crown on his head and named him, "Messiah Bringer."

He snapped awake, blinking in surprise at his French Regency desk, the familiar walls of his office, and realized he'd dozed off. He wasn't the Messiah Bringer yet, but that would come soon enough. He rose from his chair and strode around his office, forcing blood through his jet-lagged veins.

When he opened his office door, Betty Dowager turned from her computer screen with an anxious glance. "Go with God," she mumbled.

He nodded. He was utterly exhausted, but he had one more task before everything was in place. Afterward he would rest several days before heading back to Europe for the final meeting that would set the plan in motion. Messiah Bringer! The memory of his dream brought a jolt of elation, as he once again imagined the roar of a million Christian voices singing his praise.

He climbed to the third floor, praying as he went for one more sign, one more assurance. *Show me, Lord,* he beseeched. *Forgive my doubts.*

Brent Lucas was hunched over his keyboard, his back to the door. His head jerked slightly at the sound of Biddle's knock. "Yes?" he said, not looking around.

Biddle cleared his throat. "I hate to interrupt such intense concentration."

Lucas turned, and his expression changed from annoyance to surprise. He jumped to his feet and came around the desk to shake hands. "Mr. Biddle!" he exclaimed.

"I wanted to personally welcome you on board," Biddle said, thinking as he had the other times they'd met how physically imposing Lucas was and how brimming with energy. Lucas's shirt outlined his muscular chest and torso, giving him an aura of unstoppability. His aggressiveness was right there on the surface; he wasn't the kind to let anything stand in his way.

Biddle realized that his odd sense of familiarity with Lucas came from the inch-thick binder assembled by his team of private investigators. It detailed Lucas' grades and athletic endeavors, how Lucas' father and brother died, about the suicidal house fire when his mother died and almost killed her two sons. He knew everything, down to Lucas' last girlfriend and the kind of car he drove. Under different circumstances, Lucas might have been a wonderful addition to the firm.

Brent released Biddle's hand and went back to his desk, thinking his boss seemed more than a little keyed up.

"Any questions so far?" Biddle asked as he took a seat across from Brent.

Brent thought for a second. "Only one," he said, reaching for his jacket where it hung on the back of his chair and pressing start button on the recorder that sat in the side pocket. "In the research meeting . . . the unemployment report. I have to admit I've been curious."

"About what?"

"All of it."

Biddle leaned forward. "We invest according to the Word of God."

"What about earnings per share and cash flow?"

"We use balance sheets and income statements like everyone else, but when I receive signs, we act on them." Biddle smiled. "There's a higher truth than analysis, wouldn't you agree?"

"Pardon my cynicism, but you're saying that God revealed a government employment report?"

"If God puts it in one Christian's heart to help another Christian, what would you call that? Is information given in that way something to be refused? Don't God's commands transcend man's statutes? Non-believers don't understand that, but you should."

Brent remembered that he was a guy who'd supposedly sent twenty-five thousand dollars to the New Jerusalem Fellowship. He nodded. "Absolutely . . . but do you disclose that to our clients?"

Biddle's eyes narrowed. "Some of them," he said quietly.

"The reborn ones?" Brent persisted.

Biddle nodded. "Why would I share that information with unbelievers?"

An hour later, Biddle looked across his desk at Wofford. "I have no doubt. He's the one."

Wofford sat in an overstuffed chair chewing a thumbnail. "Smythe found out what happened at Lucas's old firm. He asked me why we hired him."

Biddle looked up sharply. "Tell Smythe to mind his own business."

"I did, but I'm not sure his curiosity is satisfied." Wofford looked down. A flicker of worry passed across his face. "He suspects something."

Biddle felt a spasm of anger at Wofford's caution. "Forget Smythe. Think of the opportunity. If we do our job, we fulfill the prophecy."

Wofford looked up, and his expression hardened. "What if you're wrong? We're risking everything!"

"Everything? What is everything? Are you risking your soul?"

"No, but–"

"We don't have Jesus here! We can't touch Him! We can't watch Him move through crowds, see Him heal the sick, feed the hungry! If we lack courage, how's that going to happen?"

Biddle tried to control his annoyance. After all, how could he explain his visions to someone who had never seen them? How could he explain that God's will moved inside him like an unborn child? It was part of him, indistinct, yet full of unspeakable promise. The Second Coming was a miracle, something to be trusted, an event that would unfold like a flower from the small bud of faith and possibility. And a nuclear attack on the President of the United States would be the spark. The massive reprisals would be enough to begin the conflagration.

"Armageddon," Wofford whispered, as if reading Biddle's mind. He rubbed an invisible spot on his trouser leg. "God guide us," he said.

"His will is being done!" Biddle snapped. He held up a finger and quoted from Hebrews: "Faith is the substance of things hoped for, the evidence of things not seen."

The burden of his own certainty became so much heavier when those around him were weak. Yet even as he cursed Wofford's fear, a different thought intruded–Anneliës, her name a sultry whisper in his mind. He felt his cheeks redden. His weakness, he thought, as he turned reflexively toward the window.

Anneliës was inextricably part of the plan. He hated that, just as he sometimes hated her. Nothing about her was the way he'd planned. She was different from any other creature he'd encountered - unbelievably tempting and seductive, a devil in his heart and an angel in human form. He had chosen her because her extraordinary allurements would enable them to complete the preparations with Lucas, but they had snared him as well. His gaze wandered to the corner of his credenza, to the picture of Faith, his wife. *God help me*, he prayed.

NINE

NEW YORK, JUNE 20

THEY SAT AT a corner table illuminated by wavering candlelight. Brent could hear the background murmur of other voices, but his attention was rooted on the woman across the table. His heart caught in his throat as he gazed at her, with her flashing eyes and high cheekbones, her simple black dress held up by thin spaghetti straps.

Maggie could have been a model, a fact made obvious by the way other men turned to stare, but she set little store by her beauty, just as she did by the accumulation of wealth or worldly power. Like Brent's father and brother, she valued the qualities that made her community thrive—the welfare of her fellow citizens, fairness, equality and justice.

Tonight, in spite of the romantic setting, her lovely features were creased in anger. "You're thirty-one years old," she was telling Brent. "And you still have no idea what you want."

Brent sighed. This whole topic was something he wanted to avoid.

"You want a good marriage and a life that stands for something, but you also want to be rich and powerful," Maggie went on.

"I want you."

"Okay . . . when?"

He shrugged. "You know . . . when I get some things settled."

She shook her head, and her anger seemed to dissipate, only to be replaced by sadness. A tear broke free and ran down her cheek. "You never make the hard choices. I'm sorry, but I don't think I can wait."

Brent reached across the table for her hand, but he never touched it. From somewhere nearby he heard a crashing sound as if a waiter had dropped a tray of silverware.

He opened his eyes. His bedroom was dark. From down in the street he heard the noise again, only he recognized it this time—a garbage truck compressing a load of trash. He was alone, as he had been since that last night with Maggie. His heart beat a lonely tattoo against the walls of his chest.

TEN

NEW YORK, JUNE 20

EARLY MONDAY, WOFFORD took a cell phone from his pocket and placed it on his desk. He leaned back in his chair and waited. When it rang, he picked it up, pushed the send button and listened. The voice on the other end whispered that Google's earnings would be five cents ahead of forecast. "Go with God," Wofford said, and clicked off.

ELEVEN

NEW YORK, JUNE 20

BRENT SLUMPED IN his chair and only half-listened to the morning meeting. He was recalling Saturday afternoon when he'd given Simmons the tape of his conversation with Biddle. Simmons had been unimpressed. She'd called it "smoke," not hard evidence, and said she needed more.

Brent's other problem was his growing unease about his decision to join Genesis Advisors. In spite of the money, he now realized it had been a mistake. Increasingly he simply wanted to get on with his life, and while much of that stemmed from regrets about Maggie, she wasn't the whole reason. The idea of being a spy troubled him more each day. He shot a guilty glance at Owen Smythe. It had been one thing to bust a few greedy bastards in Boston. That had been unplanned, an instinctive response to the situation, but this felt very different, coldly planning to take down an entire firm and ruin so many careers.

A sudden silence descended over the room and interrupted his thoughts. At the head of the table, Fred Wofford, once again running the meeting in Biddle's absence, bowed his head and started to pray. Anticipating what might follow, Brent suppressed a shudder of distaste but pressed the record button.

After his "Amen" Wofford looked at the expectant faces. "The Lord spoke last night," he began and went on to announce that God had told Biddle about Google's earnings.

Brent struggled to mask his incredulity—the idea that God would front-run a company's earnings report! He glanced around the room, angered now by the preposterousness of the lie and the transparent greed of the partners. No longer concerned about being unfair, he felt a thrill at having some concrete proof.

TWELVE
FRANCE, JUNE 20

ABU SAYEED HEARD the staccato of a siren and felt the van slow as Naif's foot came off the gas. He was tucked out of sight, on a folded tarp in the cargo area. It was two a.m., the roads were quiet, and they had not been speeding. "Just one?" he asked, unable to see out the van's windowless rear doors.

"Yes," Naif said, his voice calm.

"Pull off here."

Naif stopped the van on the gravel shoulder, and they waited. A second later, a motorcycle pulled to a stop behind them and then the policeman's boots crunched over gravel as he walked toward the driver's door. Abu Sayeed's pulse pounded behind his eyes as he recognized the snap of a holster flap. The policeman shined a light in Naif's face and ordered him to keep his hands on the wheel. He sounded young, nervous. Abu Sayeed knew he'd seen what he took to be an Arab face heading north. It had to mean an alarm was out.

The policeman's light shone its way around the front seats then worked gradually toward the rear of the van, finally picking out Abu Sayeed's legs and knees and the crate on which he sat. The policeman started to reach for his holster, but Naif's hand was much quicker. It moved in a blur as he plunged his knife into the policeman's throat.

Abu Sayeed opened the rear doors and leaped out. He checked for traffic in both directions and thanked Allah for the empty road. He took the dying policeman beneath the arms, dragged him to the back of the van and threw him inside. Naif took the policeman's motorcycle and rolled it down the steep embankment into an irrigation ditch. It would be invisible unless someone stood at the edge and looked down.

They drove onward, Abu Sayeed now sitting in the passenger seat. They drove slowly, appearing not to hurry, but both of them knew the policeman had almost certainly called in their vehicle's license plate. Their eyes scoured homes and businesses, but at this hour almost everything was dark. In the next small town, Abu Sayeed spotted an ambulance, its lights flashing but no siren, waiting to turn onto the main road. Abu Sayeed could see a driver at the wheel and an attendant visible in the back. "There," he said, and Naif checked the mirror for other cars. Then he pulled across the road to block the ambulance.

Abu Sayeed climbed out of the van and began gesticulating excitedly. When the ambulance driver lowered his window to ask what the problem was, Abu Sayeed shot him through the forehead. He ran around, jerked open the rear doors, and shot the nurse and an old woman who lay on the stretcher. He dragged the driver's body around to the back, turned off the rear inside lights and flashers, then followed Naif to a pull-off. There, leaving the dead policeman in the van, they loaded their precious cargo into the ambulance, positioning the driver's and attendant's bodies to make it appear that the crates were a second stretcher. They covered the bodies with sheets and resumed their drive toward Le Havre.

Two hours later on a dead-end road near the port they pulled up before a crumbling stucco warehouse fronted by a pair of scarred wooden doors. Naif killed the headlights as the warehouse doors swung outward. They drove into the dark interior and heard first the squeal of hinges as the doors closed behind them then the heavy thud of a bar being dropped into place. A second later, someone flipped on overhead lights to reveal a vast space with a stained concrete floor.

Abu Sayeed shielded his eyes from the glare then climbed out. He came around the ambulance, clasped Naif by the arms and kissed him on both cheeks. "Well done, my brother," he said, feeling the reassuring strength in the young man's biceps.

Naif smiled, his teeth flashing in his dark face. There was youth in his smile but also pain from the recent killing in his eyes, Abu Sayeed thought. Naif was an eager warrior, but his hardness was marred by the poetry in his soul.

"Praise be to Allah that we made it safely," Naif said, his voice soft with relief. Abu Sayeed nodded, as he too felt an easing of the tension that had eaten his stomach.

Across the empty warehouse floor, the two Americans stood behind their bodyguards. They had trusted the protection of their

God enough to risk coming here, and that in turn had triggered Abu Sayeed's own demonstration of faith: accompanying their lethal cargo for the nearly twelve-hour trip from Marseilles.

The man who had locked the warehouse doors opened the rear doors of the ambulance then dragged the two corpses crudely onto the warehouse floor. When he finished, he came over to stand beside Abu Sayeed. Mohammed Al-Wahani, a stocky Egyptian with moody eyes and a bad temper, crossed his thick arms and glared across the room at the Americans and beyond them at the shipping container that waited on its pallet in the far corner.

"Patience and respect," Abu Sayeed whispered, as he noted the hatred in Mohammed's eyes. "Today our enemies are our friends."

Mohammed took a deep breath, but he finally nodded. "If that is your wish," he muttered.

Abu Sayeed walked toward the Americans. The bodyguards were staring at the corpses, and they edged reluctantly aside as he drew close. "Mr. Biddle," he said.

"What happened?" Prescott Biddle asked, as he eyed the bodies.

Abu Sayeed shrugged. "Unavoidable, I'm afraid."

Biddle stared for one more second then indicated his associate, "This is Mr. Wofford."

Wofford tore his horrified eyes away from the bodies long enough to offer a sweaty hand. Abu Sayeed glanced at his swelling bag of a stomach and suppressed a scowl. He shook the hand briefly then quickly turned to examine what from the outside appeared to be a normal half-size container. It was metal, a weathered dark blue, similar to the thousands of others that were loaded onto ships and carried across the ocean every day. When he looked through the container's open hatch, he suppressed a shudder.

A Bedouin with a two-thousand year heritage of open space and arid sands, he could not imagine being locked in a tiny box and thrown into the sea, and he prayed Mohammed could survive the ordeal. Perhaps he would emerge babbling on the other end; however, it had to be risked. Mohammed's face was too well known to the western authorities to get him into the

United State any other way.

"Reinforced, absolutely guaranteed to float," Biddle said, running his hands over the seals around the container's hatch. "Everything inside will be perfectly safe and dry." He stepped in, stooping to avoid the low ceiling, and pointed to five large tanks strapped to the back wall. "Ten days' worth of oxygen. Far more than your man will need."

He clicked on a light above the built-in cot, indicated the row of batteries that provided power, pointed to several crates of health bars, dried fruit, nuts and bottled water, even a small portable toilet. "All the comforts of home," he said.

Abu Sayeed turned back to Naif and Mohammed and nodded. They went into the ambulance and emerged with the first crate, carrying it with care as if they feared waking whatever lay inside. They lowered it onto a hand truck and wheeled it toward the container. Then, neck veins bulging from the strain, they hoisted the crate inside, laying it crosswise in front of the oxygen tanks where they fastened it in place with metal brackets. A minute later, they returned with the second crate.

"Aren't you going to give us a look?" Biddle asked.

"It is not safe," Abu Sayeed replied.

"That's eight hundred million of my dollars in there," Biddle insisted. "I want to see it."

Abu Sayeed shrugged. "Be my guest, but if you open the lid, the radiation signature may signal a satellite or one of the roving detection trucks. The French and the Americans are hunting for these." Abu Sayeed nodded to Mohammed, who scowled but opened a Swiss Army Knife and started to remove the first of the screws that held the lid in place.

Biddle's eyes flickered back to Abu Sayeed. "That won't be necessary."

As Mohammed stopped removing the screw and then helped Naif finish fastening the crate in place, Abu Sayeed experienced a momentary sense of amazement at what they were about to attempt, and he wondered what Allah could be planning. Success? Failure? Perhaps something that no one expected?

Biddle interrupted his thoughts. "Which one goes?" he demanded.

Abu Sayeed nodded toward Mohammed.

Biddle turned. "You understand English?"

"Of course," Mohammed growled.

"You must remember two things," Biddle said. "First, strap yourself into the cot before they shove the container off the freighter. Second, never open the hatch." He turned back to Abu Sayeed. "When it goes in the water, the container will turn right side up and float, but it will be almost completely submerged. A locating device will signal my boat. We'll pick it up within an hour or two."

Abu Sayeed saw fear in Mohammed's eyes as he stared into the suffocatingly small box. Abu Sayeed cleared his throat. "You are certain everything will work as you predict?"

Biddle nodded. "All the arrangements have been made. We are doing God's work. He will not let us fail."

Abu Sayeed bowed his head. "God is infinitely great," he said quietly.

"He is," Biddle agreed.

THIRTEEN

OYSTER BAY, LONG ISLAND, JUNE 25

SATURDAY EVENING, BRENT got dressed and drove out to Biddle's estate for the firm's annual black-tie party, even though on a list of things he hated, attending black-tie soirees ranked just above bar fights.

He followed the directions to a secluded lane in Locust Valley and turned at a pair of tall stone gateposts. A security guard checked his invitation and identification then directed him down the winding drive through several hundred yards of manicured grounds, to a grand brick house set near the water. Brent relinquished his vintage BMW to a parking valet then followed other arriving guests through the house and onto the veranda at the rear.

He paused there to gaze at Biddle's grounds, with formal gardens to the left and the cool lights of a swimming pool glimmering off to the right. Farther to the left, across several acres of lawn, a tall hedge outlined a tennis court, while directly behind the house a series of descending walkways led to a huge white tent. Beyond the tent the calm waters of Long Island Sound glittered like a field of gems, reflecting the lights of the party.

So this was how people lived when they had the really big bucks, he thought, in a house as big as a Marriott with a yard the size of a county park. He found it strangely disappointing and thought about Maggie, knowing her reactions would have been the same. He tried to ignore the sharp pang he felt.

After another moment he joined the flow of guests down the garden path beneath a broad stone and wood trellis thick with flowering vines. Time to get it over with, he was thinking. The only people he'd know would be the other GA people, so he planned to put in a brief showing then hurry back to Manhattan for a late movie. He was nearing the tent when he heard his name and turned, surprised to see that the voice belonged to Prescott Biddle. Biddle detached himself from a cadaverous woman who lurched a little as he released her arm, until someone, maybe one of Biddle's staff, swooped in and steadied her. Biddle appeared tanned and relaxed in a double-breasted tuxedo. He smiled broadly and gave Brent's shoulder a warm squeeze.

"Delighted you could make it," Biddle said. He took Brent's arm as though they were the oldest of friends and began to walk him into the tent. "Stay with me. There are a number of people I'd like you to meet."

For the next twenty minutes, Biddle kept his grip on Brent's arm, introducing him to the quarterback for the New York Jets, the Yankees' new first baseman, a lead tenor for the Metropolitan Opera, and several Fortune 500 CEOs. During one lull in the conversation, Brent caught sight of Owen Smythe beside a pretty blonde woman. He started to go move in their direction, but Biddle grabbed him again.

"This way. I'll introduce you to your largest account," Biddle said as he towed him toward an elderly man with olive skin and an eagle's beak for a nose.

"Khaled," Biddle said. "This is Brent Lucas, the young man I told you about. He's our new young star, who now has day-to-day responsibility for your account." Biddle gave Brent a wink. "Why don't you get to know each other for a few minutes."

As Biddle spun away and disappeared into the throng, Dr. Faisal turned to inspect Brent with a pair of deep-set eyes. His bald head and concave cheeks gave great prominence to his bone structure, making him appear both gauntly ascetic and immeasurably wise. Brent might have found his gaze unnerving if not for the laugh lines that crinkled at the corner of his eyes. "Mr. Lucas," he said in a warm voice. "My new financial oracle."

"I wouldn't go that far," Brent said with a laugh. He tried to hide his nervousness at meeting the man who was entrusting him with over three quarters of a billion dollars.

Dr. Faisal gave him a wry smile. "Such a young man. You have a grave responsibility managing so large an account."

Brent nodded uncertainly and tensed for the admonition that seemed likely to follow.

"The better you do," Dr. Faisal continued, "the more money we will have for great purposes."

"Yessir," Brent replied, recalling the correspondence file, all the distributions for human need or world peace.

Dr. Faisal turned to several young women standing behind him. "Allow me to introduce my granddaughter, Amina, and her two friends from Princeton, Margot and Elizabeth. Ladies, this is Mr. Brent Lucas."

Brent nodded hello to the three young women. Dr. Faisal's granddaughter was unmistakable, tall and thin with her grandfather's prominent nose. She seemed shy as she shook Brent's hand, but then she held his gaze, and he realized that she had inherited her grandfather's quiet dignity. He chatted with Dr. Faisal and the three young women until the girls moved off toward the buffet table. Dr. Faisal moved to follow, but before he did, he turned to Brent. "I will invite you to stop by my home in Manhattan where we may speak at greater length."

Brent promised to call and set up a time then watched the old man hurry protectively after the three young women. He checked his watch. Time to hit the road if he was going to make his movie.

"That is a grave responsibility."

He turned and found himself confronting a pair of rich blue eyes set into a stunning face. A longer look revealed remarkably high cheekbones and ripe lips that seemed to pout and smile at the same time. This woman, whoever she was, emanated a sensual energy that caught him off guard and made the air around him seem to hum. Her hair was blonde, pulled close around the scalp, and a choker hung at her throat with a red gem the size of his thumbnail. A quick glance at her left hand showed no ring, as he wracked his brain for a name, thinking she had to be famous, certainly a model or movie star.

"What responsibility is that?" he asked, trying to recapture his bearings.

"Running Dr. Faisal's account," she said.

Her accent was English with a hint of German or Dutch. Her floor length black dress was cut low, and he struggled to keep his eyes from the swell of tanned cleavage and the puckered nipples outlined against the sheer fabric. "I guess," he said.

"You must think you're up to it," she said, sounding a challenging note.

"I'll just do my best and hope it's good enough," he countered, wondering again who she was, how she knew so much and where she'd come from.

"Now you're being falsely humble." She smiled. "Dr. Faisal wouldn't trust you if you weren't very good."

"I'm very new," Brent said.

She held out her hand and laughed, the sound melodic in his ears. "Nice to meet you, Mr. Very New. I'm Simone Hearkins."

"Brent Lucas." Her hand was dry and firm, her fingers strong. She held his gaze and let her hand rest in his a second longer than necessary. "Um, I'm kind of dry from talking. Can I get you something from the bar?"

"That would be lovely. White wine, please."

Brent hurried away and returned a moment later, half-expecting Simone to have changed her mind and disappeared. To his surprise, she was where he'd left her, beside one of the tent supports watching the band.

She turned, smiling, her eyes dancing with a light that seemed to suggest wild thoughts. "There you are," she said, as she took the proffered wineglass. Something in her manner suggested she'd missed him. Her voice was low and warm with an aura of restrained sexuality that made his breath catch.

They sipped wine and made small talk for a time. She explained that she lived in London and knew Biddle through her job at a British investment bank. When their conversation paused for a second she turned and glanced at the band. Her next question surprised him. "Would you care to dance?"

Brent shrugged. "I'm not much in the dancing department."

"You're being modest again," she said with a delighted laugh, as she took his hand and led him onto the floor. Her dress, cut high along one side, exposed a long sweep of thigh as she moved. She kept her eyes on him, seemingly unaware of the stare she drew from other men.

Finally, the band slowed the tempo. Brent started to thank her, expecting to leave the floor, but Simone put her hand on his shoulder and stepped close. They began to move again, and she folded her body against him, pressing her hips in a way that was more than casual and then responding when he pressed back.

Maggie flashed through his mind, but only briefly. Why should he feel guilty when she wanted nothing to do with him?

They found a small table when the band eventually took a break. Simone said it was her turn to go for more wine. Brent found her far too fascinating to mention the slightly bitter taste of the glass she handed him. A few minutes later, whatever was wrong with the wine no longer mattered because he'd started to feel more than a little light-headed, but so incredibly relaxed.

Simone was the only thing he could think about. He'd never connected to anyone so quickly. Her beauty seemed to expand as they talked, and her desire for him was as tangible as heat. When she leaned back, the fabric of her gown lay against her skin like a coat of wet paint, highlighting the perfect outline of small nipples and areolas. He imagined them in his mouth.

"Do you want to drive me back to Manhattan?" she asked, as if she'd read his mind.

"Yes," he said, his voice hoarse.

Simone took his hand and started to lead him toward the main house, but as they reached the veranda, fireworks began to rise from a string of barges several hundred yards offshore. They turned, and Simone folded against him, the mound of her mons veneris pressing his thigh. In the distance Brent saw a large yacht motoring smoothly toward Biddle's dock, its graceful lines silhouetted in the bloom of an exploding rocket. He felt rooted in place. In addition to the heat and urgency of Simone's body, the fireworks seemed overwhelming, their colors pulsing and vivid in an unearthly way, more beautiful that anything he'd ever experienced. At some point he realized she was tugging his arm, and he turned and followed her through the house.

"Can I drive?" Simone asked when the attendant brought his mint BMW 3.0Csi.

Brent waved her into the driver's seat, even though he seldom let anyone drive his precious antique. Tonight was an exception. He felt so warm, so incredibly desired. As they left Biddle's estate and wound along the darkened country lane, Brent realized that lights were dazzling his eyes so much that he couldn't have driven if he'd wanted to. They came to a stoplight and were suddenly back in traffic. Oncoming cars became twin lasers that swirled like roller coasters. Other lights, those of businesses and strip malls, kaleidoscoped into stunning patterns.

He stared, transfixed. Rather than being shocked or frightened, he felt elated, as Simone drove with easy competence. He relaxed into a hammock of comfort, as though they'd been best friends forever.

As they neared the city, Simone's hand slid onto his thigh. Lines of heat radiated from her fingertips, moving upward, igniting him. They reached Manhattan and stopped at a light, and he traced his fingers along the top of her dress then slipped them inside. She looked at him and smiled.

"Where should we go?" he whispered.

Simone's look said the answer was obvious. "Your apartment."

They parked and hurried the two blocks to his building, their hands already exploring. In the otherwise deserted elevator Simone wrapped her legs around his waist, grabbing fistfuls of his hair and pulling his lips toward her breasts. By the time they stumbled out and he unlocked his apartment door, the air in his nostrils burned, as though his lungs were full of fire.

He pushed open the door and mumbled an apology for his unpacked mess. She laughed, then disappeared in the kitchen to get them both glasses of ice water. When she emerged a moment later to hand him his glass, she was naked.

Brent's breath froze at the sight. He picked her up and carried her to his bed, struggling out of his clothes as he went. She lay on her back, knees spread apart, and watched him kick off his boxers. He stumbled slightly and felt his knees go a little wobbly but tried to shrug it off. He looked at her there on the bed, so eager for him, so extraordinarily beautiful.

"I hope we can make love all night," she murmured.

Brent nodded in agreement. He moved to the bed and took her in his arms. He felt the most amazing desire but also an immense weight that swept in like a storm cloud and seemed to press in from behind his eyes. No matter how he tried to resist, it seemed to pull his head down, force his eyes closed. In another instant he tumbled like a man falling off a cliff, downward into a dark pool of sleep.

FOURTEEN

OYSTER BAY, LONG ISLAND, JUNE 25

ABU SAYEED NOTED the change in pitch as the engines throttled back and the bow settled in the water. For several seconds the yacht seemed suspended in time, and he raised his eyes to the stars overhead. They were anemic in this part of the world, pale as sick children. In the desert he could lie on his back and almost touch their laser brightness. There the face of God was so much closer, he thought.

He had rolled back one of the sliding glass doors and was squatting in the opening where the yacht's darkened salon led onto the aft deck. It was probably unwise to expose himself like this, but he detested the ship's confinement and the sea's constant smell of putrefaction. He craved the sensation of wide-open space. He believed Allah would not deny him this moment.

Suddenly, he heard a familiar thump and whoosh, the unmistakable sound of a heavy mortar being fired. It came from someplace to his right. He reacted instantly, dropping to his belly, bracing for the explosion that would follow, while inside the salon he heard Naif and Mohammed do the same. But when when the explosion came, there was no destruction, only a huge blossom of colored sparks in the sky overhead.

All three men crawled to the salon windows on the port side and squatted, with their eyes pressed to small slits in the Venetian blinds, as the line of fireworks barges sent rocket after rocket into the air. It was beautiful, Abu Sayeed thought, even though the sound of the explosions churned his stomach.

A moment later as they approached the dock, they could see the shoreline and Biddle's mansion and a crowd of guests in a large tent. Servers dressed in dark pants and white shirts scurried like worker ants, carrying trays to and from a nearby preparation tent.

Abu Sayeed let out a tense breath. So far, the execution had been flawless. The container had been floating at almost the exact intended coordinates, the beacon had worked perfectly, and they'd picked up Mohammed and the missiles at around two that afternoon. Now, all three of them were dressed like the servers. It was a clever way to bring everything to shore.

The hundred-foot Hatteras reversed engines, the bow thrusters engaged, and they bumped gently against padded pilings. The mate and captain were the same two men who had delivered the cases of Coke in Penn Station and served as Biddle's bodyguards in Paris. Abu Sayeed had taken pains to keep them separated from his men. When they were all in the same small space for even a short time, he could feel a fog of inchoate violence start to gather.

He heard one of Biddle's men jump onto to the dock where he secured the lines and fixed the gangplank. The other one shut down the engines, and Abu Sayeed tensed as he awaited their signal.

Several minutes passed. Finally, footsteps came up the gangplank. It was the red-haired guard. "Follow me!" he snapped. As Abu Sayeed came off the yacht, he spotted Biddle's other man far ahead on the shore, positioned where he would be able to turn back curious guests.

At Abu Sayeed's soft whistle, Naif and Mohammed brought one of the two missile crates off the yacht. Abu Sayeed walked ahead of them with a tablecloth folded over his arm, his silenced Heckler & Koch MP5A3 sub-machine gun beneath. Anyone who noticed them would assume they were carrying party supplies.

The ground lights near the dock had been turned off, and when they entered the pool of shadow, Biddle's men led them away from the party. They passed through a narrow opening in a tall hedge and came into a brick courtyard between a garage and a stone cottage with a heavy slate roof.

Biddle's man unlocked the cottage and handed Abu Sayeed the key, and the three Arabs hurried inside. They put the crate in the small living room. Abu Sayeed re-locked the door before they returned for the second crate and the heavy duffel that held their extra weapons and ammunition.

When they finished unloading, the larger of Biddle's men loomed in the cottage doorway. "Keep the curtains closed and the noise down," he ordered. "Stay inside until morning.

Even then don't go beyond the hedges. Mr. Biddle has private security, and they mustn't know you're here." He pointed to a walkie-talkie on the dining table. "We'll call before we come. Otherwise, don't answer the door."

Abu Sayeed felt a cold rage in his stomach at the man's tone. He glanced around and saw calm in Naif's eyes but blind hatred in Mohammed's. He put his hand on Mohammed's arm and squeezed until a level of self-control began to return.

The bodyguard observed the exchange. He gave a little smirk then closed the door.

FIFTEEN

NEW YORK, JUNE 25

ANNELIËS KUEPER LAY in the dark and listened to Brent's breathing. A hallway chandelier threw enough light into the bedroom for her to see his silhouette as he settled into deeper sleep. Biddle had assured her the drug would take an elephant down.

She spoke his name one time, then louder, and when he didn't stir, she lifted his arm off her chest and sat up. She waited another minute on the side of the mattress, the air-conditioning raising goose bumps on her flesh.

Brent seemed nice enough, certainly a competent lover if he weren't zonked on the Ecstasy she'd added to his third glass of wine and then the tranquilizer she'd added to his ice water. She almost regretted it, and she cracked a wry smile in the darkness, wondering if it meant she still had a heart someplace inside the scar tissue. Finally, she stood, went into the living room, found her purse and removed the small plastic case Biddle had given her and shown her how to install.

Movement helped her focus because it reminded her of the danger and the opportunity. If she played this right it could mean a new life. If she played it wrong, she'd be dead. Either way, things had to change. She was finished letting people like Sayeed think they owned her, making her fuck their friends or people they were trying to set up. She shuddered, refusing to think about what was going to happen to Brent. She thought about herself instead.

Her life had been building toward this since last January when Abu Sayeed brought Biddle into the private London casino where she worked. It had been her third consecutive evening with a Kuwaiti sheik, who smelled like a pig and made love like a savage but paid fifteen hundred pounds a night for the privilege. Abu Sayeed had already told her what the proposal would be and given her Biddle's picture, so she recognized him instantly.

She watched him for a time, noting that he didn't gamble and drank only water. And when her Kuwaiti finally went to the bathroom, she approached him and started a conversation. Biddle was handsome, outwardly aloof and sophisticated. He offered her two thousand pounds to discuss his business proposition, and they left the casino before the Kuwaiti returned from the restroom. In their initial meeting there was nothing in his manner to suggest that he found her attractive or even that he liked women. Only later, once she worked her way inside his defenses, did he start to change, becoming awkward, even diffident.

That first night Biddle promised her a hundred thousand pounds if she would do a simple job for him and then swear herself to secrecy. He was associated with the U.S. Government, he told her, and she would be killed if she ever disclosed a single word. She knew he was lying, of course, because she already knew he was working with Abu Sayeed. Either way, she didn't give a damn.

After that, she met with Biddle several more times to discuss her assignment. Their encounters were always in London, in hotel rooms rented for that purpose. From the beginning Biddle's evolution was obvious but steady. He started out cold and impersonal, barely making eye contact, but by their third meeting, as though some scab of rectitude had been scraped away, he stared at her with almost desperate hunger.

By their fourth meeting, Biddle's distraction was almost painful. Finally, Anneliës stood and began to remove her blouse. With a cry that seemed part guilt and part release of his frantic desire, Biddle reached for her.

That first time, he trembled like an adolescent and ejaculated in seconds. Afterward he sat with his back to her on the edge of the bed, sobbing and begging her forgiveness. She ran her fingers through his hair and told him how good it had been. When he left, he gave her ten thousand pounds.

From then on, they met at least every two weeks. Each time, Biddle arrived with an aura of desperate need, but after they had sex he would kneel beside the bed and pray. He made her sit against the headboard, her hands folded, eyes closed and head bowed until he said, "Amen." In his prayers he called her names, like "filthy whore" and "diseased bitch," but when he finished he would hold her and stroke her hair. It was incredibly strange, but she endured it because she also sensed the opportunity.

Now, with Biddle's plastic case in hand, she went back to the bedroom, removed the cordless phone from its base, took it into the kitchen and turned on the overhead light. She pulled the back off the phone then used a pair of tweezers to remove a small chip from its foam bed. She attached it to the phone's wiring as she had been instructed, then replaced the back. With the phone once again on its stand in the bedroom, she searched for Brent's second phone, which she found in the living room on the floor between a packing box and the window.

She took it to the kitchen, installed the second chip and was about to put it back together when she heard a noise. She looked up to see Brent, naked, weaving, holding the doorjamb for support.

"What are you doing?" he croaked.

Her heart pounded, but she smiled and cocked her head. "Clumsy me," she said sheepishly, holding up the backless phone and covering the small plastic case with her arm. "I dropped your phone."

He blinked, fighting the drug. "Are you leaving? I know I had too much to drink. I've never been unable to . . . please don't go yet."

"I'm not leaving," she said, standing up and coming over to put her arms around him. "I thought of something I have to do and was going to leave a reminder on my answering machine."

He nodded. "Okay," he rasped.

"Go back to bed."

He turned and stumbled down the hall, and she sighed in relief. When she checked a moment later he was face down on the mattress, snoring loudly. Back in the kitchen, she finished putting the phone together, turned it on and dialed the number of the FBI's Manhattan office from memory.

After two rings a man answered. She recognized the voice.

"It's working," he said. "Get out of there."

Anneliës turned off the phone, found a piece of paper and wrote Brent a note saying she'd had a wonderful time and promising to call soon. She pulled on her dress and carried her shoes as she let herself out.

SIXTEEN

NEW YORK, JUNE 26

THE MOMENT THE alarm went off, Brent felt the sharp stabs of sunlight through his eyelids and his head starting to pound. He reached out and whacked the clock/radio then lay perfectly still, afraid he'd be sick if he moved another inch. A few glasses of wine—how was it possible to feel this bad?

He recalled Simone and winced. Horny and impossibly gorgeous—at least that's what he remembered—only he'd been so wasted that he wondered what she really looked like. He let his hand creep across and found the bed empty, the sheets cold.

He cracked one eye, enduring the pain, viewing the wreckage of his clothes where he'd tossed them the night before. "Simone?" he croaked. There was no answer. After another second he stood and stumbled into the bathroom. He peed, brushed his teeth then managed to hold down several glasses of cold water he drew from the tap.

Back in the living room, he looked around at his jumbled moving boxes and wondered if it had been a fantasy. Had a beautiful woman really walked out of his kitchen bare-ass naked? Then he remembered what had happened next—absolutely nothing because he had passed out. It seemed like a bad joke, he thought as he spotted the scrap of paper atop the clutter on his dining table. "Thanks for a wonderful evening. I'll call you. Love, Simone." No phone number. No kidding! Like he'd ever hear from her again. If he didn't feel so bad he might have laughed.

He stood there a moment until he remembered something else—DeLeyon, his Little Brother! Today was their monthly game of hoops! He put his hands to his head. He'd never survive. He had the shakes, the cold sweats. He'd have a heart attack if he tried to dribble a basketball.

He gave up thinking about the pain because he couldn't break a promise to DeLeyon. He staggered back into the bedroom, and five minutes later, wearing shorts and a T-shirt and carrying a fresh shirt in a canvas bag, he caught a taxi to the West Side. He climbed out at Riverside and One Hundred and Twenty Fifth Street and stumbled down through the narrow band of Riverside Park to a concrete basketball court shaded by tall sycamores and oaks and bordered by the West Side Highway. A game was in progress on one end of the court, while at the other end, a huge African American kid in a sleeveless T-shirt stood with a basketball held loosely against his hip and an impatient look on his face.

"Yo, y'all late!" he called when he caught sight of Brent.

"Rough night," Brent mumbled.

DeLeyon screwed up his face. "You wish!" he said, starting to dribble the ball. "Prob'ly went to a movie by yo'seff and overslept." He cut loose with a jump shot and swished the chains that hung in place of a net. He was sixteen, beginning to grow into his size, his arms filling out with ropes of dark muscle, his bony little kid face taking on a sculpted maturity that was still full of youth but also had a soulful depth.

The Big Brother thing had been Harry's idea. He'd said it was more for Brent than his Little Brother, that it might keep him from becoming too much of an egotistical Wall Street asshole, or at least slow the process a little. For almost five years Brent had flown down once a month from Boston and headed to the Upper West Side to meet DeLeyon, who had grown from a gangly kid to his current six-five. DeLeyon had miraculously managed to survive his boyhood on the Harlem streets, even though some of his posse hadn't. His life had been hard enough to make bad choices awfully tempting, but most times he'd managed to make good ones. He slept at his grandmother's some nights, other nights at his mother's and sometimes even at his father's—depending on where it was safe or who was sober.

No matter what else was going on in his life, Brent always showed up because these once-a-month meetings were pretty much the one constant in DeLeyon's life. Regardless of his own efforts, he gave the kid all the credit for staying on track. In addition to being a superb athlete, DeLeyon had excellent grades and the brains to go Ivy. Brent already had the coaches from Harvard, Yale and Brown looking.

Now he took a deep breath and tried to shove his pain into

the background. "Late or not," he grinned as he stepped onto the court and touched fists with DeLeyon. "I'm going to kick your bony ass."

"Keep wishin', white boy."

"It ain't wishing," he said, giving DeLeyon's ball a quick swat as he attempted a steal.

DeLeyon recaptured the ball then dribbled it easily a step or two away. Brent headed to the foul line. "Okay," he said, feeling his knees wobble. "Let's not waste time. Gimme the ball."

"Uh-uh," DeLeyon said. "We shoot for it."

Brent missed his first shot, while DeLeyon hit, giving him first possession. Immediately, he blew past Brent to score on a spinning lay-up. Brent lost the ball on his first turn, and DeLeyon took it back behind the line then swished a long three-pointer. The game went like that for the next hour and fifteen minutes, and DeLeyon won forty-four to twenty. Twice, Brent had to bend over, hands on knees to catch his breath.

"That's the worst ass-kicking yet," DeLeyon said with a broad smile as they walked off the court.

"Yeah," Brent admitted as he stripped off his sweat soaked shirt and used it for a towel on his chest and underarms. "You're getting better, and I'm getting worse."

"You bad today," DeLeyon laughed. Then he sobered and gave Brent one of those dead serious looks that made him seem years older than sixteen. "But I appreciate you coming, man."

They headed over to Broadway to a little pizza place where they bought slices and Cokes, and Brent grilled DeLeyon like he always did about his grades and everything else in his life. DeLeyon mumbled his answers, pretending to resent the intrusion, but after a bit he reached into the pocket of his shorts and pulled out a sweat-soaked report card. He handed it to Brent, who unfolded it with care and scanned DeLeyon's grades.

Brent smiled as he saw nothing less than A+. "You need to work a little harder."

"You ever quit, man?"

"Not until you get into Harvard."

"Yeah, right," DeLeyon said, shrugging it off.

DeLeyon didn't know it, but Brent had long ago determined he'd put him through college and pay whatever the scholarship didn't cover. "Okay, gotta go," he said. "Keep it up. I'm proud of you."

"You really are, aren't you?" the boy said, the tough outer layer disappearing for a brief second.

Brent nodded. "Yeah, I really am."

By twelve-thirty, after a shower, several cups of coffee and three power bars, Brent's hangover had faded to a sort of depressed exhaustion. As he toweled off, he looked around at his confusion of unpacked boxes and scowled as he realized the problem. Being with DeLeyon always left him with a feeling of vague dissatisfaction and reminded him that there were more important things to do than trying to make himself rich.

He pulled open one of the boxes and started to unpack a stack of plates, but then glanced out the window. He'd planned to spend the day getting the apartment organized, but the sky outside was cloudless, the temperature pleasantly cool. Besides, why unpack? He wasn't going to be here that long. Soon, he'd find a way to get Simmons her proof and then get on with his life, whatever that meant.

Fifteen minutes later he was in the BMW, roaring out of Manhattan on his way toward Morristown. It was much too perfect a day to be trapped inside, and he hadn't seen Fred in almost two weeks. Of course, Fred would act like his visit was no big deal, but Brent knew that down deep it mattered.

The Lincoln Tunnel's traffic was light, typical for a Sunday, and when he emerged on the other side, the summer afternoon was so delightful that even Newark's grunge didn't seem too oppressive. He sped through the Oranges and crested the Ramapo Hills where, and as it always did, New Jersey transformed itself from a wasteland of abandoned factories and ruined tenements to the green rolling hills of Morris County.

On reaching Morristown, he drove straight to his old neighborhood and parked in front of a white clapboard bungalow on a quiet street close to the town center. A few miles away grand homes sat on multi-acre lots, the estates of investment bankers and lawyers who commuted to Manhattan, but the close-in neighborhoods contained small neat homes, most built after World War II and owned by people like Fred who lived and worked in Morristown–policemen, firemen, city workers and teachers.

Brent found his uncle in the backyard, wearing dark pants and a threadbare wife-beater. He was bent over, trimming his roses and humming a little tune, and if he heard Brent approach he gave no indication. In spite of a knee injury that had forced his early retirement, Fred Lucas was big-boned and still thickly muscled. Although Brent could see places where the flesh was starting to sag, his uncle's shoulders and arms still looked powerful.

"Need some help?" he asked when he got close.

Fred turned his head just enough to see Brent in his peripheral vision. "You wouldn't know a rose from a freaking dandelion."

"Yes, I would," Brent countered. "Dandelions grow in the middle of the lawn. Roses grow around the sides." He paused. "Otherwise, I think they're almost indistinguishable."

His uncle had gone back to cutting. "You're a moron."

"Which one of us went to Yale?"

"A liberal moron. I rest my case."

Brent laughed and raised his hands in surrender, knowing Fred never admitted defeat in any contest nor gave an inch in any argument. When Fred was wrong–not an infrequent occurrence–he'd simply revert to foul language, insults and name-calling until his opponent lost focus. He'd won dart throwing, arm wrestling and beer drinking contests over more able competitors simply because he needled them to distraction. The same was true with family arguments.

"Did I ever tell you what a pain in the ass it was to grow up with an uncle who couldn't stand to lose?" Brent asked.

"You only whined about it maybe a thousand times. It was your way of thanking me for giving a wissy like you a sense of perseverance."

"That must have been it."

Fred finally cracked a smile, straightened and slipped his clippers into his back pocket. "So, how's the big shot money man?" he asked as he straightened up, limped toward his nephew, threw his arms around him and gave him a hug that left the front of Brent's shirt stained with sweat.

"Pretty good."

Fred eyed him a second, then tossed his head. "Yeah, right," he said. "And I'm rich and handsome."

"Everything's fine," Brent insisted.

Fred walked up the back steps and through the screen door, letting it slam behind him. He came back out a moment later with two cans of Budweiser and handed one to Brent. "Don't shit a shitter," he said as he cracked his cold beer and sipped the foam off the top.

"Really," Brent insisted, trying to mean it.

Fred went over and flopped into a cheap aluminum lawn chair. "Know who I saw the other day?"

"Who?"

"Maggie."

"That was quick." Brent glanced at his watch. Usually it takes you at least five minutes to bring her up."

Fred sighed. "Man, she's pretty."

Brent shrugged.

"Pretty dumb move."

"She broke up with me. Remember?"

"Only cause you were stupid."

Brent waved his beer. "'Preciate the support."

"Or decided you weren't rich enough."

Brent looked at the curling paint on the back wall of the house. "There's nothing wrong with having enough money to take a trip or paint your house."

"A–I don't want to go anyplace, and B–there's nothing wrong with letting it peel!"

Brent shook his head.

"I keep trying to tell you, and you keep trying not to believe me, but money ain't gonna make your life any better. People in this neighborhood spend their whole lives on the clock, but they still get married and have kids. Money don't make 'em nicer. It don't make 'em live longer. It didn't keep those other bastards in the Trade Center any safer than Harry."

"Maybe I'm doing something a lot more complicated than just grubbing for money. Ever think about that?"

Fred shook his head. "Nope."

Brent let out a laugh. "Why didn't you take your own advice, smart guy?"

"What? Get married?" Fred looked at himself. "Who'da put up with me?"

"Plenty of stupid women out there."

Fred became suddenly serious. He shrugged uncomfortably. "Putting out fires is dangerous–I don't gotta tell you." He turned to his flowers. "It hurts the people around you. Your mom–she wasn't evil. She just couldn't take it without your dad. Shit like that happens."

Brent swallowed. This was a subject he hated. He took a deep breath then pointed toward the stakes along the back fence. "Tomatoes look good."

Fred nodded. "Good call. Let's talk about global warming, or the Yankees and how I hope the team plane goes down right into Steinbrenner's fucking house when he's in it."

Brent sucked down about half his beer and let out a silent belch. "These conversations are always a pleasure."

"You know, before you went off to that phony-ass west coast business school, you were gonna teach. What ever happened to that?"

Brent finished his beer and crumpled the can. "You and Maggie," he said sourly. "I'll do it when I'm ready."

Fred shook his head. "You think you gotta have ten million bananas first."

"You don't know what you're talking about."

"Never stopped me before!"

"That's for sure," Brent said as he started into the house for a fresh beer.

"Get me one, too," Fred called.

They worked in the yard until six when Fred lit the grill, and then they cooked burgers and ate on the old backyard picnic table. Fred had run out of verbal steam, and by the time they finished dinner, he seemed to be in a reflective and melancholy mood.

"I give you a hard time, but I worry about you in that place," he said after a long silence, during which they each worked on bowls of vanilla ice cream with chocolate sauce.

"You shouldn't."

Fred shook his head, his eyes turning inward, giving a brief hint that he wasn't as tough as he liked to pretend. "Nobody's fine in New York. It either kills people or turns them into assholes."

"People die out here, too," Brent said. His father had raced into a burning building when Brent was twelve. Fred had been pulling hose off the truck and watched it collapse.

Fred nodded. "But lemme tell you, I put out fires in these people's houses for thirty years. I know what these Wall Street bastards're like with their slicked-back hair and German cars and wives that look like they been chained in the basement and starved. They don't say 'Thank you' when you risk your ass saving their stupid house; they ask why you didn't get there faster."

Brent stood up, wiped his mouth and picked up a load of plates to take into the kitchen. "I've got it under control."

"That's what your mother said after your dad died," Fred said with a scowl. "Anyway, you look like a goddamn lump."

Brent straightened up as if he'd been slapped. "You know, Fred, I'm not my mother!" He went into the house then came out a moment later and collected the bowls. "It's just my job."

"Not everything it's cranked up to be?"

He shrugged.

"You just remember something," Fred said when Brent came back outside again. "When you need help and those city assholes don't know you no more, you know where to come."

"I know where to come." Brent went over and put an arm around his uncle's shoulder. "Thanks for dinner."

Brent didn't drive straight back to the city. Instead, he took a detour across town to a neighborhood of similar bungalows, turned onto a familiar street then slowed toward the middle the block. To his surprise all the lights were burning in Maggie's house. Cars were parked in the driveway and along the curb. Tightness gripped his chest, a sudden wild fear. Maybe she'd met someone else. Maybe this was some kind of celebration. He knew he should simply drive away, but he had to know.

Feeling like a fool, he pulled out his cell phone and punched in her number. It rang five times, and he was about to hang up when a man answered.

"Is Maggie there?" he asked, surprised by his hot surge of jealousy.

"Is this Brent?" the guy responded. He had a hoarse voice, New Joisey accent and sounded older, maybe forty or forty-five.

"Yeah."

"Hey, kiddo, it's Spud," the guy said with a laugh. "Where you been? How come we don't see you 'round the station no more?"

Joe Spedowski, or "Spud" as he was known on the Morristown PD, was Maggie's best friend on the detective squad. "Ask your partner," Brent said.

"Women don't know shit. Ain't you figured that out yet?" Spud said. "I'll get her."

The phone clattered on the kitchen counter. In the background, the refrigerator door opened and closed, and beer bottles clinked in the door racks. The back door creaked, and over the sudden wash of other voices came the shout, "Brent's onna the phone."

A second later footsteps approached, and then Maggie's voice. "Brent?"

"Yeah," he said, finding himself at a total loss, everything he wanted to say trapped behind a wall of reserve.

"What's up?" she asked, already sounding distant.

"Nothing. I just wanted . . . sounds like you're having a party."

"Some people from work."

Another voice suddenly called out, "Call him back, Maggie. You're missing your going away party."

"Be there in a second," Maggie replied.

Another touch of panic. "You're moving?" Brent asked.

"Oh," she said dismissively. "I just got kind of transferred."

"To what?"

"This thing called Project Seahawk. It's port security. FBI, Coast Guard and different police forces, kind of a task force. They wanted another computer nerd."

"It's a big deal!" Spud shouted. "Don't let her tell ya it ain't."

"Where?" Brent asked.

"Newark."

He felt a flood of relief. "Now you're a commuter!" he said, trying to sound hearty. "Well, congratulations. I'll let you get back to your party."

"We can talk some other time."

He tried to sift her tone for some note of encouragement, but heard nothing. "Sure."

He clicked off the line then drove through the sparse traffic back to his empty apartment.

SEVENTEEN

PROJECT SEAHAWK OFFICES, NEWARK, NJ, JUNE 26

FBI AGENT ANN Jenkins grabbed an escaping strand of kinky red hair, stuffed it behind her ear, read several more paragraphs and cursed. The document before her was labeled "Top Secret," but as far as she was concerned it might as well have read "Transparent Ass-Saving Excuse." It was typical CIA bullshit, full of double-talk and equivocation and void of a single hard fact. What pissed her off most was the tone, sort of a "You're Extremely Lucky We're Sharing This With You," and its implication that the CIA was the REAL INTELLIGENCE SERVICE while the FBI was a bunch of bozos masquerading in dark suits.

The memo implied that some Russian-made Strella-18 missiles "might" have been stolen from a military base outside Kiev and "may" have been sold to some Mideastern terrorists associated with the Wahaddi Brotherhood. It concluded with the warning that what the CIA termed the "package" "might" be headed for the continental United States.

From long experience with CIA communications, Jenkins translated the "mays" into the certainty that the missiles had been stolen and sold to some crazed Muslims who wanted nothing more than to explode them on U.S. soil. The document was a political form of "tag," meaning she and her team were now "it" and therefore responsible for making sure the "package" didn't make it ashore along the northeastern coast between Maryland and Massachusetts. As Deputy Director of Project Seahawk's New York office, that area was her bailiwick, and while responsibility wasn't something she characteristically dodged, with her boss on medical leave recovering from open-heart surgery, the timing sucked.

She read the last sentence again and felt her stomach buzz with tension. Reflexively, she reached into the top drawer of her desk, grabbed some Peanut M&M's from an open package and tossed one in her mouth. This kind of crap made her die for a cigarette, but she was quitting . . . again. So, instead of smoking she was chewing through three packs of M&M's a day.

The problem was that Project Seahawk was a fairly recent invention of Homeland Security—itself a fairly recent invention—and as such was an amalgamation of all the different state, local and federal agencies that had anything to do with port security into one, theoretically, seamless entity. The key word being *theoretical* because, as Jenkins had learned after being assigned here from the FBI, the reality fell far short of the lofty goals. For starters Project Seahawk's New York office was actually in Newark, a quick shot through the Lincoln Tunnel from Manhattan's pricey real estate but a world away in terms of stature and prestige. During its short life, it had been perennially under-funded and short-staffed, and like any olio of agencies that lacked a true power base, it had become a regular source of manpower for other agencies whenever "special projects" came up in the region.

Right at that moment, Jenkins was looking at a forty percent staff reduction due to the President's upcoming visit to New York. It pissed her off mightily that highly trained professionals responsible for keeping the nation's ports safe from terrorism were sent out checking trashcans and mailboxes for bombs, especially when her staffing was pathetic to start with, but there was nothing she could do.

The CIA memo ought to be enough reason for the powers-that-be to give her back her entire team and cancel the upcoming POTUS visit, but she knew that wasn't going to happen. Next year was a Presidential election, and when it came down to politics versus practicality, politics won every time.

Beneath the CIA memo sat a list from Homeland Security of personnel newly assigned to Project Seahawk. She glanced at the single name on the list—Maggie DeVito. One bloody person, whoopie doo. Even worse, Jenkins noted, DeVito was coming from the Morristown Police Department, supposedly picked because she was strong in computers and relational database manipulation. She rolled her eyes. In her experience, rural cops were smarter than morons, but just marginally. She once again suppressed her desire for a cigarette, popped another M&M in her mouth and told herself that she was lucky for at least one thing. At least she was a skinny broad.

EIGHTEEN

OYSTER BAY, LONG ISLAND, JUNE 27

PRESCOTT BIDDLE WAS sitting alone at his dining table awaiting the soup course when an unexpected noise made him glance toward the entryway. It was Faith, his wife, leaning unsteadily against the wall. She stayed there for a time then seemed to gather resolve and made her way to her seat at the far end of the table.

"To what do I owe this surprise?" he asked in a mocking tone. On most nights his wife ate in the small room on the second floor where she spent her days smoking, drinking and watching television.

Faith did not reply, but reached out and one by one adjusted her ashtray, the silver coaster where her vodka would be placed, and the crystal and silver cigarette lighter. Her inventory check complete, she finally looked at him. "You've been so excited," she said, her voice rough as the hiss of sandpaper on wood. "I thought I'd find out what it's about."

How did she know, Biddle wondered? They slept in separate rooms. He sometimes went days without speaking to her. "Just some developments at work."

"Oh," Faith said. She stared pointedly at his left hand where it lay on the table, at the grayed webbing between the thumb and forefinger, the flesh permanently damaged by his snakebite a few months earlier. "Are you still playing with your little friend in the basement?"

Biddle felt his temper flare. He took a second to control it then folded his hands and spoke to her as he might to a child. "You used to love the Lord."

"I was once a dutiful little girl who obeyed her family . . . but then they told me to marry you." She picked up the bell beside her plate and rang it, and when the maid put her head into the dining room, she ordered vodka.

"Will you ever stop blaming other people for your lack of self-respect and devotion?" Biddle demanded, keeping his voice level.

The maid reappeared with the vodka along with two bowls of vichyssoise. Biddle bowed his head and spoke a blessing, but Faith ignored him. She sipped her drink and fished a cigarette from her pack. She lit the end, inhaled deeply then held it in the V of nicotine-yellowed fingers. "You love to list my failures," she said after another gulp of her drink. "You and God must talk together for hours and lay them all out."

Biddle had started on his soup, but he dropped his spoon and brought his hand down hard enough to rattle the silver. "You will stop mocking the Lord!"

"I'll say whatever damn thing I want!" Faith shot back.

"No!"

Faith's gaze wandered as she sipped her drink and smoked. "When I married you, I didn't love you," she said, her voice heavy with self-pity. "I didn't think it mattered because I thought children would make me happy. I didn't realize that all you love is your money, and now that you've got more than you can ever spend, all you want is your snake and your tooth fairy."

"Stop it!" Biddle snarled.

Faith waved his words away. "I know how your greedy mind works. You're excited because you think your tooth fairy's going to give you something!"

Biddle tried to ignore her, but her words ate into him. As much as he resisted, they undermined him and dragged him back to his boyhood, as if they were spoken not by Faith but by his father, Rev. Josiah Biddle. What was it about this drunken cadaver at the other end of the table? How could she do this to him? When he looked at her face, he pictured his father's instead, a razor strop in one hand, Biddle's thin arm gripped in his other. He remembered Proverbs 23:13: "Withhold not correction from the child; for if thou beatest him with a rod, he shall not die." His father would recite the words, and the strop would slash again and again across Biddle's back and legs.

In spite of all the years of abuse, he'd followed his father's urging and married Faith. She had been seventeen, thin and frail, but Rev. Biddle had selected her for her extreme devotion. Immediately after the wedding, Biddle had taken her to Boston and his new life, away from everything she had known in their

Tennessee mountain community. For a woman who'd expected life to revolve around keeping house for a man and raising children, his long hours in the graduate program at M.I.T. had left her feeling lost. It had gotten worse when, suspecting God had bigger things in store for him than mere fatherhood, he refused to have children.

Now he stared down the table at her, slumped in her chair, the burnt stub of her cigarette in one jaundiced hand and her drink in the other. Because of him, because of his disregard, she had become bitter and disillusioned and had slowly drifted, first from their marriage, and then from God. Gradually her despair had led her to drink–at first secretly but then openly and constantly. He looked away and sipped his soup, trying to push away the guilt.

A voice in his head countered, *No! He was not responsible!* The Devil was whispering lies to make him doubt himself. Faith's choices had made her this dried-up monster, reeking of tobacco and booze, her parchment skin stretched over brittle bones. Faith was his reminder of what happened when a person turned away from the Lord.

He pressed forward in his chair. "Do you even know who I am?" he demanded.

For a few seconds, Faith's glassy eyes seemed to clear, and she barked a hoarse laugh. "I have no idea who you are."

Biddle thought of his meeting earlier that day with Thomas Swaggert, the Vice President of the United States and the man who would soon accede to the Presidency. Swaggert was seventy-two, a Tennessean and fellow Pentecostal, once also a handler of serpents before his hunger for national office had led him to a mainstream church. Swaggert was one of the cornerstones of Biddle's plan, and he had gone to him seeking assurance that Swaggert's heart was still capable of Biblical vengeance.

He had found Swaggert cautious, but beneath his politican's veneer as full of hate for non-believers as ever. It had gladdened him because given the coming outrage at a terrorist attack on the President, the electorate would demand a massive military retaliation against Iran and Syria. The new President would have to be steadfast, making certain that Israel became involved. Then the Final Battle would be under way.

He looked again at Faith, fighting his desire to tell her about the coming glory, to rub her face in her failure to live up to his greatness. As if she was reading his mind Faith waved one hand, moving it like an eraser on a blackboard. "No," she slurred. "I do know what you are. You're an asshole!" She let out a drunken laugh, showing her wolfish, discolored teeth.

"The End of Days is coming!" Biddle said, leveling a finger at her. "The Son will soon return, and your soul will be judged!"

Faith put her arm on the table, shoving her untouched bowl and saucer and slopping soup over the side. "Go play with your snake."

"Be careful, woman!"

Faith pushed back her chair and stood unsteadily. "Idiot," she sneered.

Biddle watched her shuffle from the room and thought again of his great secret. When he became the Messiah Bringer, she would understand the error of her ways. He felt a thrill run up his spine–the End of Days! The Second Coming! One thing was certain–the Messiah Bringer would be rewarded. He shook his head, enraptured by anticipation.

The maid came in and took his soup then wordlessly wiped up the mess at Faith's end. Afterward, she served Biddle a plate of broiled snapper and green salad, and as he ate, his thoughts changed and drifted to Anneliës. How she transfixed him! Her existence proved that God did not intend for him to waste his life with Faith.

His mind wandered further, to the night Anneliës had spent with Brent Lucas. He tried to choke off the thought, but not before he felt the claws of jealousy close around his heart. He reminded himself that her sacrifice had been in God's service and a true Christian did not hate, but what he felt for Lucas had the dark tar-like consistence of something very close.

NINETEEN

NEWARK, NJ, JUNE 27

MAGGIE KNEW SHE should have been razor sharp on her first day at Project Seahawk, but she wasn't, not even close. Her new boss, Ann Jenkins, the Deputy Director, seemed to sense it because she'd paused several times during their orientation walk around the ops center to give Maggie a questioning glance.

"Must have been one hell of a send-off party," Jenkins sniffed at one point, apparently finding Maggie less impressive than her personnel folder and test scores indicated.

"I couldn't sleep," Maggie said. She didn't bother to add that the insomnia had nothing to do with partying but everything to do with her old boyfriend.

"Well, then," Jenkins said, giving her a cool smile. "What do you think so far?" Her skin stretched tight across her cheek and jaw in a way that suggested an eating disorder or compulsive exercise. To Maggie, Jenkins looked uptight even by FBI standards.

"A lot of different agencies and a lot of computers," Maggie said, her tone noncommittal. "Does it work?"

Jenkins tilted her head as though sifting Maggie's words, maybe reappraising her a little. "Our capabilities outstrip anything that's ever been done," she said. "But it doesn't work as well as it should. That's the reason you're here."

Maggie nodded, knowing now was the time to say something politically correct, like how excited she was to join the team, but she remained silent because she already had doubts about whether Project Seahawk was the right fit. Jenkins had made it clear that she envisioned Maggie as an inside person, meaning she'd be crunching through reams of paperwork and solving computer incompatibilities. That meant she'd miss the things she loved the most—working cases and having human contact.

Jenkins started walking again, her heels clicking on the linoleum in an unspoken demand for Maggie to keep up. They came to a locked door, and Jenkins punched in a code. Inside, through a second locked door, they entered the computer room, cooled to a constant fifty-five degrees. Jenkins talked for several minutes about terabytes and gigaflops and millions of computations per second, describing Operation Seahawk's vast data crunching power. When she finished, she gave Maggie a skeptical glance, as if questioning how much a small-town cop could have grasped.

Maggie already understood that most FBI agents assumed local law enforcement people were dumber than rocks, so before she answered she took a long look around at the gleaming rows of mainframes and servers with their flashing lights. "From what I've read, the problem isn't the size or speed of your systems," she said at last. "It's database incompatibility. For example, accommodating instance heterogeneities in large freestanding systems. I have a paper on it, in case you're interested." When Maggie looked at her again, Jenkins seemed to be suppressing a smile.

Finally, Jenkins nodded. "You're right, and in addition to database problems, our groups have interdepartmental biases and cultures that have never shared information. Our job is to make sure neither the computers nor the people prevent communication."

"Why are all the groups segregated?" Maggie asked, referring to the way the Coast Guard was housed in one group of offices, the FBI in another, the New York/New Jersey Port Authority Police in a third, the New York City Police in theirs, and so on. "Seems kind of hard to break down barriers that way."

Jenkins lowered her head and looked at Maggie through upraised eyes. "I'm the Assistant Director," she said. "I happen to have a boss."

"Gotcha," Maggie said with a smile, thinking that maybe she was being a little tough on Agent Jenkins.

An hour later Maggie was back in her cubicle starting to get organized. In addition to computer work, she was supposed to act as a liaison officer to the town and city police forces of New Jersey. Jenkins had explained that her counterparts from New York and Connecticut were out checking mailboxes and manhole covers for next Sunday's POTUS visit. When she'd asked why a port security operation was involved with a Presidential visit, Jenkins had shaken her head and growled, "Don't ask."

Maggie hoped some peace and quiet would help her sort out the feelings stirred up by Brent's call. Before last night, they hadn't spoken in months. The enforced silence had been her choice—five months and twenty-six days if anybody was counting—and during that time she'd been reasonably successful in keeping him out of her thoughts. Nonetheless, last night her fragile wall of self-denial had collapsed, and she had had to admit she missed him terribly.

Goddamn you, Brent, she said to herself, preferring anger over vulnerability. They'd dated in high school, broken up in college, dated after he graduated from Yale, broken up during his time in business school, then gone out again when he was in Boston. This last time, after nearly two and a half years, it had seemed, well . . . perfectly natural to take things to the next level. She was thirty-two, ready to start thinking about the future, but when she'd shared those thoughts with Brent, he'd pulled back.

She knew the reasons. They had a lot to do with Harry's death, with his parents' deaths before that, and Brent's irrational fear that Lucases were poorly made for parenthood or long-term relationships. Still, she hadn't been able to accept the way he'd become cold and distant. She'd told him she didn't want to force him into something, but she wasn't going to waste her life on a partner who showed no hint of changing. It broke her heart, but in the end, she'd been the one who'd called things off.

Over the past months, she'd told herself she was over him, but last night something in his voice had gotten under her skin. He'd sounded lonely and lost, and after all this time like he was finally reaching out to her. Sadly, she wondered if she could ever be there for him again.

TWENTY

NEW YORK, JUNE 28

TUESDAY MORNING BEGAN with a special firm meeting. The first thing Brent noticed when he walked into the conference room was the look of barely restrained excitement on Biddle's face. He turned to Owen Smythe, whose shrug indicated he, too, had no idea what was happening.

"First," Biddle began once the last person sat, "a reminder that I'm going to be out of touch for the next ten days on a salmon river in Siberia. I'm leaving right after this meeting. I'll have my sat-phone turned on about an hour each day, so you can reach me in an emergency. Betty will know the hours when I'll be available." Biddle smiled and looked around the room. "Call at your peril, gentlemen."

There was muted laughter, but Biddle raised his hand for silence. "More important," he said, his voice deepening. "The Holy Spirit spoke last night. The Lord told me that a moment of great darkness approaches. Because of that we're going short. I want us net flat by close of trading, and by tomorrow we will be short with ninety percent of maximum leverage. The market is going to crash, gentlemen."

There was murmur of surprise. Brent looked around at the delight etched on the faces of the other partners. What could be so important that it would change the direction of the market, he wondered? What did Biddle know?

He ran over upcoming earnings releases and government economic data but came up with nothing. Still, there was Biddle at the head of the table with a wild glint in his eyes. Why was Biddle doing this? Were Brent's clients about to be exposed to massive risk based on some delusion? He caught himself—his clients! Reminded of why he was here, he pressed the record button and cleared his throat. "Yesterday, we were unanimous in our assessment that the market would continue moving higher."

"Yes," Biddle said.

"We're going to ignore that now and reposition the entire portfolio?"

"Yes."

"I'd like to know how you justify taking that kind of risk with our clients' money."

An angry murmur came from the other partners, but Biddle held up his hands for silence. "Because mine is the way," he said. He smiled around at the others then clapped his hands, dismissing the meeting. "Have a good day, gentlemen, and God bless."

Biddle walked out, followed by the other portfolio managers. Brent remained seated. No one, not even Smythe, would meet his eye.

TWENTY-ONE

NEW YORK, JUNE 29

BRENT SAT AT his desk looking over the cash balances generated from selling out his portfolios a day earlier. His first instinct had been to refuse, but when he'd called Simmons to tell her about the meeting she had instructed him to go along. Still, it was utterly nuts.

He brought up Dr. Faisal's account on the computer and looked at the performance. The account's value had grown from seven hundred sixty five million to nearly eight hundred twenty million in the time he'd managed it. This morning the market was roaring ahead yet again; only Biddle said there was "darkness over the world" and they had to go short! He stood and started to pace, telling himself he'd be out of there soon enough.

His phone buzzed, and he reached over and jerked it off its base. It was Joe Steward, the firm's head trader. "I've got everyone else's list. Where's yours?" Steward barked, meaning the lists of stocks Brent would be shorting.

"You'll have it when it's ready," Brent replied.

"Get your ass in gear," Steward said and hung up.

Brent tossed the phone back into its cradle and resumed pacing. It buzzed again, and he snatched it up. "What?" he barked, expecting Steward again.

Instead, it was Betty Dowager, her voice high-pitched, anxious. "I need to come down and speak with you."

He assumed it was because Steward had called her to complain. She was probably going to patch Biddle through on the phone and stand there as a witness while he commanded Brent to go short according to God's holy word.

"Suit yourself," he said.

A moment later, Betty hurried into his office and shut the door. She stood as far from him as possible, pressing her plump rear end against the doorknob. Her glasses had heavy frames with arched points at the hinges. They usually gave her an aspect of slyness, but now along with the ashen color of her cheeks they simply added to her look of concern.

She put her fist to her mouth and held her other hand over the swell of her tummy as though she had eaten something bad. "Two men are here from the FBI," she said in a near-whisper. "They asked to see Mr. Biddle, but he's already out of touch. Mr. Wofford is on vacation as well, and I can't reach him. They want to talk about one of your accounts."

Brent frowned. "Which one?"

"Dr. Faisal."

Brent had no idea what it could be about, but he wanted no part of handling it alone. "Who's our counsel?"

"Spencer McDonald at Tweed, Barker and Rowe. I've already put in a call, but he's not available."

"Tell the FBI guys I'll talk to them when Mr. McDonald can be present."

Betty shook her head. "They insist on seeing you right away."

"Tell them I'm not here."

She pointed over her shoulder. "They know you are. They followed me up here," she said in a hoarse whisper. With that, she opened the door and hurried out.

Right away, a man with a linebacker's neck, square jaw and small eyes set into a flat face stepped into view. "Mr. Lucas," he said. "We need to see you, sir. Right away."

"I'll be ready in a second," Brent said.

"Please do not use your phone, sir," the man said.

Brent felt his neck grow hot. "What the hell is going on?" he demanded.

"We'll explain when you talk to us."

"Well, I'm not ready yet!"

"Please be quick, sir," the agent said, as he backed out and closed the door.

Brent looked out the window through the blur of a sudden downpour. What the hell was going on? The FBI had no right to tell him not to make calls! He grabbed his cell phone and hit the autodial.

Simmons answered on the second ring. "What?"

"Some guys from the FBI are outside my office waiting to talk to me about one of my accounts. Do you know anything about this?"

There was a pause. "No."

"What do I do?"

"Talk to them. I'll make some calls and check it out."

Brent rang off, but instead of opening his office door, he called Betty Dowager, got Spencer McDonald's direct number and dialed.

"Spencer McDonald's office," a woman's voice said.

"This is Brent Lucas at Genesis Advisors, I need to speak with him.

"I'm sorry, but he's in conference."

"Please interrupt him. It's extremely important."

She put him on hold, and after a moment a man picked up. "This is McDonald. What's this about an emergency?"

"The FBI is outside my office, wanting to talk about one of my clients. I don't want to do it alone," Brent said.

"I'm afraid I can't get there until sometime this afternoon."

"They won't wait. They didn't even want me to make this call."

"Who is the client?"

"An Egyptian. Dr. Khaled Faisal."

"Foreign national." McDonald let out a heavy sigh. "You don't have a choice in that case. Hear them out and find out what they want. Before you agree to anything at all, call me back." He gave Brent a cell number.

"Just so you know, Dr. Faisal is one of our largest accounts," Brent said.

"Be as cooperative and respectful as possible," McDonald responded. "Your first responsibility is to protect the firm. You don't want the FBI to suspect you've got something to hide."

Brent hung up, went around his desk and opened his office door to find two men in dark suits, white shirts and sober ties. The big guy who'd already stuck his head in the office stepped forward. "Agent Tom Anderson," he said in a clipped voice. He was maybe six-two, a little shorter than Brent but probably thirty pounds heavier. Brent guessed him for early forties.

The other man introduced himself as Agent Darius Stewart. He was several inches shorter, thin and wiry by comparison to his partner, and his reddish hair and freckles made his age hard to guess. Anywhere from late thirties to late forties, Brent thought.

The two agents held up wallets with badges and FBI picture ID's. "We need to speak with you about Dr. Khaled Faisal," Agent Anderson said.

The way the two agents looked at him made him feel surprisingly furtive. His mouth was dry as he pointed them to chairs.

They sat, and Agent Stewart cleared his throat. "How long have you known Dr. Faisal?"

Brent shrugged. "Not long. I've only been with the firm a few weeks."

Agent Anderson made a note of Brent's answer. "How would you characterize the relationship?" Agent Stewart continued.

"Professional," Brent said.

"Ever been to his home?"

"No."

"Have you disbursed funds to Dr. Faisal or members of his family?"

"No," Brent said. He added, "Previously money was disbursed from the account, but never to Dr. Faisal or any member of his family."

"What were the reasons for the disbursements?" Anderson asked. He leaned forward, thick forearms on his thighs.

Brent was surprised by the hostility in the agent's eyes. "Humanitarian causes and peace projects," he shot back. He barely knew Dr. Faisal, but Anderson's attitude was getting under his skin.

Anderson raised his eyebrows in mock surprise. "Peace projects?" He shook his head slowly. "Sorry, sir, but no way."

"I beg to differ! It's in our correspondence file!" Brent said, feeling his cheeks grow hot.

Stewart leaned in. "What Agent Anderson is trying to say is that we've learned Dr. Faisal has been a major funding source for worldwide terrorism." He said it in a quiet voice, with none of his partner's venom.

Brent sat back. "That's insane! I've read the whole account history. The money has gone to the International Red

Cross, UNESCO projects, Doctors Without Borders, peace conferences."

"You know that because he told you that," Anderson interjected.

"No, I know it because I can read."

"You see where you think the money has gone," Anderson insisted.

"The last I knew the Red Cross wasn't a terrorist organization!"

Agent Stewart raised a calming hand. "We've learned that money transfers can be addressed to legitimate organizations yet sidetracked through the assistance of complicit bankers."

Brent suddenly felt less certain. "You've checked with the Red Cross and UNESCO and the others?"

Anderson cut a sideways look at Stewart, who nodded. "They never got the money."

Brent felt like he'd been slugged, and he sat back and rubbed his eyes. "I don't know what to say."

Stewart removed a stack of documents from his briefcase and placed them on the edge of Brent's desk. "I'm sure this is upsetting, but I assure you we do not suspect that Genesis Advisors or its employees were aware of what was happening."

Brent nodded. "I hadn't even thought of that," he said in a miserable tone.

"And I am aware that this is also a very large account with very large fees. I'm afraid there's nothing we can do about that."

Brent took his hands away from his eyes and looked across at the agent. "What do you mean?"

"We're seizing the account." Agent Stewart pointed to the stack of documents. "That's what this paperwork is all about."

"Dr. Faisal doesn't get a chance to at least defend himself?"

Anderson sniffed as though Brent had made a joke. "If he feels that we've seized his assets wrongly, he's welcome to make his case in court. He won't though because if he loses, he'll go to jail."

Brent was thinking he and the FBI were supposed to be on the same side, but in his guts it somehow didn't feel that way. "You're taking his money?"

"Yes."

"Our attorney needs to review those documents first."

Anderson gave him a withering look. "You don't tell the Federal Bureau of Investigation when we can carry out our orders."

Rather than respond, Brent picked up his phone and dialed Spencer McDonald's cell number. After two rings, McDonald answered, his voice hushed as if he was in a meeting. "Yes?"

"It's Lucas. The FBI is accusing Dr. Faisal–"

"Are they seizing the account?" McDonald interjected.

"They want to, but I'm trying to hold them off until you have a chance to get in here."

"Do they have court orders?"

Brent took the receiver away from his mouth. "Do you have court orders?"

Agent Stewart nodded.

"Let me talk to them," McDonald said.

Brent held the phone out for Agent Stewart, who stood and leaned across his desk. "This is Agent Darius Stewart," he said. He looked off into space as he listened to McDonald's question. "Yessir," he said after a few seconds. "They were issued under provisions of the Homeland Security Act and signed by Judge Slovenski of the New York Federal Court." He listened again for a few seconds. "Yessir," he said. "Dated this morning at nine fifteen." He listened, then nodded his head. "Yessir. Thank you, sir."

Stewart handed the phone to Brent. "For you," he said as he sat back in his chair.

"Sign the agreement," McDonald said to Brent. "We won't do any good fighting the seizure order, and right now the most important thing will be keeping this out of the papers. If we cooperate, the feds will keep their mouths shut. If we don't, you'll have reporters there in another couple hours."

"What about Dr. Faisal?" Brent asked, his voice hoarse with barely suppressed anger.

"One of those court orders is no doubt a gag order, forbidding you or anyone in the firm from communicating with your client until the FBI gives permission."

"So we let them take his money, and we don't even tell him

it's happened?"

"There's nothing we can do," McDonald said. "We'll get our ducks in a row and then fight this in court. I'll call you as soon as my meeting ends, and we'll get together."

Brent hung up and glared at Stewart, who paged through one of the documents and pointed to a red tape arrow. "We need your signature," he said.

Brent's neck swelled against his shirt collar, and he stared at the arrow.

"Sir?" Agent Stewart prodded after a minute.

Brent finally grabbed the paper and signed. Stewart flipped to the next arrow, and Brent continued until the stack was exhausted.

Stewart placed half the documents inside his briefcase and left duplicates for Brent. "One of the documents you signed—which by the way would have been binding in any case—is a court order forbidding any communication about this case with anyone outside or inside this firm. Failure to abide by that order is a felony. The other documents give us permission to transfer the account's assets into a Federal holding account until this matter is adjudicated."

"You didn't need my signature on those, either, did you?"

Stewart gave him a tight smile. "No, but it makes everything neater and provides evidence of your firm's willing cooperation."

"I'm so glad we could be of service."

Stewart ignored the sarcasm. "Willing support of your country is important," he said evenly.

"We'll be in touch with your superiors."

"By the way, Mr. Biddle won't have any problem with what we've done," Agent Anderson interjected as he rose from the chair and jerked his cuffs down over his meaty wrists. "He is a patriot and an excellent Christian."

"Good day, Mr. Lucas," Stewart said with a quick nod. Brent caught the admonishing glance he shot Anderson on their way out.

TWENTY-TWO

NEW YORK, JUNE 29

AS THE VAN swung onto the cross street and picked up speed, Naif Abdulaziz glanced into the dirt-streaked side mirror at where a rain-lashed Park Avenue lay behind them, snarled with endless lines of traffic. On the sidewalks pedestrians scurried as gusts of wind whipped at women's skirts and tore umbrellas inside out. Naif nodded in satisfaction. Conditions were perfect for his task, which meant that once again Allah's blessing would assure his success.

The van pulled to the curb in front of a fire hydrant, and the transmission clunked into park. The driver glanced over. He was a Christian holy man, only tonight he wore no collar, just a dirty coat and a tan rain hat whose wrinkled brim flopped down to obscure everything but a pair of wire-framed glasses, a broad jaw ringed with fat and full lips. "It's number twelve," he said.

For several moments Naif studied the large four-story townhouse with a façade of white marble and a small portico over the front door. Then he sat back, closed his eyes and pictured his mother and two little brothers standing before the schoolhouse where he once taught and dreamed of becoming a poet. He let the images harden and tasted the scarred emptiness in the part of his soul where gentle words had once made a garden. It was because of the Americans that he'd had to leave everything he loved—his family, his home, his students and his books—and as he focused on his loss a flash of hatred raced through his body. This was the feeling he was looking for, the way he fortified himself at the prospect of spilling blood.

He opened his eyes and looked again at the elegant townhouse, thinking that these people who loved their lives and their luxuries were about to learn what it was like to meet a true martyr. He buttoned his long coat and tugged the collar up around his face. Pulling on a rain hat similar to the one his driver wore, he slid his silenced Makarov 9mm pistol into one pocket and his combat knife into the other.

Finally, he crawled into the back of the van, took the bouquet of long-stemmed roses from their box, held them high to hide whatever parts of his face the raised collar and hat didn't conceal and stepped out the back door into the downpour. Movement was like a release, and the ironbound strength of his purpose flooded his heart. He lowered his head like any poor deliveryman without an umbrella and dashed for the front door of number twelve. He crowded close, shoulders hunched against the rain that blew beneath the small portico. As he rang the buzzer, he pretended to be unaware of the security camera above his head.

A voice came over the intercom box beside the doorbell. "Can I help you?" a man's voice asked, the accent European.

"Flower delivery," Naif said.

A moment later, footsteps crossed what sounded like a marble floor, and Naif slipped the knife from his pocket and held it out of sight behind the roses. The door had a heavy metal frame inset with tall glass panels fronted with protective metal bars. An inner door opened, and the gauze curtains showed a single silhouette.

A lock clicked and the door swung inward. A short man with a balding head, white shirt and apron over dark trousers smiled up at him. He held out one hand for the flowers, while his other hand tendered a five-dollar bill. As Naif extended the bouquet, he moved beyond the reach of the security camera. He released the flowers as he struck, shoving two fingers of his left hand into the butler's nostrils, giving the man's head a savage sideways jerk and slashing the knife along his exposed carotid artery and windpipe. Blood burst across the floor. Naif stepped to the butler's other side and eased him to the floor. The kill had been soundless.

He turned, scanned the sidewalk to make sure it was still empty then quickly pushed the door closed. Once the lock clicked, he grabbed the butler and dragged him by the collar into a dimly lit dining room at the back of the house.

From here a thin slit of light and the faint sound of voices leaked beneath a swinging door. Naif crossed to the door and stopped to listen, recognizing the canned laughter of a television show. He inched the door open and saw a butler's pantry and a kitchen beyond. A middle-aged woman stood at the kitchen's center island with her back toward him, watching a television mounted high on the wall as she chopped vegetables.

Naif opened the door just enough to slide inside, his crepe soles soundless on the tile floor. He checked around the corner to assure himself that the woman was alone, then with one quick step moved behind her, cupped her chin, forced her head back and cut her throat. Afterward he returned to the foyer where he stepped across the long smear of blood and started up the stairs.

The second floor landing opened into a large living room that went from the front to the back of the house. The room was mostly dark, but a shadowy illumination came through the tall windows, delineating ornate furniture and paintings in gilt frames. A triangle of bright light spilled through an open doorway at the back of the room, and Naif crept silently toward it until he could see into a library with wood-paneled walls and crowded floor-to-ceiling bookshelves.

Khaled Faisal sat in an oversized leather chair with a pair of glasses low on his nose and a book open on his lap. He had dozed off, and his chin touched his chest, which rose and fell peacefully.

Naif watched for several seconds then stepped into the room. "Traitor," he said in Arabic.

Faisal's head jerked up, and he blinked in surprise. As his eyes focused on Naif, a flash of fear glimmered, quickly replaced by anger. "Who are you?" he demanded.

"The Wahaddi Brotherhood sends its regards. You, the traitor who besmirches the greatness of Islam with your cowardly peace."

"You are the traitor," Faisal said.

Naif raised his pistol and pumped four bullets into the old man's chest, the sound echoing off the walls in spite of the silencer. Faisal slumped over as though he had once again fallen asleep, and Naif walked up to his chair, put the barrel an inch from his forehead and fired twice more.

Naif picked up his spent cartridges then went quickly through the rest of the house, making sure it was empty. Afterward, he hurried down the stairs, and leaving the door slightly ajar as he had been instructed, walked outside.

He climbed into the passenger seat of the van, glanced at the driver and jerked his head. "Go."

"Successful?" the man asked.

Naif nodded.

"Good," the man said.

As they pulled away from the curb, Naif put one hand against his ribcage where his heart bucked like a trapped beast. His arteries burned with the rocket fuel of his anger. At that moment, he felt feral, lethal as a Nile crocodile. He dropped his hand to his pocket and fingered the hilt of his combat knife. Once the killing had started, it was so easy to keep going.

He took a shuddering breath. The man beside him had no idea. Christian, he wanted to say, only the restraining hand of Abu Sayeed lets you draw breath for one more day.

TWENTY-THREE

NEW YORK, JUNE 29

HAVING SIGNED THE documents, Brent was too full of anger to think clearly. He yearned to lash out, especially at the larger of the two agents. It took all his self-control not to slug the bastard, and he felt a burst of relief when Betty Dowager showed up at his office door. She offered to accompany the agents over to the custodian bank where they would complete the seizure of Dr. Faisal's account.

He waited for them to leave then called Simmons. "They just appropriated my client's account," he said.

"Apparently they're working some sort of terrorism case," she said. "It takes precedence over any financial crimes, so there's nothing I can do. Just go along with them and don't blow your cover."

Brent hung up then looked up the number of the Manhattan FBI office. His hope died completely when the receptionist there transferred him to Darius Stewart's line and he listened to Stewart's voice mail announcement. Until that moment he'd harbored a wild hope that Stewart and Anderson were scam artists of some kind.

He slammed the phone into its cradle then marched down to Betty Dowager's desk and waited for her to return. When she finally did, he told her to get Biddle on the phone.

"What do you think I've been trying to do," she snapped. She dialed again, then shook her head, saying his phone was still turned off. She tried to object, but Brent saw Biddle's number on her computer screen and copied it onto a scrap of paper.

His next stop was Fred Wofford's assistant, who said that he, too, was out of touch and unreachable. The woman seemed anxious, and he suspected Wofford knew about the FBI's visit but wanted no part of handling it. Typical Wofford, he thought, as he went back to his office, stared out at the rain and thought again about the old man he'd met at Biddle's party and all the money he'd spent for world peace. Records of his gifts were everywhere. Dr. Faisal was no more a terrorist than he was! Complicit bankers–bullshit! The longer he sat, the madder he became.

How was it possible that in the United States of America the Federal Government could seize a person's property then threaten witnesses with jail if they reported it? To hell with them all–the FBI, Justice Department and screw his cover. It was patently wrong, and he was equally at fault if he sat back and did nothing. With that, he stormed out of his office and burst through Owen Smythe's door.

Smythe glanced up and shot him a questioning look. "Is the rumor true?" He studied Brent's face a few seconds then nodded. "FBI?"

Brent slammed the door then collapsed into a chair. "The sons of bitches!" He proceeded to tell Smythe everything about the FBI's visit, his attempt to get Biddle and his conversation with Spencer McDonald.

When he finished Smythe sat forward and put his elbows on the desk. "We just let the FBI take it?" He sounded shocked.

"Eight hundred and twenty million. All cash because we just sold him out of the market. Nice and neat." Brent scowled and made a signing motion. "Poof, the whole thing just walks out the door with no argument."

"Sounds like a movie," Smythe said.

Brent was about to agree when there was a knock on Smythe's door and Betty Dowager put her head inside. Her glance took in both men, and her expression became severe. "Mr. Biddle is on the phone," she said in a cold voice, as if she knew he'd already violated the gag order. "The call is coming to your office."

Brent felt Betty's eyes burning into his back as he ran next door, but he didn't care. "Give me the details," Biddle barked as soon as he picked up the phone.

Brent filled him in on all of it.

"What did Spencer say?"

"To let them take it."

"Then it was the right thing to do," Biddle said without hesitation. "I trust his judgment implicitly."

"I'm glad you do. We've let the government walk out with our client's money without doing a thing."

"I'm sure Spencer realized that now was not the time to fight."

"Well, I want to know when it will be."

"When Spencer tells us. I want you to sit down with him as soon as he's available and let him review the documents."

Something about Biddle's tone troubled him, a sound of finality, as if certain unfavorable conclusions had already been drawn. "I assume we're going to support our client. Dr. Faisal is no terrorist."

"The FBI will have to tell us that," Biddle said.

"Dr. Faisal entrusted us with his money!" Brent said, feeling his temper begin to rise. "He deserves our full backing until the facts are in!"

"We also need to protect the firm," Biddle said. "We will do what is right, but for now, the first thing is for you to meet with Spencer as soon as possible."

There was a brief silence. Brent could hear the hissing of their sat-phone connection. "By the way," Biddle added, "I'm sure there's a gag order surrounding this, but in any case we don't need it getting out. You haven't told anybody, have you?"

"No," Brent lied.

At exactly three o'clock, Brent stood at the bay window in Genesis Advisors' first floor reception room and watched a silver Mercedes S500 pull to the curb. He held his umbrella over his head, rushed out through the rain and opened the passenger side door.

"Brent Lucas?" the man behind the wheel asked. When Brent nodded, he reached out his hand. "Spencer McDonald."

Brent guessed McDonald was in his late fifties. He had a pale complexion, a swelling stomach and thinning gray hair that had once been light brown. His blue eyes hid their cleverness behind wire rim glasses, and a ring of soft fat at the neck almost camouflaged the stubbornness of his jaw.

"I hope you intend to fight this," Brent fumed, "because I certainly do."

McDonald pulled away from the curb. "I understand how you feel; however, the last thing we need right now is anger or irrationality."

"I can be pissed off without being irrational," Brent snapped.

McDonald said nothing as he turned left on Fifth Avenue and followed the flow of traffic downtown. They turned right on Sixty-Fifth and headed across Central Park, then turned south again. Brent assumed they were headed to an office somewhere on the west side, but then McDonald surprised him by turning into the Lincoln Tunnel. "Where are we going?" he demanded.

"My house."

"Why?"

McDonald drew a ragged breath as he slowed behind the line of barely moving cars. When Brent glanced over he could see a line of sweat along McDonald's hairline. The man smelled as if he'd just run several miles. McDonald seemed to sense the examination. "I've had a very bad day," he said tersely.

"So have I," Brent shot back.

"Look, if this case involves the war on terrorism, I don't trust the walls of my office."

"Come on," Brent scoffed. "You can't believe the government's bugging us!"

McDonald shrugged, his eyes on the traffic ahead. "Better safe than sorry."

Out the other end of the tunnel, they drove south on the New Jersey Turnpike, then west on Route 280 to the Oranges. The real estate became fancier and the properties larger as they headed into West Orange, and McDonald finally turned between two brick gateposts into the long driveway of a multi-acre estate. They parked on a graveled circle in front of a large house with white columns.

McDonald led the way through the front door then down a long hall to a paneled library. He sat behind an antique desk and pointed Brent to an overstuffed chair. In spite of the grandness of the house, Brent found its atmosphere oddly sterile. The desk held a scattering of papers but no mementos or family photographs, nothing of an idiosyncratic or personal nature.

Also, the room had a stuffy odor, as though it had been closed up too long. The bookshelves held expensive leather bound volumes, the kind people liked to show off but never seemed to read. The paintings on the walls were bland as hotel art, suggesting nothing of what Spencer McDonald loved or did in his spare hours. Brent envisioned a guy who'd spent too many years working the brutal hours of a Manhattan attorney, who'd created enough wealth to buy this impressive house but never had the time to build a life.

Brent waited while McDonald studied the FBI's seizure documents. His hands shook noticeably as he read, as though he suffered from Parkinson's Disease. Finally, he looked up and scowled. "Well, it's tight. They did their homework."

"What's it based on?"

"Secret testimony."

"Come off it! Not in America!"

"Welcome to the war on terrorism."

"We have to fight it!"

McDonald said nothing.

"We have to fight it," Brent repeated.

"Not if Prescott Biddle says we don't," McDonald said at last.

"Did you talk to him? Is that what he said?"

"If it becomes public that one of your largest international accounts has been seized by the government, other international accounts might consider pulling out." McDonald looked at him and blinked slowly. "The losses could be significant."

"Let me tell you what would be a whole lot worse," Brent shot back. "That people find out we didn't lift a finger to stop it!"

McDonald rubbed a finger across his chin then folded his hands together in a gesture of finality. "That won't happen, assuming we can trust the discretion of everyone involved."

"So you and Biddle want to walk away from my client?" Brent asked in a stinging tone.

"Well . . . I don't know if I'd call it walking away."

Brent turned and looked through the window. He didn't know if McDonald was still talking because there was a noise in his head like a hive of angry bees. "I need to get back to my office."

"One last thing, Mr. Lucas."

Brent turned slowly and saw that McDonald had fixed him with a harsh stare. "What?" he snapped.

"You're making it very clear that you don't agree with Mr. Biddle's decision on this matter. Regardless of your personal feelings, there is the government's gag order to consider." McDonald paused, pursing his lips.

"What about it?"

"You need to obey it."

Brent shrugged. "I'll try."

McDonald's voice took on a warning note. "You need to do better than try."

TWENTY-FOUR

PROJECT SEAHAWK, NEWARK, NJ, JUNE 29

AGENT JENKINS PACED the floor of her tiny office, her heels catching on the frayed polyester carpet each time she turned. She'd been arguing with herself for the past twenty minutes—dying to pick up the phone and call her boss, but resisting because it had been only six days since the poor bastard's open-heart surgery.

Finally, deciding to spare him, she called FBI headquarters in Washington. She waited to get through to the Executive Assistant Director in charge of Counterterrorism and Counterintelligence, and then told the man in no uncertain terms that she needed her people off the POTUS assignment and back on port security. She cited the CIA memo, saying she had to assume it was serious and accurate.

The EAD sidestepped and said it was out of his control because she and her staff now reported through the chain of command at Homeland Security and Department of Justice. Jenkins swallowed her desire to tell the EAD where to stick it. Instead, she thanked him and called the Undersecretary for Border and Transportation Security at Homeland Security, someone she'd wanted to avoid because she knew from previous dealings that he was a political hack with neither law enforcement expertise nor guts.

She made the same request, but the Undersecretary coughed and cleared his throat then reminded her that the Threat Advisory System was at yellow. The President's staff wanted it to remain there, he said, and her request was not consistent with a yellow threat level. With the President's trip imminent, it was vital that her staff help with routine security checks.

Jenkins suggested that rather than worrying about the nicety of keeping the threat level unchanged, they should worry about keeping the President safe. At that point the Undersecretary's voice became icy. Did Jenkins feel prepared to stake her career on her recommendation? The Undersecretary suggested that Agent Jenkins should think long and hard. It could be a lonely position, he said.

Jenkins hung up and resumed pacing.

TWENTY-FIVE

OYSTER BAY, LONG ISLAND, JUNE 29

ABU SAYEED SAT alone in the silent cottage, perched atop the missile crate where he'd spent much of the day. The weapons fixated him, drew him with a kind of magical intensity. He felt seduced by their power, the psychological devastation they would wreak.

He yearned to lift the cover off the crate, remove one of the weapons and embrace its deadly symmetry, as if that might distract him somehow from his error in judgment. Naif! He should never have permitted him to go off with the Christian minister. Too many things could go wrong, and Naif was far too important to the mission.

He sat a while longer, struggling with his anxiety, until finally the stillness became more than he could bear and he took out his cell phone and dialed.

In only seconds he heard the welcome sound of Naif's voice. "The objective is in sight."

Abu Sayeed turned his eyes to heaven. Thanks be to Allah. "Take great care, my brother," Abu Sayeed ordered. "Allah blesses you." He clicked off.

He stood, felt the stiffness in his legs and went to the window where he moved the blackout shade to peek out at the rain-splattered courtyard, wondering at the whereabouts of his hidden sentry. This endless waiting ate at all of them but wore hardest on Mohammed, whose troubled emotions had always been too close to the surface. Unfortunately, his time in the shipping crate had only made things worse.

Mohammed's lack of control was the reason he'd had to send Naif on today's mission, a silly errand that he knew was superfluous to Allah's greater purpose. Only, it had been part of his agreement with Biddle and something he therefore could not avoid. The murder of Khaled Faisal was at best a gesture of vanity, and the killing of the other man was for Biddle's benefit alone. What did any of that matter if they failed in their holy purpose?

Unable to stand his own anxiety and the imprisoning cottage walls, he opened the door and went out. The pounding rain wet his face and hair and soaked him to the skin almost at once. He glanced around, but Mohammed was invisible, concealed in the trees where he could watch the driveway for approaching vehicles and at the same time see anyone entering the courtyard from the other side.

Abu Sayeed walked to where the opening in the tall hedge gave a view of the water. Rain dripped from his nose and ran into his eyes as he searched for the outline of Biddle's yacht. It was tied to the long dock only seventy-five yards away but nearly invisible in the mist.

He stared at its faint shape, filled with a sudden premonition that the winds of fortune were shifting ever so slightly and beginning to blow against him. Allah had blessed him to this point, but he sensed that sending Naif on a fool's errand was an insult to God and meant there would be danger now where there had been none before. Because of it, once darkness fell, they would move the missiles back onto to Biddle's yacht.

Over the past days Abu Sayeed and his men had crept over every inch of Biddle's estate. They knew the schedules of the private security detail, when they changed shifts and went on their breaks. Moving the missiles would be riskless.

Biddle had purchased another smaller boat for them to use in their attack. Of course, he assumed they would die on it like typical Arab suicide bombers. Amazingly, Biddle seemed to have no inkling that they might have another plan. The thought made Abu Sayeed smile. A month earlier he had leased a Hatteras 100' in Beirut, and his team had trained on a yacht identical to Biddle's. After all, Allah blessed the prepared and crafty warrior.

TWENTY-SIX

PROJECT SEAHAWK, NEWARK, NJ, JUNE 29

MAGGIE STIFLED A yawn as she pulled together her paperwork and sorted reports into a thick accordion file with a pocket for every agency that was part of Project Seahawk—the FBI, the CIA, the Bureau of Immigration and Customs Enforcement, the Bureau of Customs and Border Protection, the ATF, the Coast Guard, the New York/New Jersey Ports Authority Police, New Jersey State Police, New York State Police, New York City Police, the U.S. Marshal Service. It went on and on.

Her assignment was to analyze the flow of information, particularly issues of compartmentalization and data processing incompatibilities. Often, different agencies possessed bits of information on the same situation, but the data was never combined. Because no one saw the "big picture," potential threats went undetected.

Maggie sighed as she looked at the bulging folder. The task was undeniably important, but she found the endless examination of procedural details and software protocols stultifying. Her background in computer science made her an excellent choice for the job, and her superiors in Morristown considered it a huge compliment to have one of their officers chosen for Project Seahawk. However, it was only her third day, and she already missed being a real cop, getting out on the streets and working cases.

With the file packed she stood and stretched, thinking at least tonight she would get in a good workout, something she'd missed since the weekend. Exercise relaxed her, blew the dust off her brain cells, and God knew between job tedium and thinking about Brent there'd been enough "stuff" these past few days to gum up the works.

Brent had been on her mind entirely too much. She kept thinking about his phone call the other night, fantasizing that maybe he'd thought things over and wanted to get back together.

Only, she hadn't given him a chance to say it, and now maybe the moment had passed. She shook her head. Stop being pathetic, she told herself.

She was walking out of her cubicle when her cell phone rang. She stopped, pulled it off her belt and glanced at the readout. The caller I.D. showed a New York City area code and a number she didn't recognize. Her first instinct was to ignore it, let the caller leave a message, but after another second she answered.

"Maggie," Brent said, his voice unmistakable.

Her pulse quickened. She heard horns and the rasp of a bus engine in the background.

"I need to talk to you," Brent said. "I was hoping I could drive out tonight when you're done with work."

She heard it again, the same ragged tone as the other night, only worse. He sounded worried, which got her attention because Brent was one of the most self-confident people she'd ever met. Self-confident but mortally fearful of commitments, she reminded herself.

A glance at her watch showed it was already six forty-five. "I'll be home around eight," she said, deciding her workout could wait.

"I'll be there," he said.

Five minutes later, she was waiting at the elevator when the Shift Commander flagged her. "Main conference room in ten minutes. Jenkins' orders. Everybody."

Maggie could tell from his face that something was up. She started to ask how long it might take, but he'd disappeared down the hall. She headed down to the meeting room, really more auditorium than conference room with a big rectangular table in the middle and then forty or so theater-style seats facing a wall that held several projection screens. She sat with the more junior people in the theater seats, while the honchos took their places around the table. She looked around at the puzzled expressions.

"Hope you didn't have dinner plans," said a voice beside her.

She turned to see Steve Kosinsky as he settled into the adjoining seat. He was a Lieutenant in the New York State Police, a nice-looking guy with big shoulders, crunch-toned stomach, and an earnest face. She knew he was divorced with no kids because he'd asked her out to dinner twice. She'd turned him down, refusing to date people from work.

"The one night when I'm supposed to meet somebody," she groaned.

"Word has it Jenkins has a major hard-on about something," Steve said. "The last time this happened we didn't get out of here for two days."

"You're not serious?"

He shrugged.

Maggie glanced at her watch and remembered Brent. He was probably on the road by now. She went to the last call on her cell phone and hit the callback button.

"Where are you?" she asked when he answered.

"Stuck in traffic on the West Side Highway."

"Something's come up," she said. "A meeting. I don't know how long it will last."

"I can wait."

Maggie glanced at Steve. "I'm told it may go very late," she said.

"Right," Brent said.

She heard the disappointment but also disbelief. He thought she was blowing him off.

"I'm sorry," she said. "I really am."

"Yeah, me too."

Just then Ann Jenkins stepped to the podium and the overhead lights began to dim. "Gotta go," Maggie whispered. "Maybe we can do it tomorrow night?"

"I can't wait 'til tomorrow night," Brent said, cutting the connection.

Maggie sat there feeling helpless. There was nothing she could do.

"We've received a threat warning from CIA Europe that the Wahaddi Brotherhood may have gotten their hands on some dirty weapons," Jenkins announced, causing the room to fall silent. "Previously, the CIA claimed these guys had no more money because their bank accounts were seized, but it looks like they might have missed a billion dollars or so. French police reported the disappearance of a motorcycle cop and an ambulance a couple hours outside of Paris, and a few hours ago they discovered the ambulance and some bodies in a warehouse outside Le Havre. They also picked up trace radioactive readings in the ambulance. There's concern in London and Paris that the weapons may be there, but my gut tells me they're headed here." She paused and looked around.

"My superiors don't agree. Homeland Security is holding the threat level at yellow, and we still have a POTUS visit in three days." She scowled when she said this as if POTUS was a communicable disease. "I don't know what the other Project Seahawk districts will decide, but as of now we're going to Condition Red, meaning double shifts on all port and ship inspection teams. I'm sorry, people, but I believe we have no other choice."

"If this is such a big deal, how about pulling our guys off the POTUS security teams," somebody suggested.

"Already tried," Jenkins snapped. "Request denied."

Muffled groans came from several of the Ports Authority cops in the back row because Jenkins's announcement meant they'd get almost no sleep for the next few days. Maggie glanced over her shoulder, giving one of the men—the father of a new set of twins—a sympathetic grin.

Beside her, Kosinsky snorted. "She's just climbed out on a skinny limb," he muttered.

Maggie shrugged. In spite of the inconvenience, she felt a grudging admiration at how Jenkins had just taken full responsibility for an unpopular decision. "You have to give her credit. She's got a set of brass balls."

"Balls don't look good on women," Kosinsky whispered.

He groaned a second later when Maggie's elbow caught him in the ribs.

TWENTY-SEVEN

NEW YORK, JUNE 29

BRENT BROKE THE connection, dropped his cell phone on the passenger seat, then glared at the stagnant river of brake lights ahead. He wasn't sure what to think. It wasn't like Maggie to make phony excuses.

He glanced toward the passenger seat where Harry slouched against the door and gave him a disgusted look. *What you expect, bro?* Harry asked. *You had your chance. She's a beautiful woman. You think she's gonna hang out for a bonehead who won't commit?*

"It wasn't gonna work anyway," Brent countered. "She wanted kids."

So?

"So, bad idea."

Bullshit!

"Okay, then why didn't you get married?"

Harry shook his head. *Sooner or later you always bring it back to Mom.*

"I didn't even mention Mom, but as long as you bring her up, I guess women who try and toast their own kids are completely normal?

She was trying to kill herself, idiot! She wasn't thinking about us!

"Okay, you made my point for me. Lucases never think about their families. What did you think about when you ran up those stairs? What did Dad think about?"

Are you just stupid on purpose?

A horn sounded behind him. Brent blinked and saw the cars ahead already moving. He threw a glance at the empty seat beside him and, feeling a fresh blast of resentment at his brother for letting himself get killed, he began to inch forward.

After a half mile, he exited the highway at West 136th Street. Southbound traffic on Riverside Drive was light, but he took his time. He'd already made up his mind that he wouldn't go along with the FBI's gag order; however, he'd hoped to talk it through with Maggie before he actually went to Dr. Faisal. Now there'd be no chance.

Twenty minutes later, he looked up at the dark windows of his client's house. It appeared no one was home, but he went to the door and rang the bell. He waited then pushed the button a second time, hearing the muted chimes through the thick, barred glass. A security camera looked down from just overhead, and he tilted his face so anyone inside could see him.

He rang a third time, then put his face to the bars and saw a glimmer of light coming from the back of the house. As he pushed against the door, it moved slightly.

He looked around instinctively, but the sidewalk was empty—no dog walkers or pedestrians, no one watching. He pushed the heavy door, and it swung inward a few inches. "Hello?" he called, as he stepped into the darkened entrance, half expecting an alarm to go off or someone to start shouting, but there was only silence. He tried to tell himself that someone had simply been careless, but people in Manhattan never left their doors unlocked, especially people in ten million dollar townhouses.

"Dr. Faisal?" he called. His voice echoed back out of the emptiness. He stepped through an inner door then inched his hand along the wall until he found a light switch and flicked it on. An overhead chandelier lit the room and drew his eyes to the jagged smear of dried blood on the marble floor.

His pulse began to hammer. He touched his belt, but he'd left his cell phone on the car seat. He considered going back, but he'd parked nearly a block away. Instead, he pushed the outer door closed and followed the blood trail into a dining room with a long formal table. Light and the sound of a TV came from a doorway to his right.

He crept ahead and looked through the butler's pantry at a pair of legs splayed on the kitchen floor. He moved closer, seeing the body of an Asian woman. She was wearing a white cook's smock, her head in a pool of congealed blood. Her eyes were open, staring, her skin almost the color of paste.

He took several steps back through the butler's pantry, and when he turned he spotted a hand sticking out from behind one of the tall dining room doors. He walked around the door and saw that the second corpse was a middle-aged man with a gaping wound at his throat.

He braced his hands against the wall and sucked air into his lungs for a moment then went back to the entry hall and forced himself up the marble staircase. He found a light switch on the second floor landing and moved through a pair of double doors into a large formal living room, toward the lighted doorway at the far end.

His pulse thundered in his ears, as he came around the corner and spotted Dr. Faisal in an overstuffed chair, an open book at his feet. A reading lamp behind the doctor's head carved a bright circle of light and highlighted the bloodstains on his white shirt and the two holes in his forehead.

Brent stared, unable to move, his mind filled with wild conjectures but also a feral outrage that anyone had done this to an old man who'd spent his fortune making peace.

Finally, full of fresh fear that Dr. Faisal's granddaughter might also be there, he went back to the landing and climbed to the top two floors. He walked through a large master suite with an office and small sitting room as well as four other bedrooms. Thankfully, they were empty.

As his brain slowly calmed, one question remained. Was this some terrible coincidence, or was it somehow connected to the seizure of the doctor's account? He was sure he knew the answer—there were no such things as coincidences.

He was walking down the stairs when it hit him. His hands! He'd touched everything—doorknobs, light switches, the wall in the dining room, woodwork and banisters! He'd even looked into the security camera when he rang the bell. Was his face on film?

His mind began to race as he walked out of the house and down the sidewalk toward his car. He was bonded like everyone in the financial industry, his fingerprints filed with the FBI. The minute the police dusted the house they'd have a match. What if the real killers had been more careful and left no trace? If that was true—since there was no sign of forced entry and since he'd known Dr. Faisal—he would be the only suspect.

He tried to slow his brain and think rationally. A number of old classmates from Yale had gone to law school, but they were almost all securities, tax or estate lawyers. One was doing legal aid work in Texas, but otherwise he didn't know a single criminal attorney, not one, and besides, only guilty people ran straight to lawyers. Nobody had even accused him . . . yet.

Next, he thought about Simmons. She would be his alibi! She could tell the FBI and the police why he was working at Genesis Advisors!

He reached his car, fumbled for his cell phone and punched in the emergency contact number Simmons had programmed into it. The number rang and rang. He killed the call and dialed a second time. Again no answer. How was that possible?

He shook off the panic he was starting to feel and decided to contact the two FBI agents, Stewart and Anderson. He'd talk with them before the police found his prints, explain that he was working for Simmons, that he'd found the doctor already dead. The agents would understand. Ironically, their testimony might be the only thing that could clear him.

TWENTY-EIGHT

NEW YORK, JUNE 29

BRENT HUNCHED IN his darkened car and punched out Agent Stewart's number on his cell phone. As it rang he looked up the block at a couple walking their black lab in front of Dr. Faisal's front steps. The dog pulled against its leash and began to sniff. Brent froze, fearing that it would smell dead bodies and start to howl, but the owner gave the leash a tug and moved off. Brent let out the breath he'd been holding then realized that the phone was still ringing and no voice mail had picked up. He checked the number and redialed. No answer. Same result as Simmons. Government inefficiency, he thought. Probably it would be fixed by morning, but he couldn't wait.

He considered his options. He could call the FBI's central number, but the night duty officer wouldn't put him through to Stewart's home, not unless Brent disclosed the reason for his call, which he wasn't about to do. Even if they promised to relay his message, it might be hours before Stewart got back to him.

He checked Stewart's business card. The address was Avenue of the Americas somewhere in the high Fifties. If he showed up in person, even if they wouldn't call Stewart's house, he could at least demand to see another agent. He needed a face-to-face meeting with another human being to tell his story. One way or another, the FBI had to understand that he was innocent.

Twenty minutes later, he parked in a loading zone on a side street less than half a block from Stewart's building. As he climbed out of his car, a light-colored van cruised slowly past. He would have paid no attention, but he caught the guy in the passenger seat giving him an intense stare. It made him feel strangely furtive, but he shook it off then hurried up the block and through the front doors to the night security desk in the lobby.

"Fourteenth floor—FBI," he told the guard as he prepared to sign in.

The guard put his hand over the sign in book. "FBI?"

Brent nodded.

The guard shook his head. "Ain't this building."

Brent reached for his wallet and extracted Stewart's card, pointing to the address and floor number. The guard looked at it then shook his head. "Don't care what it says. We ain't got no FBI."

Brent took back the card. "Who's on the fourteenth floor?" he demanded.

"Law firm."

"Which one?" Brent challenged, certain the guard was mistaken.

The guard pointed impatiently at the tenant listing on the wall beside the elevator banks. "Tweed, Barker."

Brent stepped to the roster, which confirmed that Tweed, Barker and Rowe occupied floors ten through sixteen. His stomach went cold at what appeared to be such an odd coincidence. Could a printing company have made a mistake when Agent Stewart ordered new cards? It seemed a ludicrous explanation.

He asked the guard for a Manhattan phone directory and looked up the listing for the FBI. Their only address was 26 Federal Plaza in lower Manhattan. He pulled out his cell phone and dialed the main number. Again, there was no answer. "Is there a pay phone?" he asked.

The guard pointed across the lobby to several phones beside a shuttered magazine stand. Brent went over, dropped some change in the slot and re-dialed the number.

A night operator answered immediately, and Brent asked for Agent Darius Stewart's extension. The operator put him on hold, and when she came back she told him there was no Darius Stewart in the Manhattan office.

Brent took a deep breath, a fresh flame of panic burning in his guts. There had to be an explanation. Maybe Stewart worked out of Washington. When he asked for Tom Anderson's extension and got the same response, he asked the operator to check the national record. She typed for a time before telling him that there were a number of Stewarts, but no Darius. The only Tom Anderson was a programmer, not a field agent.

Brent hung up. Back at the security desk he said to the guard, "I need to go up to the reception desk at Tweed, Barker and Rowe."

"It's after hours. You got business?"

"My attorney works there." Brent heard the lack of conviction in his tone.

The guard's expression was careful. "Why don't you call 'em in the morning?" he asked, raising his voice a little.

The second guard had been casually flipping through pages of *The New York Post*, but now he raised his eyes and cast Brent a wary glance. At six-four, two-twenty, even in a suit he undoubtedly looked threatening to a couple of overweight security guards. Fearing they'd call the police if he pushed any further, he walked outside, ignored the rain and headed toward a pay phone on the corner.

A call to information gave him Tweed, Barker and Rowe's number, and a second later he asked the firm's night receptionist for Spencer McDonald. Manhattan lawyers worked the same crazy hours as investment people, so it would be nothing unusual for McDonald to be there at eight o'clock on a weeknight. The extension rang until McDonald's voice mail answered. "This is Spencer McDonald," it said. "I will be out of the country for approximately three weeks beginning . . ."

Brent's breath caught. He gripped the receiver as if he could choke out the truth. He wanted to call back and listen to the recording again, but nothing would change. Spencer McDonald had a deep baritone and a thick southern accent, very different from the flat, slightly nasal tone of the lawyer who had taken him to New Jersey.

He knew it was fruitless, but he called the firm's main number one more time. "Mr. McDonald's still out of the country?"

"Yes, Europe for two more weeks."

"And you couldn't have more than one Spencer McDonald?"

"I'm sorry," the receptionist replied.

Brent knuckled his eyes. How was it possible–three people dead, Faisal's money seized, the FBI agents vanished, Spencer McDonald . . . what? . . . an imposter?

He felt a surreal dread in his guts as he hurried to his car and fumbled for the scrap of paper with Biddle's cell number from his briefcase. He dialed, got Biddle's recording and left no message. Wofford was the only other choice, so he looked him up in the firm directory and dialed his mobile number.

On the third ring, he heard Wofford's drawl. "Hello?"

"Fred!" He took a deep breath, struggling to sound calm because what he was about to say was so unbelievable. "It's Brent Lucas. I need to talk to you about–"

"Lucas!" Wofford snarled. "What the hell have you done?"

Brent opened his mouth, but at first no words came. Could Wofford already know about the bodies? "What?" he managed at last.

"We're onto you! We know you wired Faisal's money out of the country! How long have you planned this?"

Brent was too stunned to reply.

"This is how you repay Biddle's trust?" Wofford continued. "You're not going to get away with this! Where did you send the damn money, Lucas?"

Brent's hands were shaking. "I didn't send it anywhere! I swear! The FBI took it!"

"According to Betty, you gave wire instructions!"

"Betty's lying!" Brent shouted. "I released the money to the FBI! It was their wire instructions! I talked to Prescott! I–"

"Lucas!" Wofford said sharply. "You're a wanted man! Turn yourself in!"

Brent clicked off and knuckled his eyes. His lungs couldn't seem to get enough air. This had to be some kind of hallucination. He tried to think analytically, but his brain refused. Wofford's words echoed in his ears–Faisal's account transferred out of the country on his signature!

He thought of Betty Dowager. Had she planned this? Otherwise, why would she lie? He looked up her number and dialed.

A man answered on the first ring.

"Betty Dowager, please."

"Who is this?" he demanded.

"Brent Lucas. It's urgent."

"You!" he exclaimed. "You've put her through a terrible time! Mrs. Dowager is extremely upset! She isn't well enough to come to the phone."

"Look, I'm innocent, and she may be the only one who can help me! It's extremely important."

"She's sedated. She's already asleep, and I'm not about to wake her."

"Please!"

The man's voice went up several octaves, betraying his tension. "I just told you, she's not going to talk to you! Now don't call here again!"

There was a click, and the line went dead.

TWENTY-NINE

NEW YORK, JUNE 29

FROM THE BENCH beneath the sycamores on the west side of Fifth Avenue, the Genesis Advisors' building appeared stately and peaceful, an island of stability in the midst of New York's bustle. What crap, Brent thought.

It was eight forty-five, about the time he'd hoped to meet Maggie in Morristown, but he was perched here instead. The rain had stopped, and now a gentle wind fingered the leaves overhead. Evening strollers and dog walkers had come out, and they filed slowly past along the wet sidewalk. Behind him, Central Park lay vast and silent, filling the night with the peaceful smell of wet earth. Brent was immune. His mouth was dry, and his pulse jack-hammered as he stared at the light burning in Owen Smythe's office.

He was praying Smythe was still there. He hadn't seen him come out, even though most nights Smythe left around now. Of course, tonight he was probably doing damage control, making calls to warn clients in advance of tomorrow's headlines. Brent pictured front-pages of *The Daily News* and *The New York Times* reporting that a portfolio manager at Genesis Advisors had stolen eight hundred and fifty million dollars. The entire world would assume his guilt. Once they found the bodies he'd be a murderer, too.

He thought again about calling a lawyer, but what would he say? I'm a victim of mysterious people who killed my client and stole his money. Without a shred of supporting evidence, who would buy it? He rocked back and forth on the bench, and his anger hardened into an almost physical pain. Somebody had set him up. He had no idea who, but he was going to find out. There'd be plenty of time for a lawyer after he'd made them pay.

A little after nine, the front door opened and a tall figure came down the steps and turned east. Brent stood then dodged several speeding cars as he hurried across Fifth. He trotted along the opposite sidewalk until Smythe reached the middle of the block, then he crossed the street and came up behind him, thankful there was no one else nearby.

"Owen," he said. "Wait!"

Smythe spun, his eyes wide going with fear. He gripped his briefcase and held it to his chest as if Brent were an assailant. "What do you want?" he demanded.

"I need to talk to you."

"They said you'd left the country."

"Why would I leave?"

Smythe's mouth opened and closed, but no sound came out.

"Why would I leave?" Brent repeated.

Smythe shrugged.

"I didn't take that money."

"Okay," Smythe said. He dared a quick look at Brent's hands.

"You think I did?" Brent demanded.

"I . . ." Smythe gave another helpless shrug. He threw a desperate glance over his shoulder toward Park Avenue with its stream of pedestrians.

Brent grabbed Smythe's arm. "I started to tell you what happened when I came into your office. You remember that?"

Smythe tried to twist his arm free. "Let go or I'll yell for the police," he hissed. "They're looking for you!"

"I didn't do it!" Brent snapped, keeping his grip. "If I'd stolen the money, I would have gone straight to the airport and gotten the hell out of the country, but I didn't! That's why I'm talking to you now!"

Smythe seemed to take that in, and then after a few seconds he nodded. "Wofford told everybody that the FBI guys were fakes, that you masterminded it."

"No!" Brent gave his head a violent shake. "I thought they were real until just a little while ago. Same with the lawyer that Biddle told me to call."

Smythe had lowered his briefcase by now and was listening with a puzzled expression. "What lawyer?"

"Spencer McDonald? You've met him, right?"

Smythe nodded.

"What's he look like?"

Smythe shrugged. "Tall, thin, patrician."

Brent shook his head. "Not the guy who came to meet me." He finally let go of Smythe's arm. If he still wanted to run, Brent wouldn't stop him.

"This is unbelievable," Smythe said, rubbing his arm where Brent had gripped it. "You've . . . you've been set up."

"It's a lot worse." Brent hesitated, but then he told about finding Dr. Faisal and the other two bodies.

Smythe listened with a stunned expression.

"I wouldn't be telling you this if I were guilty," Brent said. "You're logical enough to realize that." He paused, hoping for some sign of acceptance in Smythe's eyes. "I've got to find a way to clear myself."

"You need to get a lawyer then go to the police."

"I've got nothing, other than the knowledge that I've been framed. I need some kind of proof."

Smythe shook his head, finally getting it. "If I help you I'll go to jail, too."

"I helped you when you needed it!" Brent cried. "You could be dead right now if those guys had knifed you."

Smythe glanced back at Park Avenue again, as if part of him wanted to run before he heard any more. Finally, his shoulders slumped. "What do you want me to do?"

"All I have are phone numbers that the FBI Agents and the lawyer gave me. I need you to check to see if any of them are on Biddle or Wofford's or Betty Dowager's computers."

"Jeez, at least you don't ask for much," Smythe said with a sardonic smile. "You actually believe someone at GA set you up?"

Brent shrugged. "Betty Dowager brought the FBI guys to my office. She gave me the attorney's number, and she's Biddle's assistant."

Smythe stared disconsolately toward the Genesis Advisors building and sighed. "No damn promises," he muttered.

"I really appreciate it."

"Yeah," Smythe muttered as he started back. After a second, he turned. "Where are you going to be?"

"Around, staying out of sight."

Smythe nodded. Brent watched him head westward into the last fiery glow of sunset, his shoulders slumped, his briefcase almost dragging the ground like an unsupportable weight.

THIRTY

NEW YORK, JUNE 29

NAIF SLUMPED LOW in the van's seat and watched through the passenger side mirror. The rain had stopped. A thick mist still hung in the air, but it didn't matter because there was no mistaking the guy on the bench. He hadn't gone to Faisal's immediately the way Biddle had predicted. Instead, he'd started out of the city, where they'd only managed to follow him up the crowded highway thanks to the tracking bug in his cell phone.

For a time it had looked like everything was going wrong, but then Lucas turned off the highway and went to Faisal's, then to the supposed FBI offices on the West Side. The Christian had wanted to take him then, but Naif refused. Nothing must jeopardize the main mission. Allah would create the right opportunity.

For some time, Lucas had been sitting and staring like a cat about to pounce. Now, Naif saw him stand and trot across the avenue toward where they were parked on the cross street. A moment later Lucas approached a man who had exited the corner building. When the man saw Lucas, he seemed about to run, but Lucas grabbed his arm. They were almost near enough for Naif to crack his window and overhear their conversation.

After several minutes the second man turned and went back toward his office, while Lucas crossed to his parked car. He pulled out and drove down the street, past their van.

The minister followed, turning left at the light, heading uptown on Madison. He punched his cell phone buttons as he drove, his voice tense when he told the person on the other end about Lucas's meeting, and how the man on the sidewalk had gone back toward the office.

Naif kept his eyes on the tracking device, and when Lucas turned and started down a side street in the nineties, he hit the minister's shoulder and pointed.

They turned east, staying sixty or seventy yards back.

After three blocks, the tracking device showed another change in direction, and then Naif caught sight of Lucas's BMW disappearing down the ramp of a parking garage. This was a safer choice than the street, and when the minister gave him a questioning glance, Naif nodded. With luck the garage would be almost empty, and the kill would be silent. They would put his body in the van and dump him someplace where he'd never be found.

They turned into the garage and crept down the ramp. Around the turn at the bottom they spotted Lucas standing beside his car, talking to the parking attendant.

"Stop," Naif said, wanting the van where it would prevent other cars from coming in or out.

He opened his door, climbed down and walked nonchalantly toward the two men, noting that Lucas kept his back turned as if he feared being recognized. Naif's hand went to his knife in the pocket of his long coat. He stopped a few steps behind Lucas and cast one more look around. No one else in sight.

He slipped the knife from his pocket, ready for the attendant to take Lucas's car and disappear down the next ramp. Only, the man turned, glanced at Naif and then seemed to notice the van. "Can't park that here!" he said.

Naif glanced back. The minister shifted the van into reverse but Naif shook his head. The attendant caught the signal and stepped between Naif and Lucas.

"No vans, man. Too high. Gotta back it out."

Lucas still had his back turned. Naif stepped sideways, trying to keep open space between them, but the attendant stepped with him.

"Move it right now," the attendant said, raising his voice. "I'm gonna have people wanting to get in."

The attendant seemed to have forgotten about Lucas's car. Naif could wait no longer. He turned slightly, masking his right hand. When he struck, the speed and force drove the blade deep into the man's abdomen, and he ripped upward. It happened so fast there was barely a sound, only a wheeze before the man's knees buckled and he started to fall.

Naif jerked the blade free and stepped over the body, angling for a clear shot at Lucas's kidney. Lucas seemed to sense something because he started to turn, forcing Naif to go for his midsection instead. Lucas jumped back as the knife slashed toward him, his movement blindingly fast for such a big man. Naif felt his blade strike and tried to move in closer, expecting Lucas to freeze for a split second and look down, stunned that he'd been cut by a stranger.

Lucas did neither. Instead, he stepped forward, pushed Naif's knife arm wide, then lashed out with his foot and caught Naif in the hip.

The blow had staggering power. Naif reeled sideways and tripped over the dying attendant, going down hard on his elbow. An arc of pain shot through his arm, and his knife skittered away. Naif plunged his hand into his other pocket and grabbed his pistol. There was already blood on Lucas's shirt from the gash in his abdomen, and Naif knew the sight of a gun would make him run. It would be an easy shot.

He started to jerk the pistol free, but the silencer snagged on the lining. Contrary to reason, the sight of the gun didn't seem to frighten Lucas. Instead of running, he stepped around the fallen attendant and kicked again, this time catching Naif beneath the armpit. With another shot of blinding pain, the kick turned him all the way over. He sprawled hard on his stomach and lost his grip on the gun.

At the same moment, Lucas's knees landed on his back. Hands seized his dreadlocks, and he felt his nose break as his face was slammed repeatedly into the concrete floor. He was beginning to black out when he heard the shot, and the hands released him.

He looked up, half blinded by blood that ran from his forehead and saw the minister now out of the van, holding the pistol he'd just fired. Lucas was running, having put the van between himself and the minister, and he was quickly disappearing up the ramp. "Shoot him!" Naif shouted, but it was already too late.

THIRTY-ONE

NEW YORK, JUNE 29

BRENT MADE IT only to the top of the ramp before he slowed to a walk. He could go no faster. Blood soaked his shirt and pants, and his wound was a bar of hot iron against his abdomen. Even if his would-be killers didn't catch him, some bystander was liable to call the cops. No taxi would stop for a bleeding man, and he couldn't go back for his car. He'd been planning to ditch it because the police would be looking for the license plate.

He turned left toward Second Avenue, heading past a line of dilapidated brownstones. He picked one that appeared deserted then descended the steps to the basement entrance beneath the stoop. The space was unlit, littered with blown trash and garbage bags. It smelled of rot and urine, but at least he was hidden. He lifted his blood-soaked shirt and looked at the ugly diagonal tear that gaped from the bottom of his ribcage to his opposite hipbone. He put his hand into the cut and probed, wincing at the pain but grateful nothing bulged through the muscle wall.

He pulled his shirt closed and buttoned his suit coat. His mind rattled with questions for which he had no answers. Who were those guys? Where had they come from? Why were they trying to kill him? He remembered the garage attendant. The poor bastard might still be alive. He took out his cell phone, dialed 911 and reported the knifing.

He ended the call then started up the steps. His eyes drew level with the sidewalk, and he paused to search for any sign of the van. The street looked clear, so he went up the rest of the way and started walking west this time, as fast as he could, against the traffic. If the van came back around, he'd see it up ahead.

The first siren approached as he reached Third Avenue, and he quickened his pace in spite of the pain. He pulled out his cell phone and hit the auto-dialer to call Simmons. He needed her to get him to a doctor.

The phone continued to ring. By the time he reached Park there was still no answer. It was riskier walking here because there were more people and the light was better, but he had no choice. He stepped off the sidewalk and stayed just outside the line of parked cars, the way he would if he were trying to flag a taxi. He hit the auto-dialer a second time. Nothing. Desperation surged. He walked as fast as he could. With traffic approaching from behind, he prayed no one would notice the blood. Up ahead a doorman stepped out and whistled for a cab. Brent stopped and backed between two parked cars until a taxi stopped, a passenger got in and the doorman went back into his building.

He resumed walking, pain causing him to stumble several times. He was light-headed from shock or blood loss. After another couple of blocks he saw his chance: a woman arriving back at her apartment, unloading a Volvo station wagon with help from her doorman. Brent slowed and waited. The doorman came out, grabbed several pieces of luggage and hurried inside, as the woman, late fifties, overweight and slow-moving, with several shopping bags in one hand and her dog leash in the other, led a golden retriever from the car toward the building entrance.

The car's tailpipe was coughing exhaust. Brent pushed the tailgate closed, rushed to the driver's door, jumped inside, slammed the shifter into gear and accelerated. He was out in traffic before anyone noticed. He shot north on Park then turned west. New York City had a famously rapid response to human tragedies such as muggings, knifings or rapes, but a notoriously slack response to basic property losses like car thefts. Every New Yorker had stories about reporting stolen cars, how the Manhattan police literally yawned. If the stories were wrong, he was a dead man.

He crossed Central Park and made it onto the West Side Highway. Traffic was light, and he headed north to the George Washington Bridge, knowing it was the longer route to where he was going but needing to avoid the cops at the Lincoln Tunnel.

He jerked out his wallet as he drove and counted sixty-two dollars. That was all he had because his credit or ATM cards would be like drawing arrows for the police.

On the other side of the Hudson, he followed signs for the

New Jersey Turnpike. He saw a police car parked on one side of the turnpike ticket booths, but fortunately the cop never spared him a glance.

He was thinking only about his Uncle Fred now, remembering what he'd said—how he'd help out when no one else would. He had to get to Morristown, but he was so sleepy. Twice he felt the tires thump on the warning strip before his eyes snapped open. Come on, he told himself! Just a little farther! He focused his thoughts on the two guys who'd just tried to kill him. They'd knifed an innocent garage attendant and maybe shot Dr. Faisal. Slowly, his rage began to boil again. He used it to keep going.

He looked over at the passenger seat where Harry sat, his face smeared with soot, his clothes smoking from recent flames. *Hang in there, bro. Don't let those bastards get away with this.*

Brent grunted and set the cruise control. His vision was blurring, but he was on fire himself now and he held the wheel in a death grip.

Forty minutes later, he was on the quiet back streets of Morristown, nearing his uncle's neighborhood. His movements had become sluggish. It was hard as hell just to stay on the road, but he'd almost reached safety.

With two blocks to go he suddenly slammed on the brakes. The FBI and police would have figured out that he was running, and they'd have his uncle's house staked out for sure! Why hadn't he thought of it before? He let his forehead bang the steering wheel, finally overcome with hopelessness. It occurred to him that maybe he ought to just go ahead and surrender.

Then what? Harry's voice came to him. *How you gonna get proof from jail? You want to end up a scapegoat for whoever killed your client and stole his money?*

"I've got sixty-two dollars," Brent said. He glanced down at his bloody stomach. "I need a doctor."

Only one other place to go, Little Bro.

Brent scowled, but he turned around in the next driveway.

Maggie's lights were off, but the sight of her house brought a strange combination of hope and futility. She was a cop, sworn to uphold the law, but maybe she still cared about him enough to listen to his story. Maybe she didn't—but he was too near to blacking out to make another choice. He drove into her driveway, turned off the engine, staggered to her back door and rang the bell. After another minute he rang again, but nothing stirred inside.

The garage door squeaked on its hinges as he raised it and saw that Maggie's car was gone. He backed the Volvo into her garage, lowered the door, then sat behind the wheel, unable to fight his exhaustion. His eyes closed, and he felt himself drift. Numb with pain and worry, with no more strength to resist or run, he knew he'd tried his best, but tomorrow he'd be in custody.

Strangely, the only thing he could still focus on was a lingering sadness about Maggie, about how he'd let the two of them grow so distant when he still loved her. As he fell into oblivion, he thought about Harry charging up the fire stairs, loving his job and his mission, probably smiling even at the end. Harry wouldn't have backed away from Maggie. Harry had always embraced everything in his life to the best of his ability. His last thought was that he felt oddly jealous of his dead brother. It was strange how his own life had been so full of promise and opportunity, yet how he'd wasted it, never seeing the things that mattered until it was too late.

THIRTY-TWO

MANHATTAN, JUNE 29

NAIF KEPT ONE hand pressed to his forehead to staunch the bleeding as he turned to glare at this soft American who was the reason he had failed. He felt a hot rage rip at his stomach.

"I should kill you," he hissed.

"It wasn't my fault, " the fat Christian said, even as the sour smell of fear oozed from his pores.

Naif shifted position to try and ease the pain that wracked his body. He had bruised ribs, a bleeding elbow and a broken nose, but worst was the knowledge that he'd so badly underestimated his prey.

Now a new problem loomed. They had driven up and down streets, scanned unlit doorways and the spaces between parked cars. Lucas was wounded. Naif knew a man with a wounded gut couldn't go far. Still, they hadn't found him.

They were parked at the curb a block from the garage, where they could keep watch in both directions. When Lucas appeared, they would go after him. Naif took his bloody knife from his pocket and placed it on the minister's knee. "When we find him, you finish it."

The minister's eyes widened, and he shook his head. "No!" he exclaimed.

Naif reached into the pocket of his coat and brought out his pistol. He put the silenced muzzle against the minister's chest. "Kill him," he said, speaking very slowly. "Or die."

The minister made whimpering sound and seemed about to refuse, but before he could speak, Naif's cell phone rang.

It was Abu Sayeed. "Status?" he demanded.

"There have been complications," Naif said.

"He is alive?"

" . . . yes."

There was a pause. "We have a change of plans. Go to the following address."

Naif took a pen and notebook from a rubber band on the visor and wrote it down. Afterward, he programmed the address into his portable GPS. He read the directions then turned to the minister. "Go to the Triborough Bridge."

THIRTY-THREE

MORRISTOWN, NJ, JUNE 30

A SLIVER OF light showed on the eastern horizon as Maggie pulled her Toyota Corolla into her driveway. She climbed out, stretched, then shivered at the cool dampness of the night air. High in an oak tree an unseen bird began to sing. The sound reminded her of how little time she'd have to sleep and brought a twinge of sadness as she thought about promises she'd made to herself–that someday she'd learn the songs of all the local birds and have a vegetable garden and a great big backyard and some kids to tear it up. So many things seemed to be sliding farther and farther away.

Now, even those simple desires seemed self-indulgent, perhaps ultimately impossible to achieve given what she'd heard the previous evening. She could still picture Ann Jenkins as she laid out her response to rumors of eight Russian air-to-ground missiles and several pounds of spent nuclear fuel.

As the impact of Jenkins' Condition Red began to spread, things in New York would soon be a complete mess. Tankers would back up in the Atlantic as they waited to unload, and local business owners would be screaming as their goods accumulated, food rotted and the shelves of New York's stores grew bare. Then, in the absence of quick irrefutable proof, politicians would slam Project Seahawk for unrealistic, heavy-handed tactics. Maggie had to admire the woman's guts.

However, as if Jenkins's announcement wasn't troubling enough, it wasn't even the worst thing. Brent's name had come over the law enforcement network at around eleven-thirty, a flicker on her computer screen, one more green line of print among thousands of others, but her eyes had gone straight to it. He was the subject of a detain-for-questioning order regarding the disappearance of client funds and possible violations of RICO and anti-money-laundering statutes.

She'd been stunned because the idea of Brent stealing

anything was preposterous, but she also remembered his phone call, the troubling undercurrents in his voice, his need to meet with her. Had he been reaching out for help?

Her teeth chattered in the morning air, but she ignored the chill and stepped through her backyard gate in the hope that movement would diminish her anxiety. The eastern sky was growing paler, and the outline of her flowerbeds began to emerge. There were roses along one side and at the rear a perennial bed with a thick phalanx of iris stalks, their blooms already past. Overhead, more birds were starting to sing, and the scent of fresh dew rose from the grass.

As soon as she'd seen his name on the wire, she'd called Brent's cell phone, letting the number ring until she got his recording. Around one a.m., Brent's name had come across her screen a second time. His client, a Dr. Khaled Faisal, had been found murdered along with two other people in a Manhattan townhouse, and the detain-for-questioning order had been upgraded to an arrest warrant. According to the report, police had found the bodies after a butler's wife alerted them that her husband hadn't returned from work. This time the bulletin had included Brent's picture.

At three a.m., a third bulletin said Brent's car had been located in a Manhattan garage, along with the body of a slain garage attendant. Until then, all of it might have been a terrible mistake, but now she knew it was much more than coincidence or mistaken identity. By four a.m., she could no longer keep even the simplest thoughts in her head, and she had made an excuse that she was ill and gone home.

In spite of the hour she'd almost stopped to see Brent's Uncle Fred on her way home. She knew Fred couldn't be sleeping. First losing Harry and now this—he had to be beside himself. Nothing about the accusations made sense to her, yet she hadn't stopped. Emotionally she was in complete denial, but as a cop she'd seen people, even wonderful people, sometimes go over the edge. It seemed incomprehensible that Brent could have become homicidal, but regardless of her emotions she needed to admit to the possibility.

Now, on a sudden whim she kicked off her shoes, hiked up the skirt of her navy blue pin-striped suit and pulled off her pantyhose. The grass was long and needed mowing, and the wet blades licked the tender skin between her toes with shocking coolness. She closed her eyes, thinking it felt good to be here, so peaceful! For a few moments she wished she could be a little girl again, back in that perfect age of innocence where the dew could wash away her worries and make all the bad things disappear.

She crossed her arms and looked overhead at the last pale wash of the night's stars. *Where are you, Brent*, she wondered? *Where would you run?* She sighed and started toward her back door, thinking she'd go inside and try his cell phone once more before she tried to sleep. Maybe he was already in custody. If he wasn't, even if she managed to talk to him, what could she say? *Give yourself up?* She shook her head. Not him.

She was so tired that the squeak of her garage door hinges barely registered, but in another instant her training took over. In one motion, she unsnapped her holster, pulled her Glock, spun and crouched. She thumbed off the safety, and in less than a half second held a rock steady aim on the dim outline framed in the blackness of her now open garage door.

"Police!" she barked. "Raise your hands and come forward! Move slow!"

A man took several slow steps forward. "Maggie?"

She knew the voice. "Keep moving!" she commanded, then watched him stumble and go to his knees.

"Lie face down on the driveway with your hands out to your sides. Now!"

"Maggie," the voice said again. "It's Brent."

"I know who it is!" she said, only now her hands were shaking, her breath coming short. She kept the gun aimed but clicked the safety back on because she no longer trusted her control.

"What the hell have you done?" she demanded.

He wasn't lying down. He stayed on his knees with his hands over his stomach. "I didn't do it," he mumbled

She took two steps closer. "On your face, Brent! Now!"

He looked up at her and shook his head, and that was when she saw the blood. His shirt was dark with it where his suit coat came apart.

"Jesus," she said, coming closer but staying out of reach.

"How bad are you hurt?"

"Not as bad as I could be," Brent said. "A guy tried to kill me in a parking garage."

Maggie felt sick. "The attendant?"

"No, another guy."

"Who?"

Brent shook his head. "I never saw him before."

She looked at him hard. She saw no sign of lunacy, not on the surface at least; instead she saw fear and vulnerability and isolation. Her instincts told her this was Brent, the man she'd loved and trusted, but part of her brain demanded: *What if I'm wrong? What if he's guilty?* She pushed it back and came another step closer. She could see him clearly now in the gray light, exhausted and haggard, like he'd aged ten years.

"I'm sorry I came here," he said, his voice little more than a whisper. "I'm not going to involve you in this."

"I have to arrest you, Brent. I don't have a choice."

He looked at her, and something like Brent's old determination emerged. "Yeah, I know," he said. He winced then struggled uncertainly to his feet. He turned and lurched back toward the garage.

"Stop!"

He shook his head and kept going.

"Stop!" she cried a second time. She felt tears well in her eyes, but she thumbed off the safety.

"Shoot me or let me go," he said over his shoulder.

"Why are you doing this?"

He turned halfway around. "Cause I'm innocent."

"So give yourself up!"

He shook his head. "Got no proof." He stumbled, put his hands on his knees. "They did too good a job," he said, then crumpled to the ground.

Thirty minutes later, Maggie was slumped on one of the chairs at her kitchen table with her head on her folded arms. Brent lay asleep on the couch in her small den, where he'd half-walked and she'd half-dragged him. She'd pulled off his shirt and pants, washed and disinfected his wound then used all the butterfly bandages in her police-issue first-aid kit to close the cut. She knew the wound probably called for stitches, but the butterflies would do for now.

She hadn't made the call to turn him in, but it had to be done. There was no rush. Brent wasn't going anyplace. He'd been barely coherent when she bandaged him, babbling names she'd never heard and something about being set up.

After several minutes she raised her head, glanced around her kitchen and gave up any pretense of sleeping. She stood, loaded the coffee maker, took eggs from the refrigerator, then pulled bacon and English muffins from the freezer.

She defrosted the bacon in the microwave and put the muffins in her toaster oven to thaw. A few minutes later the bacon was soft enough for the frying pan, and shortly afterward the kitchen filled with its mouthwatering aroma. She split the muffins once they softened then cracked eggs into a blue crockery bowl that had belonged to her grandmother. Her ability to do something simple and physical was like a balm. Twenty minutes later, she took two heaping plates of scrambled eggs, toasted muffins and crisp bacon into the den.

"Wake up," she ordered.

Brent opened his eyes. His lips were dry and cracked.

"Sit up and eat," she said in a deliberately cold voice.

Brent winced, but he struggled into a half-sitting position and took a plate. He glanced down at the blanket she'd thrown over him, then lifted the corner and peeked at his boxer shorts. "Did you take advantage of me?"

Maggie ignored the comment as she fixed him with her toughest glare. "Who is Spencer McDonald?" she demanded, repeating one of the names he'd babbled as she bandaged him.

At her mention of the name, Brent's attempt at humor vanished. He took a few bites, then began telling her a convoluted story about how he'd gone to work at Genesis Advisor at the request of the Justice Department, how some bogus FBI agents and a bogus lawyer had embezzled his client's money, and how he'd found bodies in his client's townhouse. Finally, he told her about the assailant with the knife in the parking garage.

"You're working for government?"

Brent nodded. "For a woman named Ruth Simmons."

"You have anything in writing that proves it?"

"No," Brent said.

Maggie made a mental note to call Ruth Simmons, then asked, "How about the FBI agents or the lawyer. Could you pick them out of a lineup?"

Brent nodded, as he continued to shovel food.

"What about the guy with the knife and the driver of the van?"

"The guy with the knife," Brent nodded. "But I never saw the driver's face."

"You think they're all tied to the money?"

Brent nodded, some of the old spark returning. "If they made me disappear, the Feds would keep on thinking I took the money, but they'd never find me."

"How did they set this up?" she asked.

"I'm guessing through somebody I work with." His gaze turned inward, and his shoulders slumped. "Only I've got no way to prove it."

Maggie nibbled at her eggs and thought for a minute. "Have you considered the possibility that this is why you were hired?"

"Only about a hundred times in the past few hours. I tried to call Simmons on the cell phone she gave me. It's supposed to reach her twenty-four seven." He shook his head. "She hasn't been answering."

On an emotional level Maggie believed him. As she listened to his story the rational part of her brain was becoming persuaded as well. His story triggered another association deep in her subconscious, but she pushed it aside because the extrapolations seemed too fantastic. "Is there anybody else who might be able to help you? Someone at work?"

"One guy, and I should have heard from him by now." Brent's head shot up, and he patted his shirt pocket. "Shit!" he said. "He may have been trying to call me. I turned my cell phone off to save the juice."

He tried to swing his legs to the floor, then groaned and fell back. "Stay here," Maggie commanded. She stood and headed out the back door. The sun was over the trees, and in the early light the dewdrops in the grass glistened like tiny diamonds. The air had a foggy, romantic quality, and for a few seconds she could almost imagine that it was a weekend morning and she and Brent were still together.

She raised the garage door and saw the Volvo, and her spirits plummeted. She knew the car was stolen even before she pulled the registration from the glove box. It hammered home the fact that Brent was wanted for murder. It didn't matter that she loved him. She had an obligation to uphold the law, and she couldn't escape it.

She grabbed his cell phone off the seat then leaned against the car roof with her face in her hands. She let out a quick sob, but after a second she bit her lower lip and straightened. Get a grip, she told herself as she headed back to the house. She knew what she needed to do.

THIRTY-FOUR

MORRISTOWN, NJ, JUNE 30

BRENT SAW THE change the moment Maggie returned with his cell phone. Her eyes had grown murky, her expression distant, and he knew it had been the discovery of the Volvo. He was too exhausted, his brain too full of sand to try and explain, and he watched her turn and walk out of the room.

He checked the phone, cursed himself for having turned it off and saw that he had six missed calls from Ruth Simmons and three messages from Smythe, the first from around eleven-thirty last night. In it, Smythe's normally superior voice betrayed an anxiety he'd never heard.

"We're more than even, you sonofabitch," Smythe said. "I went back and pretended there was some work I'd forgotten to finish up. Betty had already gone home and Biddle's office was locked, but Wofford's assistant was there. I chatted her up and got her a Coke, then I stood in the stairwell 'til almost ten o'clock."

Brent smiled as he pictured Smythe hovering in the shadows. His pulse quickened as he heard what came next.

"She finally went to pee, and I snuck onto Wofford's computer. One of the phone numbers was in his trash file. Lucky for you he forgot to erase it. The name that went with the number is Howard Turner. I've got more, but it's too long to leave on a message. Call me!"

The second and third messages had come in at midnight and one a.m. "Where the hell are you? Call me!" Smythe said both times. Brent lay back on the couch and allowed himself his first breath of hope.

He checked his watch and saw that it was already six-fifteen. Smythe would be up and just about to leave for the station. Knowing his cell phone could be traced, he dropped his feet to the floor and sat up. His stomach had stiffened, and movement brought a tearing feeling. He looked down and saw that the butterfly bandages seemed to be holding. Then he gritted his teeth and stood.

He hobbled into the kitchen and saw Maggie slumped at the small table, her eyes unfocused. He took her cordless phone from the wall, shuffled back to the den and dialed Smythe's cell phone. The number rang until he got a recording. He hung up, found Smythe's home number on his BlackBerry and dialed. The number rang, only this time there was no answering machine. Probably Smythe's wife on the computer, he thought.

He waited five minutes and tried both numbers again. Still no answer. "Damn," he said. He felt a huge surge of gratitude for the risk Smythe had taken. He couldn't wait to hear the rest of his message and then offer to take him to New York's best restaurant by way of a thank you. Hell, he'd take the Smythes to Paris if that was what they wanted!

He heard Maggie's chair scrape the kitchen floor. A second later, she stood in the doorway, her face grim.

"It's time," she said, not meeting his eyes. "I'm turning you in."

Brent looked up and saw exhaustion and worry carved in her face but also determination. "Not yet!" he said. "I've got a name!"

Her face flooded with anger. "You come back into my life and expect me to risk everything for you?"

"I'm just asking for a little time."

"You're wanted for murder. You stole a car." Her voice shook with emotion. "I can't keep you in my house."

Her vulnerability struck him. It made him want to go over to her and cup her face in his hands, but he held back. "Give me a few more hours," he said. "Please!"

"I've already given you too much time!"

"A couple hours! These guys have been flawless! If they even suspect I've got a lead, they're liable to vanish completely!"

"What do you expect to do?" she demanded.

"Get something!" he shouted, sitting up, ignoring the pain. "You've got to let me try!"

She turned away and looked into the kitchen. "I just hope you're worth it," she muttered.

Brent slumped back on the pillows. "So do I."

THIRTY-FIVE

OYSTER BAY, NY, JUNE 30

FRED WOFFORD STOPPED at Prescott Biddle's gates, took a deep breath and tried to punch the entry code into the keypad. His hand shook, and he hit the wrong numbers. He cursed, took a rattling breath and tried again. He messed up again. He tried a third time, and the gates finally swung back. He headed down the driveway then braked at the small guardhouse located around the first curve, just out of sight of the road.

A man wearing a blue blazer and gray flannels stepped toward the car. He had an earpiece in one ear and a small microphone at his lapel, and even though he recognized Wofford, he walked around the car, peered through the windows, then tapped the rear hatch. Wofford hit the unlock button, and the guard opened the hatch and glanced at the boxes inside. "Mrs. Biddle order all this?" he asked.

"I believe they're expecting guests in the cottage for a few days," Wofford replied. He tried for an easy smile, as though delivering cases of foul-smelling stuff purchased from a Middle Eastern grocery was nothing out of the ordinary.

The guard raised his eyebrows and shrugged. He closed the tailgate then bent to his lapel mike. "Clearing Mr. Wofford," he said. "Silver Mercedes SUV, New York plates, one passenger. Going to the cottage." The man listened then nodded. "Roger." He saluted Wofford. "Have a good day."

Wofford started moving again, leaving his window down. The sea air was soft against his face, the bright morning light adding an extra touch of splendor to Biddle's acres of lawn and flowers, but the beauty was illusory. Dread chewed the lining of his stomach as he thought of what was hidden just ahead.

Clearly, Biddle's security people remained ignorant of the three men in the little stone cottage. Thank God. Only a tiny group knew—Biddle, Wofford, their two secretaries, Rev. Turner, and the two sheriff's deputies from Turner's church. Each of them had sworn a sacred and holy oath to the prophecy and the promise of bringing Jesus back into the world!

Wofford tried again to focus on that one supreme goal and prayed that Jesus would banish his fear. Only, it didn't work. Panic squeezed his insides. He stopped the car in the middle of the driveway, opened the door and hung his head out the side. He retched—only a few drops of clear liquid because he'd thrown up everything hours ago.

He closed the door and wiped his lips with the back of his wrist. His own vision was so different from Biddle's. It always had been, but Biddle's revelations had overpowered him—just as they had all the others. Only, when he was alone he had such horrible doubts. Would a loving God really want this?

At times he suspected Armageddon was meant to signify a war fought in people's hearts, as the religions of the world struggled to find one God together. But Biddle insisted otherwise. It needed to be an actual war, with millions dead. Anything less, and Jesus would not return.

Well, Biddle was getting his way, he thought bitterly, as his recollection of the orders he'd given the previous night made him want to vomit all over again. The call from Rev. Turner had set everything off. It had come in around nine o'clock, followed by a second call an hour later from the firm's security people.

He hadn't been able to reach Prescott, so it had been his decision. Yet again he had begged God for courage, but those prayers had not been answered, not last night and not today. Nonetheless, he'd called Turner and given the order he knew Biddle would have given. Sometime around dawn, after hours of sleeplessness, he'd swallowed some Valium and finally nestled within its soft comfort. Only now, a little over four hours later, the drug was a faint memory.

Yesterday everything had been going perfectly—even his phone conversation with Lucas. Wofford knew he'd done well. He'd sounded angry, even felt angry, as he'd focused his anxiety and let it pour out. Only now . . . he lifted one hand from the steering wheel and made a fist. His fingers felt sticky. It was irrational, but he imagined them covered with blood.

How could Biddle insist this killing was God's work, unavoidable, the only way to the prophecy? How had he let himself get pulled into this? Already it was out of control. The original plan called for only Faisal and his butler to die, but the news reports said a third person had been in the house, a woman. And then that poor man in the garage! Ironically, Lucas, the greatest threat to them all if they hoped to stay out of jail, was still on the loose.

But young Smythe! He'd had a wife and child! That had to be a sin beyond forgiveness. He put his face in his hands and let out several convulsive sobs. He'd accepted Biddle's vision as far as he could, but now he knew he'd run out of strength.

He raised his head and looked around. How long had he been there? He had stopped where the driveway forked, the right fork leading to Biddle's house, the other to the stone cottage and the dock. This surely was a sign from God—the fork of the drive, the fork of the serpent's tongue, the choice. He needed to move, but it took every ounce of his will.

A moment later he drove into the stone courtyard and used his shirtsleeve to dab the sweat from his scalp. His bowels were water. A blast of resentment ran through him directed at Biddle, safe in Russia right now, his alibi ironclad. It was Biddle's job, not his, to handle these animals. *Fuck*! Wofford thought, uttering an unaccustomed silent curse.

He climbed from the car then froze when he heard a sound at his back. He turned slowly and spotted a man hidden in the deep shadow of a pine tree. A scarf wrapped his face, covering everything but delicate eyes and what looked like a narrow band of bruised, bandaged flesh. However, Wofford's gaze went straight to the machine gun aimed at his stomach. He raised his hands. "Please! I only brought the food," he stuttered.

The man looked back down the driveway. "You were supposed to call first."

"I know," Wofford said, nodding, appalled at his mistake. "I forgot. I'm very sorry."

The man stepped over to the SUV, opened the doors and looked inside. He said something into a small microphone on his shoulder, then with one hand pressed to his earpiece, he listened. After a second he jerked his head toward the cottage.

Wofford looked around as the cottage door swung open, and Abu Sayeed stepped out. "Mr. Wofford," he said in cultivated

English. He wore dark trousers and a white shirt with the sleeves rolled up to expose thin but muscular forearms. A machine gun dangled carelessly from his hand. His chiseled nose had the inhumanity of a raptor's beak, and his dark eyes blazed with ruthless certainty, as they seemed to drill into Wofford's heart and extract the tender meat of his innermost secrets.

"You have our food?"

Wofford nodded weakly, knowing Biddle would slap his face if he could see him now and demand that he show pride and strength as a servant of Christ. He couldn't. He wasn't made to face people with machine guns and the hearts of savages. "It's in . . . it's in the back of the car."

Abu Sayeed turned back to the cottage, snapped his fingers and said something in Arabic. A moment later a third man emerged, the one who had ridden in the container. He glanced at Wofford with eyes as roiled as thunderclouds, then opened the SUV's hatch and began to carry the boxes of food into the cottage.

Abu Sayeed continued to inspect Wofford, making no effort to hide his scorn. "I trust everything is still on schedule?" he asked after several long seconds.

Wofford could not bring himself to meet the man's eyes. "Yes," he said, directing his unfocused stare toward the cottage roof.

"Of course you would tell me if anything had changed," Abu Sayeed said.

"Yes." Wofford looked at his car. The stocky man was back already, getting the last carton of food. There were still two cases of Coke and Mountain Dew waiting to be unloaded. He prayed for the man to hurry.

"Do you think of us as merely your servants who will bloody our hands whenever you order it?"

Wofford forced himself to meet the icy stare. He wanted to say it was the Arab's fault, that things had started going wrong when his man had failed to kill Lucas, but his courage failed. "Of course not, but it had to be done," he said in a faltering voice.

Abu Sayeed's lip curled. "Why don't you do your own killing?"

Wofford looked at the ground and pictured the three charred corpses. He swallowed as bile edged into the back of his throat. He was no soldier, especially no general like Biddle . . . and the thought of what he'd done. "We had a problem," he managed after several seconds. "We needed to take care of it."

"You did nothing!" Abu Sayeed said, his voice soft but full of acid. "We took care of it."

Wofford felt small and helpless. "The man was . . . our security cameras caught him snooping in our computers. He might have ruined everything . . . for all of us." His cheeks burned. He had made the error by leaving that phone number in his computer's trash file. The deaths were his fault.

"We are not murderers," Abu Sayeed said, his voice like a lash. "As mujahideen, we kill for the glory of God not the protection of blunderers. You have dishonored us."

"I apologize," Wofford said in a near whisper. He glanced at his SUV, flooded with relief as the stocky man unloaded the last two cases of soda from the back. "I have to go now," he said.

Abu Sayeed eyed him with a derisive smile. "Of course."

Wofford slammed the SUV's rear hatch, climbed behind the wheel and began to drive. He boiled with humiliation and rage and wanted to stop and shout that all infidels would die when God's prophecy was fulfilled. However, he kept driving.

THIRTY-SIX

MORRISTOWN, NJ, JUNE 30

BY TEN THAT MORNING, Smythe still hadn't answered his phone. Maggie, having decided to give Brent another reprieve, had gone to work. He dozed intermittently on the couch and dialed Smythe's number each time he awoke. His last attempt had been seven minutes earlier. Smythe should have been at work for several hours already, so why the hell wasn't he picking up?

Brent's body screamed for sleep, but his concern kept him from anything more than catnaps. He tried to convince himself that Smythe had only snooped a phone number, but he couldn't deny that whoever had murdered Dr. Faisal and stolen his money would kill to cover their tracks. He glanced at his watch. How much more time would Maggie give him?

Not much, he thought, and there were other loose ends to pursue. After a second, he gritted his teeth against the pain, rose and hobbled slowly upstairs to the guest room. Earlier, he had called information and learned there was no Spencer McDonald in West Orange, either listed or not. Now, on a hunch, he logged onto Maggie's computer then searched real estate listings in West Orange. He estimated that "Spencer McDonald's" house had six or more bedrooms and would probably cost at least two million dollars. Seven listings met his criteria, and his breath caught when the third one showed a picture of the house.

He called the realty company, and an agent told him the house was available but couldn't be shown because a movie company had rented it for several weeks. He could see it as soon as the lease expired, the agent said, but not before. In the meantime she could show him a number of other listings. He thanked her, promised to call back and hung up.

This discovery only deepened his anxiety because it reinforced the idea that people had gone to a great deal of trouble to set him up. It also sharpened his fear for Smythe. He went down to the den and dialed yet again, letting the number ring until voice mail picked up. He ended the call, as he had all the others, without leaving a message.

He dozed for a short time, but the phone woke him. He let it ring, waiting for the answering machine in the kitchen to play its message. Once he heard Maggie's voice on the other end he grabbed the receiver.

"Have you seen it?" she asked.

"What?" Something in her tone made his stomach turn to ice.

"Owen Smythe died in a house fire last night along with his wife and child."

For several seconds he couldn't breathe. He threw an arm across his eyes. This was his fault! He might as well have struck the match! Instantly, no matter how he tried to turn it off, his mind began to replay the terrible scene from his childhood–burning embers falling into a room where the walls had turned to solid flame–only this time it wasn't Brent and Harry in the room but Owen Smythe and his family. "They killed them," he whispered.

"We don't know for sure," Maggie said, her words sounding hollow.

"This is no coincidence!" Brent snapped.

Maggie's reply was soft but firm. "It's not your fault. You asked for a favor."

Suddenly he felt a new fear. What if his pursuers learned about Maggie? They'd managed to find out everything else. Even if he went to jail they might still come after her. He should get out now, immediately. He wouldn't make it far in a stolen car, but maybe far enough to keep her safe.

"Brent," Maggie said, as if she was reading his mind, "stay there. You can't do this alone, and you have no place to go."

He said nothing.

"I stopped by Fred's this morning," she continued. "Two plain-clothes guys are watching the house."

"How is he?"

"He needed to know you're alive. I took him a loaf of olive bread and slipped a note inside the bag. I just handed it to him, gave him a kiss and left. If I'd talked to him those guys could have heard every word. In the note I told him you're okay, but he's under surveillance and not to call my house or come by."

Brent groaned. "Fred doesn't listen to anybody."

"Like somebody else I know. Anyway, he'll listen this time," Maggie said. "I told him it's life and death."

When he hung up, his mind was racing again. In addition to sorrow and guilt, a desire for vengeance burned in his guts. He wanted to find his enemy and smash his face to pulp. Only he didn't even know who that person was, not for sure.

He went to the kitchen and rummaged furiously through the kitchen drawers for a legal pad, raging at the knowledge that even if he knew where Howard Turner lived, he was too weak to go after him. Worse, time was running out. Seven people were now dead, and he was the only common denominator. Even if Maggie continued to give him more rope, the police were already searching under every rock. Any hour they were liable to figure out that he and Maggie once dated, and then they'd tap her phones and watch her house. Before that happened he needed to figure out who had done these things.

He started a list on the legal pad and put down every relevant fact he could think of since he'd been approached to go to work at Genesis Advisors. Despite his fatigue, he felt strangely clear headed, powered by his anger.

When he finished, he looked down his list and groped for the invisible links.

- Gov't suspects GA of insider trading, drafts Lucas
- Simmons donates money to Biddle's church
- GA hires Lucas
- God gives Biddle tips on employment data, Intel
- Biddle gives Lucas Faisal's account
- Biddle's party - introduces Faisal
- Simone Hearkins???
- Biddle leaves for Russia
- Wofford leaves for surprise vacation
- Impostor FBI agents seize Faisal's account
- Lucas meets with impostor attorney
- Dr. Faisal murdered
- Lucas goes to Faisal's house, finds bodies

- Owen Smythe agrees to help
- Lucas attacked in the parking garage
- Smythe finds name – Howard Turner
- Smythe and family killed in fire

Whoever took the money had been careful, methodical and utterly ruthless. Also, it seemed clear that it wasn't just about the money—otherwise why kill Dr. Faisal? Kill Smythe because he snooped, maybe. Kill Lucas so he could disappear and take the blame along with him, yes. But don't kill three unnecessary people. Faisal's killing wasn't rational, yet the rest of it was too highly choreographed for irrationality. Therefore, the motive had to be more than greed, but what? Revenge? Politics? Religion? He dug the heels of his hands into his eyes. Think!

He went down the list again. The one entry that didn't seem to track was Simone Hearkins. He'd never seen again her after the night of Biddle's party. Did she have a role in this, or was she just coincidental?

He shook his head. There were no coincidences. It meant everything was premeditated, and he needed to discover how far back it went. He took out his cell phone and turned it on. There was one more call he hadn't made. He feared having his location triangulated, but he had no choice.

He auto-dialed the number. After several rings, Simmons's voice came on. "Brent, thank God! Where are you?"

"Why didn't you answer the other times I called?" he demanded.

"I know . . . I'm sorry. I was in high-level meetings. Where are you?"

"That's not important."

"We . . . I heard that you were wanted by the police!"

"I'm being framed!"

"But you're okay?"

"Mostly."

"Tell me where you are. I'll have someone come and get you."

There it was again, the third time she'd asked the question and the wrong note in Simmons's voice. "I'll call back," he said.

"Brent! Don't hang up. Tell me where you are!"

He killed the call and turned off the phone. Maybe he'd become totally paranoid, but shouldn't Simmons have asked different questions? She cared only about his location. Why? He felt sick at the likely explanation. Could things really go this deep? Had he been hired only because someone at Genesis Advisors needed a scapegoat? Had they even predicted his reactions? Intended for him to go to Dr. Faisal's house, intended for him to run!

He felt a renewed shot of rage at how he'd been suckered. He'd taken Simmons at her word, with nothing in writing, and how he was trapped between the police and his would-be assassins. His enemies had made only two small mistakes—leaving a single phone number in a computer's trash file and failing to kill him. He prayed those would be enough.

THIRTY-SEVEN

NEWARK, NJ, JUNE 30

SHADOWS HAD GATHERED in Newark's trash-littered streets when Maggie finally rolled her chair back from her computer and rubbed her exhausted eyes. Thankfully, with so many people assigned to the POTUS visit or working the docks because of Jenkins' Condition Red, the rest of Project Seahawk had been eerily quiet. It had allowed her to concentrate on Brent.

Now, even as she arched her back in a yawn, she kept her eyes on her computer screen with its constant stream of bulletins from different law enforcement organizations. Earlier, a communiqué from the Westchester County Medical Examiner had attributed the deaths of Owen Smythe, his wife and infant daughter to gunshot wounds. The fire had been an attempt to cover evidence.

The bulletin helped prove Brent's innocence, but even so her duty remained clear. She needed to pick up the phone, call the FBI and report him, but just as she hadn't done it the night before or earlier that morning, she wasn't doing it now. *What the hell was she thinking*, she asked herself? She was risking everything in her life for a guy who'd broken her heart once already.

"A penny for your thoughts," came a voice from the entrance to her cubicle. She looked around to see Steve Kosinsky's freshly sunburned face, his arms almost lobster red where they stuck out of his short-sleeved shirt.

"Ever heard of sunscreen?" she asked.

Steve scowled. "I've been out on the docks since before sunup doing container inspections. It's so jammed up you wouldn't believe it." He looked down at his arms and cracked a rueful smile. "I finally put some goop on after lunch, which was the first chance I had to sit down. Guess I was a little late."

Maggie shook her head. "Not if you're hoping for skin cancer."

Steve stepped inside and plopped into a chair. "If you care so much, why won't you have dinner with me?"

"Nothing's changed. I don't date guys at work."

Steve shook his head. "That's old-fashioned. It's the Phantom Boyfriend."

Maggie couldn't help smiling. Unlike most guys who were persistent, Steve had a way of making it light, so despite the turndowns, it wasn't awkward. "He's top secret. If I told you about him I'd have to kill you."

"Would I get to die the way Nelson Rockefeller did?" he asked hopefully.

"In your dreams."

Steve gave a wry shrug, but then he spread his hands, his gesture taking in the whole of Project Seahawk. "This is great, huh? We're at Condition Red, and half the troops are out looking under manhole covers." He shook his head. "My bet's with Jenkins. She's got solid instincts." He tipped his chair back until it leaned up against the cubicle wall.

"Then why don't they listen to her?" Maggie grumbled.

"Cause she's a woman. Cause she's a hard-assed bitch."

"So am I."

"Actually, I would guess your ass is anything but hard, but I wouldn't have first-hand experience."

"You're not going to get any, either."

Steve took a deep breath and let out a long-suffering sigh. "Life isn't fair." He took one finger and touched the burned flesh of his forearm, making a pale dot that went quickly back to angry red. "We've got half our guys doing the wrong thing because the President wants to kiss babies, and the other half getting skin cancer looking for those missiles." Steve planted his hands on his knees and brought his chair forward onto all four legs. "Jenkins is going to get nothing but shit for making the tough call. They treat this place like it's a joke."

"Why don't you go back to being a cop?" Maggie asked.

Steve shot her a look out of the corner of his eye, and he shrugged. "I don't want some shithead setting off a bomb in my country or poisoning the water supply or doing whatever those idiots do in the name of what they believe in. What about you?"

"I might if they don't let me get away from this paperwork," Maggie said. She grabbed a pencil from behind her ear and tossed it onto her desk. "Why not let me go out and do something?"

Steve tipped his chair again and thumped his head against the wall. "We work for the government, and you have to ask a question like that?" He paused, becoming serious. "I saw your resume. Somebody's got to figure a way to coordinate all this information. You're the right person."

Maggie scowled. "Jenkins just doesn't know what else to do with me."

"Nope. You're good," Steve insisted.

"Rumor has it you are, too," Maggie said.

"I'm the best!" Steve gave her a wink. "But you've never seen me work."

"You ever quit?"

"Not until you show me the Phantom Boyfriend."

"You're smoking dope."

Kosinsky shook his head and gave her a rueful smile. "I want to meet the lucky sonofabitch." He kicked his feet out and let the chair crash forward again.

"You break my chair, you're going to pay for it."

"On my massive salary? No problem." Kosinsky stood, put his hand on the cubicle partition and gave her a careful look. "Let me know if there's anything I can help you with. I'm serious."

As soon as he was gone, her thoughts swung back to Brent, and her mood darkened anew. She should do it right now–pick up the phone and turn him in. That was her sworn oath, her duty. Only the current situation went against all the rules. Part of it was the extraordinary amount of money and also the number of seemingly connected murders. Big thefts almost always avoided unnecessary violence, but not this time. Why? She thought yet again about the CIA's warning. It was a wild connection, but weren't the cost of the dirty weapons and the amount of Faisal's stolen money awfully coincidental?

Maggie propped her elbows on the desk and put her chin in her hands. Would anyone else even consider the possibility that people in Brent's company were involved with terrorists? What could be the motive?

She'd already pulled a listing of Genesis Advisors' employees from the New York State Department of Commerce. Other than Brent, they'd all been there for years. According to the Social Security database, on the surface at least, none appeared to have a Middle Eastern or Muslim association. To the contrary, business articles suggested that most if not all of the partners were fundamentalist Christians.

She reached into her desk and brought out the stapled pages from the search she'd done on the name Brent had gotten from Owen Smythe. There were eighty-two Howard Turners in New York, New Jersey and Connecticut alone. There was no telling how many she would find if she widened the search area to Pennsylvania, say, or New England. No doubt there would be thousands if she looked nationwide. There was no time to follow up on such a huge number, but at least these names were something, maybe a chance for Brent to come up with another connection.

Tomorrow at the absolute latest she would call the FBI, but for now she'd give him a little more time.

After another minute she stood. Her mind was too distracted to negotiate the subtleties of database architecture. As she turned toward the exit her thoughts returned to Jenkins. Her boss was intuitive, a player of hunches. Wasn't there a possibility she'd think outside the box and agree that the coincidence between the stolen money and the price of the missiles was intriguing and that the murders made no apparent sense? Maybe she'd even be willing to ignore all the political reasons not to put the spotlight on Prescott Biddle and his rich partners.

Yeah, right, Maggie thought. And maybe cows would fly. Still, she had to give it a shot. She pulled the memo she'd written from her drawer and glanced over it once more. She'd laid out her case as well as she could. It was at least worth a try.

She dropped it on Jenkins' desk on her way out.

THIRTY-EIGHT

MORRISTOWN, NJ, JUNE 30

THE MOMENT BRENT snapped awake he knew something was wrong. He was on the couch. It was early evening.

"Brent?"

Maggie stood in the doorway. He hadn't heard her enter. If she'd been one of the killers coming to finish the job, he'd be dead. With his mouth full of cobwebs, he glanced down at the list he'd been going over when he'd fallen asleep. He'd made no progress.

"I've got to get out of here," he said.

Maggie leaned against the wall and folded her arms beneath her breasts. "Where to?"

He shook his head, thoughts jumbled. "Just . . . away."

He stood and hobbled into the bathroom, brushed his teeth with his fingers. When he came out she was sitting at the kitchen table sipping a bottle of water. "You're wanted for murder," she said matter-of-factly. "If you're recognized and you try to run, you'll be shot."

They locked eyes. "Why haven't you turned me in?" he asked.

She said nothing for a time. Finally she looked away. "I've been asking myself the same question. Maybe I'm afraid you'll go down for the crime, and whoever did it will go free." She shrugged. "I have a wild hunch it may be related to something much bigger. It's probably self-justification, but I've decided maybe it's a good thing you're still on the loose."

He continued to stare at her. Her shirt was open at the top, and a vein pulsed near her collarbone. He wanted to put his arms around her, kiss her, feel the life inside her, smell her scent. "Maggie," he began, looking for a place to start, his voice going soft. "I've been thinking about you a lot, and—"

Her eyes grew wide with sudden alarm. "I've got something here," she said, cutting him off. She reached for her briefcase and removed several pieces of paper. "The Howard Turner list," she said.

For several seconds Brent struggled to pull back from what he'd been about to confess. His words had taken him by surprise. Had he really been about to say that he loved her? True or not, what right did he have to say it? Finally, he managed to focus on what she held in her hand. "Why a list?"

"There are over eighty Howard Turners in Connecticut, New York and New Jersey."

"What about the phone number? Can't you get his address from that?"

She shook her head. "It's a prepaid cell phone registered to a Richard Jones, supposedly from Philadelphia. Only problem is the address and social security number are bogus. Richard Jones doesn't exist."

She handed him the list. "Better look it over and see if anything stands out."

He glanced at the names, struggling with what suddenly seemed the enormity of the task. As if it proved the impossibility of finding the truth, he told her about his computer search earlier that day for the house in West Orange. "Howard Turner could also be a phony name, or the one we're looking for could live in California."

Maggie gave him a cold look. "You want to do nothing? Would that make you feel better?"

"I didn't say that."

She stood. "I'm going upstairs to log into the Project Seahawk system," she said. "You can check the list while I take a shower. Just type in the name and address and hit the search button." She walked toward the stairs.

After a few seconds Brent followed. He felt a little more sure-footed after his long nap, the cut on his stomach no longer hurting as much. He sat at the computer and started through the names. Connecticut came first alphabetically, and he ran down the list checking the towns where each Howard Turner lived. He waited for something to trigger his subconscious, but all he saw was the same name over and over—Howard A. Turner in Hartford, Howard C. Turner in Watertown, Howard H. Turner in Meriden. He checked their occupations, but nothing differentiated them. The process seemed ridiculous.

New Jersey came next, and he started with a Dr. A. Howard Turner in Rutherford. He ran quickly through the names, becoming ever more certain the whole thing was a waste until one name jumped out—Rev. Howard Turner in Lambertville. He sat with his hand poised over the keyboard, certain he was grasping at straws, but he thought about Prescott Biddle's fundamentalism.

"Hey!" he shouted.

"Be there in a minute," Maggie called from the bathroom.

While he waited, he finished New Jersey then went through New York. No other name struck him. A second later, Maggie hurried into the room.

"Find something?"

Brent glanced over his shoulder and took in the bath towel knotted over her breasts that covered her to mid-thigh. The air was suddenly heavy with the scent of soap and shampoo and clean female flesh.

"What have you got?" she prodded.

He tried to focus, but the towel intruded. One gentle tug would pull it loose. Finally, he swung around and put his arms around her waist.

"What the hell are you doing?" She stiff-armed him, pushing him away. "I'm putting everything on the line for you, but my ass isn't part of the package!"

"You never heard of a special favor for a condemned man?"

"Turn around!" she snapped in her best cop voice.

He nodded contritely and spun back to the monitor, but he felt a sudden lift. In spite of her reaction, he'd caught the hint of a smile in her eyes. "This Howard Turner is a reverend," he said. "It's not much, but it could be a connection."

Behind him, Maggie moved closer and rested her hand on his shoulder. "What's the name of Biddle's church?"

"The New Jerusalem Fellowship."

"Check for a Web page."

Brent googled and found the church's home page. Beneath the title it read, "Where God's Word is Literal Truth." Down one side was a Church Locator. He typed Lambertville, NJ, in the box. A second later, the computer listed the address and phone number of the local New Jerusalem Fellowship Church. It said the pastor's name was Howard Turner.

Brent felt a thrill shoot up his spine. For the first time since the FBI agents had appeared in his office, he felt he was onto something real.

Maggie's fingers tightened on his shoulders as she bent over to read the screen. Brent didn't move. He let the heat of her touch wash through him. It calmed him and warmed his bones as though he was a traveler who'd been lost a long time and was finally home again. She finally pulled her hand away and pointed to the service schedule on the screen. There was evening church that night.

"I'll get dressed," she said. "We can be there by dark."

An hour later they were in Maggie's Toyota, nearing the outskirts of Lambertville. The last daylight was fading, the sky quickly going gray, but even so, the area's beauty was evident. The countryside was surprisingly bucolic, the roads having narrowed from four lanes to two, the subdivisions and strip malls that pocketed areas around Morristown or Somerville replaced by graceful farmhouses set on undulating acreage. Young corn was ankle high in the fields, and cows and sheep stood along roadside fences placidly chewing the rich grass.

The traffic in town meandered, drivers slowing to gaze at the ancient fieldstone houses with their swaybacked roofs and well-tended gardens. The place was a tourist magnet, with hotels, guesthouses and restaurants that looked prosperous along the main streets. It seemed too secular a place for something like the New Jerusalem Fellowship Church, Brent thought, but clearly looks were deceiving.

They stopped at a gas station, got directions then headed west, out of town on a back road. The church was fairly new, a nondescript clapboard building with none of the grace of the two-hundred-plus-year-old buildings that dominated the town. Lights burned inside, and a number of cars sat in the gravel parking area. Maggie pulled into the lot and parked.

She reached into the backseat, took a small pair of binoculars from a canvas bag and handed them to Brent. "I'll go to the door and act like I'm lost. You stay out of sight and check the people inside."

"What do we do if it's him?"

"Nothing. If we don't make him suspicious, he's got no reason to run."

Brent was afraid suddenly. Turner might be his only link to the truth. What if he got away somehow? He took a deep breath and nodded, knowing he had to trust her instincts. "I guess you know best."

"I'm a cop."

"And you're smart."

"Well, I am a woman."

In spite of his anxiety, he smiled, realizing how good it felt to be with her again.

A pickup truck was parked directly in front of the church door, and he climbed quietly into its bed and moved to where he could kneel on a hay bale and steady the binoculars on the cab roof. Maggie went up the steps to the front door then turned and looked at him and held up one thumb, her gesture indicating he was out of sight. After another second, she opened the door. She waited like that, seeming bewildered, holding the door wide. Brent could see a number of people in the pews on either side. One by one heads began to turn as parishioners looked back.

"Excuse me!" Maggie said to no one in particular, her voice carrying faintly to where Brent knelt. "Is this St. John the Evangelist?"

Brent saw one man shake his head.

"I didn't think so!" Maggie grabbed a handful of hair, as though she was some kind of ditz. "I'm so sorry to bother you, but somebody told me St. John the Evangelist was out of town. Is it in town?" Several parishioners nodded.

"Come on, come on," Brent muttered, a cold sweat breaking out from his armpits as he scanned the strange faces with growing desperation.

"I'm so sorry," Maggie persisted, even as the heads started to swing back to the front of the church. "But I'm kind of lost." Someone seemed to be trying to wave her forward, but she seemed too embarrassed to go any further, too confused to leave.

A second later Brent felt his breath catch as Spencer

McDonald–at least the man he knew as Spencer McDonald–walked down the aisle wearing a black clergyman's shirt and white collar. He led Maggie out onto the porch and let the door swing shut behind them. His voice was a low rumble as he gave her directions back to town.

Just before she turned to leave, Maggie asked, "May I ask your name, sir. I want to tell my friends about the nice man who helped me."

"Reverend Turner."

Brent stayed out of sight in the back of the truck. After a few seconds, the church doors opened and closed again. Finally, he heard Maggie's footsteps coming toward him.

"Well?" Maggie asked when she came abreast of the pickup.

He nodded. "It's him!" he whispered.

THIRTY-NINE

LONG ISLAND, JUNE 30

ABU SAYEED GLANCED at his watch, spoke a silent prayer to Allah, then nodded to Mohammed. It was time. They had gone over his instructions yet again. Mohammed's job was to erase their tracks, but if he was stopped and could not escape, he was to kill himself and the woman. It would be a necessary loss so the plan could still go forward. The American President's visit was two days away, but Abu Sayeed had no interest. His attack was scheduled for tomorrow.

They stood in the open door of the cottage. The night was moonless. Mohammed licked his lips, and Abu Sayeed noted a trickle of sweat at his hairline. Not good, he thought. Mohammed checked the silenced Marakov 9mm pistol he wore strapped across his chest and gave it a tug to make sure it was secure, then Abu Sayeed handed him the Heckler & Koch submachine gun. Mohammed nodded once then set off through the trees.

Abu Sayeed watched him disappear into the shadows. He would scale the wall at the front of Biddle's property, where Anneliës would pick him up. With Allah's blessing he would return within three or four hours.

FORTY

GREENWICH, CT, JUNE 30

FRED WOFFORD PUT the last of his clothes in the suitcase then held it closed while he zipped it shut. The act felt like a milestone, and he let out a sigh of relief. His wife's clothes were still strewed over the bed as she hurried to pack and at the same time understand what had possessed her husband, who by his own admission had never done anything spontaneous in his life, to book the Queen Mary Suite on the new QM2.

She was still selecting jewelry and formal dresses when the doorbell rang. Wofford glanced at his watch, thinking it must be the limo driver. The man was at least an hour early, but then better that way than late. It was probably the driver's intention to bill him for waiting time, but he didn't care. He just wanted to leave. The sooner he was on the ship, the better. He wanted to be protected by distance, insulated by deniability.

At some level he felt a terrible sense of disloyalty, but his visit to the terrorists had tipped some invisible scales. He'd finally admitted to himself that he couldn't go along with Biddle. In the final analysis, the wild hope for Armageddon, the belief that an unforgivable act might result in a miracle—none of it made sense. They led Christian lives, and they had every single thing a person could want, including great wealth. Why should they throw it away on a fantasy?

He pulled on a shirt, buttoned it on the way down the stairs and flipped on the porch light. He opened the door intending to tell the driver to wait in the car, but then he froze. A different man, his face terribly familiar, stood on the porch smiling up at him.

Ten minutes later, wanting her husband's help in deciding between several dresses, Wofford's wife called his name. When she heard no answer, she went to the bedroom door and shouted again. Again, there was no response. She went to the top of the staircase and called his name again. Typical Fred, she thought.

"Fred!" she shouted, starting to become angry.

She went down and looked in the kitchen, then in his library. Finally, she went out onto the front porch and looked at the empty driveway. Her husband was gone.

FORTY-ONE

OVER THE PACIFIC OCEAN, JUNE 30

PRESCOTT BIDDLE PEERED out through his jet's thick window at the night. He'd been flying for twelve hours, having left Murmansk at ten p.m., and throughout the entire flight darkness had gripped the world. This constant blackness reminded him that he was the avenging Angel of God, racing through the heavens toward his ultimate meeting with the agents of Satan.

His return would surprise no one. He was cutting short his fishing trip because of Dr. Faisal's murder and the theft of his assets. It was tragic Biddle would tell the press. After their exhaustive background checks and psychological profiles, they had trusted that young man, but obviously they'd failed to find the hidden character flaw. It was heartbreaking, doubly so since Lucas had also killed Owen Smythe and his young family.

The one flaw, of course, was that Rev. Turner and the Arab had failed to kill Lucas. Right now, he could be dead or dying of his wounds, but they couldn't be sure. They had to assume he was alive, and therefore dangerous and unpredictable. There remained the possibility that Lucas would go to the police, but with what? A preposterous story about fake FBI Agents and a fake lawyer who had all . . . disappeared? No, with Smythe gone, there was no way for Lucas to garner any proof, which also meant that instead of running, he was more likely to attack.

Biddle shook his head as he sipped a Diet Coke. He wouldn't let that happen. He'd found out where Lucas was, and this time his own people were going to kill Lucas and dispose of the body. Even if they had a problem, who would question two sheriff's deputies who killed a murder suspect? No, he thought, in a country that cared more about abortion rights and gay marriage than the truth of the Holy Bible, it wouldn't surprise anyone. Brent Lucas would be one more American tragedy, like O.J and Columbine. Yes, Biddle thought, God was looking down into the muck of modern America and watching His Angels of Prophesy. God knew they were taking great risks in His name, and He would ensure their success.

He tried to retain the purity of his focus, but he felt it slip. Try as he did, he was helpless to prevent the next image that took shape in his mind. It was Anneliës again, dancing before him in a smoky light. Shadows ran across her stomach and breasts as she moved, caressing the parts of her that his tongue and fingers had explored so often.

He believed that the holiness of his mission should have lessened his need, but the opposite had occurred. His hunger had grown and raged inside him now, as if his every molecule of sinfulness had been compressed into desire for this woman's flesh. He'd spent many hours on his knees, praying for strength, but it did no good. Now, he glanced at his left hand where the snake venom had rotted the skin between his thumb and forefinger, leaving a permanent disfigurement as though he had been bitten by the Devil himself.

The plane hit some turbulence, and Biddle turned again to the outer dark and tried to shake off these feelings. He bent his thoughts back to his mission, to Beddington and McTighe and the job they were doing in God's name. He closed his eyes and said another prayer, asking God to speed their progress, give them steady hands for aiming and strong hearts for killing.

The turbulence ended. Suddenly, the clouds beneath the aircraft gave way, and the full moon reflected off the black void of ocean fifty thousand feet below. As he watched, the reflection appeared to change shape, narrowing into a flame, as if the first fire of Armageddon was already igniting the world. The jet streaked across the sky, and he kept the flame in view as long as he could, counting it as one more sign from God that he would be victorious.

FORTY-TWO

CENTRAL NEW JERSEY, JUNE 30

DARIUS MCTIGHE HAD worked hard to keep the pickup tucked out of sight, but the traffic had thinned and now the only car ahead of him was a VW bug, one of the old ones tricked out with wide tires and mag wheels. The driver was right on the woman's tail, and if he hung a quick pass and got around her, it would leave McTighe's pickup sticking right out there naked. They were on 202 North, heading into the 287 merge. He prayed the woman's eyes were too taken up with road signs to notice they'd been on her tail ever since she left Morristown.

Originally, they'd been parked down at the end of her street waiting for her and Lucas to go to sleep, intending then to slip in and do their job. They'd planned to leave the woman's body there, making it look like Lucas had continued his murder spree, then they would dump Lucas where the Arab should have in the first place, about fifty miles straight out from the Barnegat Light where they'd wrap him in chains and sink him in about five hundred feet of water.

Only instead of staying home and going to bed, Lucas and the woman had left the house and—to McTighe's growing horror—they had driven all the way down to Lambertville, right to his own neighborhood church. It had to mean that Lucas and the woman were close to the truth. Just in case they'd already figured it out and were heading to the cops, Beddington and McTighe had decided to nail them before they got back to Morristown, whenever they came to a deserted stretch of road. Their story would be that Lucas had taken the woman hostage and killed her when she'd tried to escape. There'd be no questions. After all, they were sheriff's deputies.

Tom Beddington seemed to be thinking the same thing because he said, "This is going to be easy."

McTighe glanced over. Somehow hearing Beddington say it only made the reality worse. He'd been a police officer for nearly twenty years, but he'd never fired his gun in the line of duty, much less killed people in cold blood. Right now his nerves were firing off like popcorn. "Oh yeah?"

Beddington swung his head on his thick neck and gave him a disgusted look. "Where's your faith?"

"I got plenty." McTighe could feel Beddington's small eyes cutting holes in him, but he didn't care.

"Mr. Biddle set this up. He's got grace."

"He's a human being. People make mistakes."

"You gotta believe."

McTighe said nothing, but he started to worry maybe Beddington had a point. Maybe he did lack faith.

"It's your attitude, man. You need to pray more."

"Killing a cop's got nothing to do with faith," McTighe shot back, finally putting words to it.

"Man, it's got everything to do with faith."

McTighe hit the steering wheel with his hand.

"If you've got faith, you don't worry. You just do it," Beddington insisted. "You gonna do it, or not?"

McTighe gritted his teeth until his fillings hurt. "Yeah, I'm gonna do it, but I don't like doing it. I hate doing it."

Beddington shook his head and smiled. "It's God's will," he said.

"And what if it goes down wrong?"

Beddington shrugged. "Then maybe we die and go to Heaven right now, tonight. That's okay with me, man. God understands I'm laying my life on the line for Him."

"Personally, I'd like to be around for a few more years," McTighe said, feeling a combination of resentment and shame that he couldn't muster Beddington's apparent selflessness.

"You will be," Beddington assured him. "I mean, look what God's given us to help us do our job. Amazing stuff on this guy!" Beddington picked up the file that sat on the seat between them then reached up and flipped on the overhead light.

Right away McTighe reached up and turned it off. "No light!" he snapped, thinking that with Beddington he could never be sure where faith ended and stupidity began. "We already know what it says."

The file held almost everything a person could want to

know about Brent Lucas, including his schools, his test scores, the sports he'd played, names of his friends, pictures of him taken from different angles. It also had the name and address of Lucas's old girlfriend and listed her occupation as cop. That one detail in particular, McTighe was thinking, was way more than he wanted to know.

That information, plus the bug in Lucas' cell phone, had led them to him after the Arab screwed up. Lucas had turned the phone on for only a few minutes, but it had been enough to confirm his location. Tonight, with the cell phone turned off, they were having to tail him the old-fashioned way.

After they'd followed him all the way down to the Reverend's church, they'd parked the truck behind an old barn down the road. McTighe knew if they stayed in plain sight, some meathead friend might recognize the pickup and come over to shoot the breeze. What excuse do you use when you're waiting around to kill a couple of people?

What McTighe couldn't understand was how fast Lucas had managed to track the Reverend. It had even freaked Beddington out, and he had wanted to pop the both of them right there, on the road between the church and town. It would be easy, he'd insisted, and they could dump the bodies down near Camden. No way, McTighe had said. He wasn't killing anybody that close to his wife and kids.

It kept eating at him that the woman was a cop. He tried to think on what Rev. Turner had said, how true Christians had a duty to the prophecy. It was a grave responsibility, the Reverend had said, and if they didn't do it, they could be pushing back Jesus's return by five hundred or even a thousand years. Would that be right? Would God want that? It was tough to argue with the Reverend.

His thoughts were interrupted when the VW ahead of them put on its blinker. "Shit," he mumbled. One of his front parking lights was broken, and he hadn't gotten around to fixing it. If Lucas's girlfriend had been checking for tails, that broken light would be easy to pick out. He took his foot off the gas and let the space between the Toyota and the truck widen to the point where he could barely see her taillights.

"Don't lose her!" Beddington snapped.

"I don't want her to spot us."

"She ain't going to," Beddington said.

"I'm glad you're so sure."

Beddington nodded. "We're invisible to the sinner. We are enclosed in the blinding cloak of God's grace. No way they can see us."

McTighe shot him a sideways glance, hating the smug expression Beddington always wore when he talked about God. McTighe knew that God helped those who helped themselves, so it seemed just plain foolish not to be careful.

After another mile, Route 202 merged into Route 287, and the traffic became heavier. McTighe sped up again but managed to get a delivery van between him and the Toyota. They were eating up the distance to Morristown.

"We gotta find our chance," Beddington said.

McTighe winced and rubbed his hands on his trouser legs to dry the sweat. "Maybe we just ought to wait."

As if in response, Beddington took out his automatic, slid a shell into the chamber then clicked on the safety. "We already talked about this. What if they're not goin' back to her house? What if they're goin' to the cops to report the Reverend?" Beddington glanced at him.

McTighe felt none of Beddington's confidence, only fear. He thought about their alibi. They'd sure as hell need God to make it hold up because the whole thing sounded like bullshit—especially the part about how they'd driven fifty miles to meet a friend at a bar for a couple of Cokes. Maybe other people did stuff like that, but not him. Other than his jobs for Mr. Biddle, he generally hung out close to home.

He went over everything in his head again, looking for comfort in the details. He had to admit Rev. Turner had thought it out pretty good—even had a waitress at a Morristown restaurant who'd claim she'd waited on them if anybody asked. But nobody would. He and Beddington were cops. They'd be heroes for nailing a murderer.

"Hey!" Beddington said suddenly.

The Toyota's turn signal was on. There was an exit just ahead, and McTighe tried to recall what the last sign had said. Basking Ridge, that was it. "Shit," he muttered as he slowed down.

FORTY-THREE

BASKING RIDGE, NJ, JUNE 30

"TELL ME AGAIN why we didn't drag that sonofabitch out of his church and beat the truth out of him right on the spot?" Brent demanded.

"Other than feeling good," Maggie said, "to what point?"

"To make him admit he's working with Biddle!"

"What if he denies it? What do you do then?"

Brent threw his hands in the air. "I'll break his arms!"

"That would be persuasive to a jury. An accused murderer and embezzler beats up a minister!" Maggie nodded. "Good thinking."

"So we're just going to leave him there?"

"He won't run if he doesn't think he's a suspect," she said, even as something in her rearview mirror caught her eye. She was once again seeing the set of headlights she'd been seeing intermittently for the past twenty miles. They'd gone under some bright arc lights a while back, and she'd seen they belonged to a pickup truck. The truck had a burned out parking light down on the bumper.

"Can you at least tap the guy's phone?"

In her rearview mirror Maggie could see a delivery van now sitting directly behind her, screening the pickup. "We'll probably need more evidence than we've got, especially when it concerns somebody like Biddle."

Brent slapped his door in frustration.

She ignored him, staring now at the rearview mirror. "Somebody's been following us, probably ever since Lambertville. I should have paid better attention."

Brent turned his head and looked through the back window. "Police?"

Maggie put on her turn signal. "Police would have stopped us already. It's a pickup truck."

"So where are we going?"

"The back way," Maggie said.

"If he doesn't follow us maybe we can park and make out," Brent said.

"Funny." Maggie glanced back and chewed her lip. "Hopefully I'm just paranoid, but I don't think so." She thought about the narrow road through the nature preserve that led eventually to Morristown. She knew it well enough to drive it at high speed and was pretty sure she could lose somebody who didn't know where they were going.

"If those are the guys who killed Smythe, a deserted road is about perfect for them," Brent said. "This is a bad idea!"

They were off the highway, approaching the turn for the nature preserve. "You'd rather lead them to my house?"

Brent's face was creased with worry. He glanced over his shoulder at the lights of the pickup about a hundred yards back, then he gritted his teeth. "Do it," he grunted.

She swung left, and immediately the road narrowed and became uneven. The houses and lights disappeared, replaced quickly by empty darkness stretching on all sides.

The driver of the pickup seemed to sense that they would try and lose him because he roared up on their bumper. Maggie floored the Toyota, but its soft suspension slammed through the bumps. "Shit!" she said as the far more powerful truck stayed on their tail. There were no other headlights in either direction, and after a half mile or so a blue police light began to flash.

She glanced at Brent, who already had one hand on the door handle. She grabbed his arm. "Stay put and keep your head turned forward," she ordered. She struggled to think as she slowed and pulled to the side, careful to leave two of her wheels on dry pavement for traction. She shifted into neutral, then snatched her holster from the space between the seat and console.

She was sure these weren't cops, but what if they were? A voice in her head screamed that she couldn't risk shooting a fellow officer, but it all smelled wrong. No cop would make a stop like this without backup, so if they stayed in the truck and waited, they were real, she decided. If they got out, they were something else.

She unsnapped the holster, pulled out her Glock and chambered a round. She reset the safety and slipped the gun beneath her thigh, knowing if things got tight she'd have only a split second to decide.

She heard a door open. Her rearview mirror showed two men climbing from the truck. They edged cautiously toward the Toyota, taking small steps, staying to either side. She lowered her window and strained her ears for the sound of a police radio. Cops would have handhelds or the volume turned up in the truck so they could hear, but the only sound was the peeping of frogs in the nearby marsh. The man on the left stepped in front of the truck headlight, the silhouette of a pistol outlined beside his leg.

These guys had waited to make their stop until they were someplace where there'd be no witnesses. They weren't cops!

She leaned out and called back to the man on the left side, "Hold it right there! Who are you and what do you want?" She said it with enough force that the man stopped.

"Police. The two of you step out of the car," he barked. "Hands where I can see them."

"Where's the guy on your side?" she whispered to Brent.

He was slouched in his seat, staring intently at his side mirror. "Couple feet behind the car."

"I'm not stopping here," Maggie shouted. "I have the right to drive to a well-lighted place. You can follow me." She felt Brent coil beside her, again ready to bolt. She gripped his thigh. "Don't move," she whispered.

"I'm afraid that won't be possible, ma'am." The man's shoes crunched gravel as he took another step. "Turn your engine off. You and your friend just get out of the car with your hands in plain sight."

She took her hand from Brent's thigh and gripped her pistol. She was out of time, but could she shoot? What if these were stupid cops who were breaking all the rules?

Suddenly Brent let out a gasp as he stared at the side mirror. "I see his face! It's one of the FBI guys!" he said in a choked whisper. In the next second his door was open, and he exploded from the car.

Maggie heard a gunshot, but she had no time to think. She jammed the shifter into reverse, stomped on the accelerator and cut the wheel. The rear bumper slammed the guy on her side with a loud thump. She immediately hit the brakes, her automatic already out the window. "Freeze," she shouted at the man who was on his knees, groping for his gun. "Freeze!" she shouted again. The man glanced up and saw her Glock aimed at his chest, and he raised his hands.

"Brent?" she screamed as she opened her door, rolled out and squatted beside the car.

"I'm okay," he shouted.

"Are you hit?"

"No."

"Do you have his gun?"

"No, but I've got him," Brent answered. He appeared around the rear of Maggie's car struggling with a large man. He held him in a throat lock and had one of the man's arms twisted up behind his back.

Maggie straightened, went forward and kicked the first man's pistol away. "On your stomach," she commanded. "Hands behind your back. The man obeyed, lying face down in the road. She placed the barrel of her gun against his spine, pulled a pair of handcuffs from the pouch on her belt and locked them around his wrists.

Brent's prisoner suddenly began to struggle wildly. He was as tall as Brent and more thickly built. Brent's face knotted in pain as he struggled to keep control. Maggie approached, then kicked the man hard in the crotch. His eyes bugged, and then the air left his lungs in a rush. He sagged abruptly, appearing to lose all resistance and almost taking Brent down.

"Get him on his stomach," Maggie said, as she reached into her car for a spare set of cuffs in the door pocket.

She handed Brent the cuffs just as the man started to struggle again. He outweighed Brent by thirty or forty pounds, and it was clear from Brent's expression that the fighting must have re-injured his wounded stomach. Nonetheless, Brent knelt on the man's back and gripped one meaty wrist as he managed to fasten the first bracelet. He seemed to have things under control, but then the man moved suddenly, raising his shoulder and bringing one leg up as he jerked his other hand free.

Maggie saw what was happening. "Watch out!" she cried.

Brent grabbed for the man's arm as it snaked down to his

pants cuff and a second later reappeared with a small revolver. Brent was off the man's back now, holding the man's gun arm in a desperate grip. The man swung his other arm, lashing the loose cuff savagely into the back of Brent's head. Brent lost his grip momentarily, but grabbed the wrist again and shoved the gun away just as the man pulled the trigger. The gun was waving toward Maggie, and she dove to one side as a second shot boomed out.

She aimed her own gun, looking for a chance to return fire. The man continued whipping his handcuff into Brent's back and head until he once again jerked his gun hand free. He rolled away from Brent and onto his knees, bringing the gun to bear on Brent, his arms locked in a two-handed shooter's pose.

"Drop it!" Maggie commanded, her finger tightening on the trigger.

The man's gun stayed locked on Brent, but he looked at her, then past her at his companion. His eyes widened.

"Drop it!" Maggie shouted. "Now!"

The man looked back at Brent, his face now oddly contorted. "McTighe!" he shouted, but his partner didn't answer. "Oh Jesus," he whimpered.

"Drop it," Maggie repeated.

He kept the gun on Brent, but he cut her another sideways glance. "I can't," he said.

"You can't win," Maggie said. "Drop it, now!"

"I am one of the chosen!" he said, his voice cracking.

"Put down the gun," she said, struggling to sound calm and steady.

The man shook his head.

Brent was on his knees, holding his stomach. "Who are you?" he grunted.

"One of the chosen," the man repeated.

"Why did you steal the money? Why did you kill Dr. Faisal and Owen Smythe? Is Prescott Biddle your boss?"

Sweat was streaming down the man's face, and his hands shook. "I am one of the chosen," he said for a third time, as he thumbed back the hammer.

"No!" Maggie screamed as she saw the man's finger tighten on the trigger. She fired twice, knocking him backward even as his gun went off. She looked at Brent, who was frozen in shock, staring at the twitching body.

"Are you okay?" she asked in a trembling voice.

Brent only nodded. All around them the world had fallen deathly silent. Maggie's pulse thundered against her eardrums. After several more seconds, as frogs resumed peeping in the swamp, she turned to look at her other prisoner. He lay motionless. She went over, knelt beside him, then put her hand over her mouth upon seeing the jagged wound where his partner's wild shot had blown the corner of his forehead away.

Brent stood, hobbled over and touched her shoulder. When she finally glanced up, she saw blood in his hair from where the handcuff had lacerated his scalp. Without a word he took the corpse by the ankles and dragged it into the deep grass beside the right front tire of the truck, out of sight of a passing car. He pulled the larger man behind the tire as well, then collapsed against the truck's hood, his head bowed. "Who the hell were these guys?" he mumbled.

Suddenly, headlights appeared in the distance, and a car approached out of the misty dark. Maggie was still frozen, but Brent recovered his senses enough to scuttle into the road for the pistol that lay a few feet from the slick of wet blood. He shoved it into his waistband, jerked his shirttail to cover it, then he pulled Maggie to her feet and back to a safe spot. They waited by the front fender of the truck as the car slowed.

"Car trouble?" a man's voice asked.

"This lady just hit a deer," Maggie heard Brent say. She waved to show that she was unhurt. "We thought it was dead," Brent continued, "but then it jumped up and ran off."

"Happens all the time around here," the man said. "As long as everybody's okay, I wouldn't worry. Those damn things have an amazing ability to live."

"Yeah, thanks for stopping."

"Okay, 'night."

Brent waved as the car drove away, then he let out a moan. He turned toward Maggie, his eyes tight. "This has gone too far," he said. "I've got to turn myself in."

"No!" she said, the heat of her emotion catching her by surprise. She was operating purely on instinct, but she felt no doubt whatsoever. "We've got to hide all of this and get out of here."

"No!" Brent said. "We've got two more guys dead! This can't go on!"

"If you quit, they win!" Maggie shouted. She forced herself into motion. She had several plastic evidence bags in her purse, a holdover from her detective days in Morristown, and she used one as she bent down and hurriedly removed the contents of the first man's pockets. She repeated the process with the second man, then sealed both bags, wrote "passenger" on the first one and "driver" on the second. She wasn't sure the distinction mattered, but she was pleased that her brain still worked on some level.

Brent watched her for a few seconds then pulled open the pickup's door and searched the inside. A moment later he climbed out holding a manila file and the truck's registration papers.

Another car materialized out of the mist, coming faster than the last. Maggie stepped into the truck's headlights to make herself visible, but as this car passed it did not slow. Maggie glimpsed a woman passenger's face turned toward them for an instant, her expression a worried frown. Was it possible she would call the police and report two suspicious vehicles stopped in the wildlife sanctuary?

"Hurry," she called to Brent.

He tossed the file in the Toyota then came around to where the bodies lay. Without another word, Maggie took the nearest one by the ankles while Brent grabbed it under the armpits. Together, they hoisted it into the truck bed where it fell with a sickening thud. The second body was much heavier, but they managed it, as well.

Brent lifted his shirt, pulled out the gun he'd picked up and started to toss it into the bed.

"Don't," Maggie said, her voice tight. Her mind was leaping ahead. She was operating on a cold certainty now, not only of Brent's innocence but that all the usual rules had been put on hold. "You'll probably need it."

He hesitated and looked at her as if she were some stranger he'd never met, but then he tucked the pistol back in waistband.

"Find a place where the truck will be out of sight," she said. "I'll follow you."

Brent nodded, then climbed behind the wheel of the truck and started off. As Maggie followed in her Toyota, her mind raced. This wasn't just a theft. It wasn't even a theft/murder. It was a complex operation of some sort, and it pointed right back to Prescott Biddle. So, why would a billionaire steal a billion dollars?

She thought she already knew the answer, but others would say it was a wild supposition, pregnant with political risk. She hadn't even shared her thoughts with Brent because they seemed so improbable. She'd put them down in her memo and left it on Jenkins's desk, but that was as far as she thought it would go. She estimated zero probability that anyone at Project Seahawk would want to follow it up.

However, her gut instincts told her she was absolutely right and that she was looking at a full-blown national crisis—all of which brought her back to Brent. Two more dead bodies were even more reason for him to remain at-large. If he turned himself in, the police and FBI would consider the problem solved, and it might be weeks before anyone could persuade them differently. By then it might be way too late, which meant Brent had to remain on the loose until the two of them could build a credible argument. What were the odds, with the police and FBI coming from one direction and these would-be killers coming from the other?

She'd been following Brent as he searched for a turnoff, and now she noticed a strange sound, something halfway between a moan and a voice. It took her several seconds to realize she was the one making it. She was a lapsed Catholic and hadn't been to Mass in over a year, but she'd been saying, "Oh, Jesus, oh, Jesus," over and over through gritted teeth.

FORTY-FOUR

GAS STATION, SOMERVILLE, NJ, JUNE 30

BRENT SLUMPED LOW in the Toyota's passenger seat, using a paper towel to dab at the gashes on the back of his head while Maggie filled the tank with gas. His hair was matted with dried blood, and he had a pounding headache, but at least the bleeding had slowed. A moment earlier he'd unbuttoned his shirt and checked his abdomen. Amazingly only one of the butterflies had popped. A thin trickle of blood oozed from the wound, nothing serious.

He glanced up when Maggie slid behind the wheel, studying her face in the halogen glare of the service station's lights. Dark shadows pooled in the hollows of her cheeks, and the olive tone of her skin had turned a sickly yellow. Her eyes that normally sparked with energy and intelligence were dull and lusterless. It made what he had to tell her even more difficult.

The last several hours had been a descent into madness, but a moment earlier things had gotten infinitely worse when he'd opened up the dead men's wallets only to find the Sheriff's Deputy badges. The sight had sickened him.

It must have shown in his expression, because Maggie cocked her head. "What?"

Without a word, he took one of the wallets and heard her sharp intake of breath as he flashed the badge. She surprised him when her expression immediately grew hard. "It was self-defense. They were going to murder us."

"Yeah, but why? What the hell does, 'I am the Chosen!' mean? Chosen for what?"

Brent shook his head as he thought again about the truck with the two bodies. They'd left it at the end of an overgrown dirt track, rammed deep in some high bushes, but the wildlife refuge was public. In a day or two someone would stumble over it, and there would almost certainly be microscopic evidence—blood or hair samples, something that would link him to the killings. Then he'd be a cop killer on top of everything else. Even worse–Maggie had been there. He balled his fists, wishing he'd been able to keep her out of this.

As though reading his mind, Maggie put her hand on his forearm and squeezed. "I make my own choices."

He nodded and turned away. He knew she was strong and independent, that no one could force her to do anything she thought was wrong. It didn't make any of this right, but he couldn't worry about it now, not the lack of fairness, not his feelings for her, not the future. There'd be time for those things if they succeeded. His job right now had to be pushing past their problems and giving her strength while they planned their next step.

He put the wallets aside and handed her the folder he'd found in the pickup. "This helps explain how those guys managed to find us," he said, referring to the collection of intimate details about his life, down to Maggie's home address, even quotes from his employment interview with Genesis Advisors' consulting psychologist.

Maggie shook her head in disbelief as she skimmed the pages. "This cost someone thousands of dollars."

Brent glanced at the truck registration showing the Lambertville address. "Reverend Turner's liable to disappear when he learns these two guys are missing," he said. "I'm going back."

Maggie looked at him, her eyes glazed with exhaustion. After a second, she found enough energy to nod.

He reached across the seat and took her hand. "Alone," he said. He didn't know how he could succeed by himself, but it didn't matter. "I can't thank you enough for . . . everything."

Maggie seemed to come awake. She slapped the steering wheel with her other hand, as a bit of her old spirit glimmered. "Not a chance. You've got the world's worst sense of direction. You'd never even find his house without me."

FORTY-FIVE

LAMBERTVILLE, NJ, JUNE 31

BRENT BRAKED TO a stop on the gravel road then used Maggie's flashlight to check the number on the mailbox–75 East Elm, though the five lacked a nail and tilted at an angle against the seven. The house was small, like the others in this area that was not quite suburb and not quite country. It stood back maybe fifty yards from the road, well separated from the neighbors on both sides.

Brent checked his watch, twelve-thirty. Lights still burned downstairs, although the front porch light was turned off. A van and an older model Volvo sedan sat in the unpaved driveway.

"Looks like somebody's still awake," he muttered. Was it the Reverend awaiting a phone call from the two deputies? He glanced toward Maggie and saw she had finally dozed off. He watched her chest rise and fall with deep respirations and wished he could leave her there undisturbed.

"Hey," he said after a few seconds, giving her shoulder a gentle squeeze. "We're here."

She sat up and blinked. "You okay?" he asked.

"I'll make it," she muttered.

"You wouldn't have any wire cutters?"

She looked at him and wiped at her eyes. "Phone line?"

Brent nodded.

"I'm glad one of us can still think." She jerked her head. "In the trunk."

He found the wire cutters in a wooden box along with a crowbar, several screwdrivers and a slip bar for unlocking cars. He closed the trunk softly then tapped on Maggie's side window. "Got it," he whispered.

She climbed behind the wheel and waited there while he circled the house and prayed the Reverend wasn't a dog lover. He reached the backyard without incident and heard the hum of an air conditioning unit in an upstairs window. The overhead wires came from the rear of the property and attached to the house beside the kitchen porch. Enough light spilled through the kitchen curtains to outline a wooden railing about five feet below.

He crept toward the porch and glanced up, guessing the thinner, lower wire had to be the phone line. The faint sound of a television came through the wall, and he hoped it would mask his footsteps as he climbed the steps and mounted the railing. The wood protested but held, and he pulled out the cutters. A thick coating of rubber covered the handles, but he tensed as the blades gripped the wire, wondering if a few hundred volts were about to blast his body.

He squeezed, and the wire snapped away from the house with a loud click. He let out a slow breath, stepped gently off the railing then retraced his steps. He checked the houses on both sides, but they were still dark. In some distant yard a dog barked.

Maggie met him on the Turner's front porch. "Any problems?" she whispered.

He shook his head. "Ready?" He waited for her nod then knocked on the door.

A few seconds later, they heard heavy footsteps. "Yes?" a familiar voice asked.

Brent nodded to Maggie. "Reverend Turner?" she said. "This is Special Officer Margaret DeVito with Project Seahawk. I wonder if I could have a word with you on a matter of national importance?"

"Uh," the Reverend's voice came back, suddenly ragged with anxiety. "Well, I don't know. It's very late. Could you come back in the morning?"

"I'm afraid not. It concerns the death of two local sheriff's deputies and several murders in New York City. I am sure you can appreciate the need for your immediate cooperation."

"Uh . . . just a minute." Brent heard the hiss of hurried whispers and words that sounded like, "Call Mr. Wofford." A second later a woman's voice came back, "It doesn't work." More whispers followed, something about a cell phone and the van, the rest indistinct.

"Reverend, I have to ask you to open up right away. This will only take a few minutes." As Maggie spoke, Brent jumped off the porch and raced toward the rear of the house, drawing the pistol from his waistband. As he came around the side, he saw light spilling through the open backdoor and a woman on the porch, wearing a bathrobe. Something about her seemed oddly familiar.

"Mrs. Turner!" he shouted.

She swung her head toward him so that the light caught her face. His breath caught as he recognized Ruth Simmons. Panic etched her features as she turned, ran into the house and slammed the door. A second later, Rev. Turner called out through the closed kitchen door. "You can't just come barging in our house like this! It's the middle of the night! We have rights!"

Brent stepped onto the back porch and rattled the doorknob. He heard a sound like someone choking, and then footsteps. Thirty seconds went by. He fought the urge to check on Maggie. "Open up!" he called, then used the pistol barrel to break a glass pane in the door.

As he reached through and flicked the lock, a shotgun blast came from another part of the house. Thinking only of Maggie, he threw open the door and raced inside. He ran through the kitchen, small dining room, and living room, but the downstairs was empty. "Maggie!" he shouted.

"Out here!"

He ripped open the front door and saw her, gun drawn, down in a shooter's crouch. "You okay?" he shouted.

Before she could answer, there was another shot followed by a hollow thump. Brent jumped back and aimed up the stairs.

"Reverend Turner, Mrs. Turner," Maggie shouted. "Throw down your weapons and come to the top of the stairs with your hands up."

Brent held his breath. Seconds passed. The same dog still barked. Had the neighbors heard the shots?

"Reverend Turner!" Maggie called again. "Come down stairs with your hands in the air."

Silence.

"Reverend Turner," Maggie called. "I'm going to count to ten."

She began to count. When she finished, Brent put his foot

on the first step. "I'm coming up," he shouted.

He crept up the narrow staircase, his gun gripped in both hands, finger brushing the trigger. He paused, listened, shoved his fear into the background. Harry's voice was right there with him, as though the two of them were climbing the stairs together. *Life's best when you're on the edge, bro!* Brent shook his head. Harry had his head up his ass.

At the top of the stairs, his pulse slammed his eardrums. Otherwise, there was a deathly stillness. A strong metallic odor came from an open door on the right.

He risked a peek around the corner, half-expecting a shotgun blast in the face. Instead he saw the bodies and the blood. "Oh, my God," he choked, as he sagged against the wall.

"What?" Maggie called.

He shook his head, unable to describe the sigh—Rev. Turner in the middle of the floor, most of his jaw missing, a double-barreled shotgun inches from his outstretched hand, Ruth Simmons, or more likely Turner's wife, sprawled across the bed. Blood and brains splattered the far wall.

"Oh, Jesus," Maggie said as she came up and looked inside. Brent watched her double over and take several breaths, then quickly open the other two doors on the landing and sweep the empty rooms with her gun.

He crushed the heels of his hands against his temples. "Can someone tell me what the hell is going on?"

Maggie ignored him and went back in the bedroom. She was all business as she pulled a pair of rubber gloves from her pocket, slipped them on and pointed at the woman. "There's something here," she said.

Brent didn't move. After a second Maggie looked back at him.

He pointed. "That was Ruth Simmons."

"The Justice Department lawyer?"

He nodded.

"Well, hurry up. We don't have much time."

Brent held his breath and rolled the nearly headless body so Maggie could pull out what she'd seen.

"Family Bible," she said. "Opened to the Twenty-Third Psalm. She must have been reading it when he shot her."

"'The Lord is my shepherd.' It's like they were prepared for this," Brent said. He shook his head in disbelief.

Maggie began opening drawers and searching the dresser. She found a thin pair of men's socks and tossed them to him. "Put them on so you don't leave prints," she said. "Check the other rooms."

Brent glanced in the bathroom then searched a guest bedroom. A cluttered desk stood by the window, and he flipped through piles of magazine articles, partly finished sermons and stacks of correspondence. He took the letters with return addresses outside Lambertville and a black address book he found on top of the stack of sermons.

"Time to go," Maggie said from the door. Brent checked his watch, twelve-forty-five. It hadn't even been five minutes since the first shot, but if neighbors had heard it, the police could arrive any moment.

He hurriedly jerked open the desk drawers and the cheap two-drawer metal filing cabinet that sat beside the desk but found only manila folders with tax records and files of past sermons. He followed Maggie down the stairs and out the front door, where the cool night air shocked his lungs and the odors of grass and damp earth were like perfume. The neighboring houses remained completely dark.

As they reached the car, he paused for a second to listen. The dog still barked, and somewhere far away a train sounded a single lonely note.

FORTY-SIX

MORRISTOWN, NJ, JULY 1

THEY'D DRIVEN THROUGH sparse late-night traffic all the way to Morristown before Maggie broke the silence. "I have something to tell you," she said. "It's been on my mind for a while, but it seemed too crazy like . . . a tangent or crazy extrapolation."

"Let me guess—you want to have sex with me?"

She looked at him in utter amazement. Four people were dead tonight, and he was making jokes. "You really are a sick human being."

Brent shook his head. "Uncle Fred always said that humor is the only defense against the unspeakable."

"Imagine, a four-syllable word coming from Uncle Fred."

"I thought you liked him."

"I do, but you're all crazy, Brent. Everybody in your damn bloodline."

"I tried to explain that to you a long time ago."

"Well, try to get your brains out of my pants for five seconds because I want to explain something." She told him about the CIA's alert and the seeming coincidence that the stolen money approximated the cost of the missiles and the nuclear material.

Brent shot her an appraising glance. "That's why you didn't want me to turn myself in."

She nodded, "But I don't have the slightest clue how to prove it."

"Biddle is the key," Brent said. "We have to get to him and make the bastard talk."

"Kidnapping," she said with a nod. "Once again, the sophisticated approach."

"I can't afford to sit around with my thumb up my ass."

"Spoken like a true male."

"What the hell would you do?"

"Get evidence."

"Spoken like a true cop."

A short time later, she walked into her house, tossed her keys on the table and filled two glasses with ice. Exhaustion and stress had put her beyond the reach of caffeine. Cold water was a last resort.

Brent followed her, collapsed in one of the kitchen chairs and rested his head on his arms.

"Don't fall asleep," Maggie said. "We have to go through the address book."

"I'm just resting my eyes," he said.

"Like you were on the road," she said, a reference to when he'd dozed and almost run off the soft shoulder.

"Exactly like that." He yawned, shooting his arms across the table so that he sent his cell phone crashing to the floor.

Maggie bent down to pick up the phone and saw that the back had come off. As she started to put the two pieces was hanging by two thin wires with tiny clips. She put the phone on the table and pointed. "Does that look like it belongs there?"

Brent stared at the chip and tried unsuccessfully to push it back into the rest of the tightly packed innards so that it fit. "Give me your phone," he said after a second. She handed it over, and he removed the back. Together they looked at its symmetrically fitted guts. "I wondered about this the other night, but I was in too much of a panic to focus."

He turned his phone on then pulled a scrap of paper from his wallet. He dialed the scrawled phone number, pressed "send" and listened. "No answer," he said. He picked up Maggie's cell phone, dialed the same number and held it out so she could hear. After several rings she heard a voice say, "FBI."

He hung up then stared again at the small chip that dangled from his phone. "I bet this redirected my calls."

"It probably also tracked you," Maggie said.

"I bet all my phones were fixed. My office would have been easy, and my apartment . . ." He glanced up at her then away.

Something in his eyes told her that whatever happened in his apartment had involved another woman. She felt a sudden, hot flash of jealousy. To cover it, she stood and went to the sink.

Brent gripped the chip in his fingers ready to pull it out. "We have to assume they can still track us."

"Don't!" she said. "There's a better way." She told him she'd be right back then took the cell phone outside, climbed in her car and drove six blocks to Joe Spedowski's house. It was three a.m., but Spud was recently divorced and lived alone. She went up on his porch and rang the buzzer. He jerked it open a moment later wearing threadbare pajama bottoms and scratching his hairy stomach. "DeVito!" he grumbled. "This better be good."

"I need a favor." She handed him the cell phone and said she needed him to keep it with him on his rounds.

"Lemme guess," he said, as he turned it over and eyed the dangling chip. "It's bugged."

"I think it's a tracking device."

"If I should run into the trackee?"

"Wear your body armor. Call for backup."

His eyes opened wide. "You gonna give me any more information?"

"Can't."

"You owe me one."

"I owe you more than one."

He scowled and closed the door, and she got back in her car. A few minutes later when she walked back into her kitchen, Brent was going through the entries in Rev. Turner's address book. He pointed to one under the letter G, the initials, 'GA' and a number with a 212 area code. "Fred Wofford's direct line at Genesis Advisors!" he said triumphantly.

Maggie came up behind him and rested her hands on his shoulders. She let them remain there. It felt selfish, almost wrong, but his muscle and bone felt so substantial and reassuring beneath her fingers. Suddenly, all the things that had pushed them apart seemed insignificant. "Come on," she said, making her decision.

"Where to now?" Brent asked.

"Upstairs to bed. We need sleep."

He looked up at her and raised an eyebrow. "I didn't think I was allowed."

"I think you're pretty harmless tonight."

He managed a curious smile. "If I'm not?"

"Well . . . either way you're at least going to hold me until the damn alarm goes off."

He stood and put his arms around her. Neither of them spoke, and she folded her head into his chest and listened to the insistent thumping of his heart. They stood like that a long time. In spite of the night's horrors Maggie felt courage and strength begin to seep back into her bones, as though a rundown battery had suddenly been plugged into its charger.

FORTY-SEVEN

PROJECT SEAHAWK, NEWARK, NJ, JULY 1

ANN JENKINS SAT with her arms folded, her fingernails tucked out of biting range beneath her armpits, as she glared at the papers arrayed in neat piles on her desk. She'd been sitting this way for the past hour and a half, struggling to ignore the fraying tempers and the exhausted faces of people working double and triple shifts, trying to understand what was happening.

She sat there in perfect stillness, back straight, trying to open her mind. Screw it, she decided, after a few more minutes as she stood and started pacing. Nobody had invented the mantra that could take the place of a strong cigarette or at least a Hershey Bar with Almonds.

Of course—her typical luck—the candy machine downstairs was on the blink. At two a.m. nothing was open except for an all-night place about four blocks away, and she'd need an Uzi to shoot her way through the zombies on Newark's streets at this hour of the morning. Since she didn't have time to waste filling out paperwork on the resulting body count, she was staying put.

She stuck a finger in her mouth and tried to chew a piece of nail, but no luck, not even a sliver left to bite. She gave up and focused her eyes again on the pile topped by the CIA memo. Beneath it was everything she'd been able to dig up on the Wahaddi Brotherhood, which, considering the CIA's extremely negative view of the organization, wasn't much. What she had, however, detailed the gradual choking off of the Brotherhood's bank accounts in the years following 9/11, also the strong suspicion that a major Saudi family with strong U.S. economic and political ties—name deleted—had been responsible for much or most of the funding.

The second pile, not really a pile but a single sheet of paper, contained the names of all the people she'd spoken with over the past day and a half, as she tried to drum up support for

DeVito's thesis. She'd been rebuffed by her old compatriots at the FBI, by her superiors in Homeland Security and the U.S. Attorneys Office, by the White House staff, by members of the Committee to Re-elect the President, by the New York Mayor's Office, the New York Chief of Police, as well as by the Boston and Charleston commands of Project Seahawk. Her barrage of phone calls had finally brought a harsh response from her superiors at Homeland Security, and now she was expressly forbidden to communicate her Condition Red to anyone else.

The third pile, and the one that troubled her most, consisted of several news items: the theft of over eight hundred million dollars a few days earlier, the murder of a wealthy Egyptian, an arson/murder in Rye, and a murder in a Manhattan parking garage. Underneath the clippings lay Maggie DeVito's memo.

It was damn creative detective work, Jenkins thought, but her requests for wiretaps and surveillance had been turned down. The connections were too tenuous–pure speculation someone at the U.S. Attorney's Office called them–and Biddle was too powerful. Still, Jenkins respected the way DeVito had followed her gut. All her instincts told her that DeVito was on the right path.

Unfortunately, it led straight into a political minefield. Anybody who went that way risked getting blown to pieces. Shit! She shook her head, continued pacing. She tried to bite another nail.

FORTY-EIGHT

LAMBERTVILLE, NJ, JULY 1

MOHAMMED CIRCLED THE small house for the third time and listened to the sounds of the night all around. A dog barked in a yard somewhere. Once, a car sped past, not slowing. Mohammed's own car was parked over a mile away, and he moved silently and carefully. The faint sound of a television leaked through the walls, as if someone was still watching, but he didn't think they were. Maybe they'd fallen asleep, but he doubted that, too. Something felt wrong.

He'd noticed the broken pane in the back door on his first circuit, and he'd gone around twice more to make sure he wasn't missing anything else. Now, he went up onto the back porch and tried the knob. The door was unlocked. His Marakov 9mm was already in his hand, and he stepped over the broken glass and tiptoed through the kitchen.

The downstairs was empty, and he crept up the stairs, his pistol centered on the landing. At the next to last step, the smell hit him, and he glanced to the right and saw the two sprawled bodies. He looked quickly at the other two rooms, found only emptiness, then backtracked and left the house through the back door. On his way to his car he used his cell phone to call Abu Sayeed.

"The holy man and his wife are dead," he said.

Abu Sayeed said nothing for several seconds, then finally, "What about the other one?"

"I have him."

"Come back."

"What about the bodyguards?"

"They'll come with Biddle."

FORTY-NINE
TEETERBORO AIRPORT, JULY 1

ANNELIËS TOOK A series of deep breaths to calm her nerves as Biddle's Gulfstream touched down on the far end of the runway. The jet reversed thrusters, then a few seconds later, braked just short of where she waited with the car.

The engines wound down. A door swung back, a metal ladder unfolded, then Biddle hurried off the aircraft wearing wrinkled khakis and a plaid shirt with the sleeves rolled to the elbow. He stopped just short of the Range Rover and cast a searching look for his two bodyguards. He continued to glance around while the co-pilot loaded his luggage in the Range Rover's cargo compartment. Finally, he thanked the pilot for a safe journey then climbed in the car. He gave Anneliës a curt nod, and she started through the gate that led to the airport exit road.

They went several hundred yards in silence before Biddle demanded, "Where are they?"

She braked and turned to face him. It was after three a.m., so there were no other cars on the airport exit road. "I don't know," she said, presuming their absence meant Abu Sayeed had already dealt with them.

Biddle looked exhausted and worried, but he seemed to shake it off. "Come here," he said, his voice rough with pent-up desire.

She leaned into him and felt his kiss, as awkward as always, lips tentative and stiff. She responded, opening her mouth and sliding her tongue between his teeth. Biddle's mouth was nearly dry, stale with the taste of his long travel, and she resisted the urge to pull away.

The kiss finally ended, and Biddle straightened, breathing heavily. "You don't know how long I've wanted to do that," he said.

His fingers caressed her cheek. He didn't grab at her breasts or thighs, as other men would have done. She found his inhibition a relief. "I've suffered too, my darling," she murmured. "Even a day is too long."

Biddle gave her a tender smile then sagged against his seat. "Thank God it won't be much longer."

Anneliës resumed driving, turning out of the airport and heading toward Long Island.

Biddle put his hand to his mouth and stifled a yawn. "The boat is ready?" He was referring to the Chris Craft she'd purchased on his orders at a pre-owned boat sale. It was the exact model the Coast Guard used, and it now had false registration numbers and a repainted hull with wide bands of white tape along both sides that could be peeled off to reveal the diagonal red Coast Guard markings. Biddle's plan called for the Arabs to use the disguised boat to penetrate the protective perimeter, where they would then fire their missiles at the President's helicopter. Even if the President survived, he believed the United States' retaliation would precipitate Armageddon. There would be no one to point the finger of guilt, because he fully expected the Arabs to die in their attack.

"It's in position," she said. Two days earlier Anderson and McTighe had moved it to an industrial pier in the Red Hook section of Brooklyn. Biddle had leased the pier through a series of dummy corporations with untraceable ownership.

"Thanks be to God," Biddle said.

Anneliës nodded, but her pulse quickened. She knew Abu Sayeed had no intention of using the disguised boat or sacrificing his life. His plan was to fire the rockets into the middle of Manhattan then disappear before anyone realized what had happened. To Abu Sayeed, Biddle had been a tool to transport weapons and people into the United States, and soon he would become a bargaining chip to ensure their escape.

She chewed her lip as her anxiety spiked. It was time to make the ultimate decision, and the risks were terrifying. If she warned Biddle about Abu Sayeed's plan, how would he react? Would he choose survival or martyrdom? If he chose the latter, he'd give them both away, and Abu Sayeed would kill her at the first hint of betrayal. Yet if she didn't warn Biddle, her life would never change.

She reached into her pocket, and her fingers grazed the

small syringe Abu Sayeed had given her in case Biddle seemed suspicious and refused to return to his estate. All she had to do was lean over and stick him in the neck, and her own safety was assured. She could deliver Biddle, then go to JFK, board a flight to Europe and disappear. However, her money would eventually run out, and once it did, she'd be on her back again for any pig that wanted her body.

She held her breath and made her choice. When she finally withdrew her hand from her pocket, it was empty. She'd come too far, especially when Biddle could give her everything.

"Darling," she said. "I'm frightened."

Biddle had been resting, but now he opened his eyes and turned.

"Those Arabs are animals," she said.

"They are infidels," Biddle corrected. "They have never seen God's light as you have."

"I don't think we should go to your estate without protection."

Biddle seemed to think it over, then shook his head. "The Lord is all we require."

Anneliës looked away, trying to hide the desperation in her eyes. She thought of Biddle and Abu Sayeed, both men brilliant and analytical yet each ruled by his own childish superstition. Perhaps she should get away from both of them, but where to go and how to do it?

Biddle had closed his eyes again. "We're almost finished, my love," he murmured. He rested his hand on her thigh. "Soon we can be together."

Now, as she steered through the light traffic and tried again to make her choice, she thought back over fifteen years of whoring, ever since the German police had crushed the anarchist group she'd joined at the University of Heidelberg. She had fled and gone underground, where her looks had been her ticket to a living.

That was how she'd come to work for Abu Sayeed—sometimes as his courier, sometimes as a personal amusement, sometimes as his gift to others—and how on his orders she met and seduced Biddle.

Therefore, what choice did she really have? In ten more

years, who would want her? And Biddle treated her well and paid her lavishly. For the first time she no longer had to sleep with other men for money. She had a hold on Biddle and believed he would make the arrangement permanent—if he survived the next forty-eight hours.

"Are you sleeping?" she asked.

"Just resting my eyes."

She gripped the wheel tightly. "I think the Arabs intend to kill you."

Biddle's eyes opened and he turned his head. "Why?"

She shook her head. "I hear them whisper things."

Biddle said nothing, but she thought she detected a hint of uncertainty.

"I know they're treacherous," he said after a moment. "That's why I wanted Beddington and McTighe here tonight."

"Maybe we should go someplace safe until you can talk to them."

"They don't answer their phones." His voice betrayed his rising doubt. "I don't know what's going on."

"We shouldn't go back there alone."

Biddle shook his head then put one hand over his face. "Sometimes I fear that God will abandon me," he whispered. "That my sins have made me unfit."

Anneliës took one hand off the wheel and caressed Biddle's neck. "What you're doing is sacred."

"But what if I'm wrong?"

She felt him tremble, and his growing doubt alarmed her. "Prophecy is not wrong," she insisted. "You're not wrong. But if you can't reach the bodyguards, you need to stay away from the Arabs."

Biddle sank back. When Anneliës looked at him again, his expression was distant. "Sometimes," he began in a soft voice, "I know God will send me to Hell for my lust. Other times I believe you are the reward for my faith."

Anneliës forced a certainty into her voice she did not feel. "I am your reward, darling," she said.

Biddle looked at her and gave a sheepish shrug. "I'm sorry to be weak," he said.

Anneliës shook her head. "You're just confused, but it's very understandable. That's why I'm taking you to a hotel. You'll feel better when you've had some sleep."

FIFTY

MORRISTOWN, JULY 1

MAGGIE WOKE TO the Saturday morning traffic report on the clock/radio, but her very next awareness was Brent, the weight of his encircling arm and the warmth of his naked body spooned against her. She experienced a few blissful seconds until reality hit.

She tried to shrug out of his grasp, but his arm tightened. "Let me up," she muttered. Brent relented, and she kicked off the covers and staggered into the bathroom, feeling the leaden staleness in her body. For a time she leaned against the sink without moving, and finally, fighting the heavy pull of exhaustion, she began to brush her teeth.

After too many days with hardly any sleep, her brain seemed to run in slow motion while the rest of the world hurtled by in real time. In the harsh light of morning, her theory about a connection between the terrorists and the theft and murders—and the memo she'd written to Jenkins—all seemed hopelessly ineffectual, an attempt to connect the unconnectable. Only, last night when the pieces had seemed to fit together so perfectly, she'd opened her big mouth and told Brent. It had felt right at the time, but now she realized the inevitable consequence—that when the authorities refused to take her ideas seriously, Brent would go after Biddle on his own.

When she stepped out of the bathroom, Brent was already out of bed. "Try and go back to sleep," she said.

He shook his head. "No way."

She put her hand on his cheek, feeling his impatience like an electric motor beneath his skin. "You have to stay put," she said. "Give me time to pull a few more things together."

Brent stiffened. "Wait for the bureaucrats to allow you to take Biddle down?" He shook his head. "They'll never do it."

She sighed because she couldn't argue with his logic nor deny that time was running out. She thought about tomorrow's

POTUS visit. "Just stay put," she said again.

She stood on her tiptoes, gave him a quick kiss and felt a surge. Was it love, she wondered miserably? Probably. "Be tough," she said, speaking to herself as much as to him.

Ninety minutes later and most of the way through her third cup of coffee, she was searching through the previous night's police reports for any mention of the Turners, or Tom Beddington and Darius McTighe when an overwhelming wave of guilt slammed her anew. Four more people dead! And she had shot Beddington herself. It had been clear self-defense, but she had pulled the trigger on a cop. A very, very dirty cop, but still . . .

So far there was nothing in the reports, but she rubbed her eyes and forced herself to read to the end. Finally, she shoved back from her computer and ground her knuckles into her eyes. She had no time for pointless recrimination. She needed a plan, only what? She couldn't seem to think. Ideas refused to string together, but she was desperate for a strategy–one that had a hope of working with just herself and Brent.

"Wow," a voice said from the entrance to her cubicle. "Looks like somebody had a rough night."

She glanced up, sweeping a handful of barely combed hair from her face, and saw Steve Kosinsky leaning against the partition with a large cup of coffee in each hand. She forced a smile. "That bad?"

Kosinsky shrugged. "You're still gorgeous. You're just tired gorgeous." He stepped into the cubicle and put one of the cups on the edge of her desk. "I can only hope that it means you finally came to your senses about the phantom boyfriend."

"You mean dumped him?"

Kosinsky smiled and cocked his head. "Anyway, everything okay?"

She waved a hand, taking in her cubicle. "My favorite way to spend Saturday."

Kosinsky stood on his tiptoes and glanced around at the empty cubicles and offices. "They need a few brave souls to hold down the fort. POTUS' speech is much more important that finding out whether a bunch of towel heads have a nuke."

"That's politically correct."

"I care."

"Are you going back to the docks?" she asked.

"Nope." Kosinsky scowled. "Everybody in my unit's out checking parked cars and trash bins today, so it's my turn to man the phones while we let commerce grind to a halt."

"Have you seen Jenkins?" Maggie asked.

Kosinsky shook his head. "Somebody said she was here most of the night. She's probably gone home to catch some sleep."

Maggie narrowed her eyes and studied him, wrestling with the beginnings of a desperate idea. With nothing left to lose, she plunged. "Do you have time to help me with something? I have a wild hunch I'm trying to check out."

Kosinsky shrugged. "Yeah," he said. "What is it?"

"You've got to keep it to yourself."

He hesitated for a beat. "Why?"

"Because it's pretty far-fetched. I sent Jenkins a memo on it, but she hasn't said anything, so . . ."

"You don't want to embarrass yourself?" He smiled. "Not a word will escape my lips."

"Thanks," Maggie said. "If you could run some background checks, arrest reports, give me everything we've got on a few people." She wrote the names on a yellow pad: Prescott Biddle, Fred Wofford, Rev. Howard Turner, Owen Smythe and Betty Dowager. She briefly considered adding the two deputies, but held off.

Kosinsky picked up the paper and read the names. "You're too busy?" he asked.

"Yes," she lied. She felt bad about bringing him into this, but she couldn't afford to bring suspicion on herself, not right now.

He read the names and smiled. "If I get you the stuff on these people will you have dinner with me?"

Maggie slapped her hand on her desktop. "Do you ever quit?"

Kosinsky gave her an innocent look. "Moi?"

Two hours later, she was on the phone trying to explain to an irate police chief in Port Chester, New York, why nobody at Project Seahawk had followed up on a report of suspicious boating activity he had made several days earlier.

"You're telling me it's this POTUS visit?" the chief demanded.

"Yessir."

"Tell the sonofabitch to stay in Washington and let people do their jobs."

"I'll pass that on, sir," Maggie said. She hung up as Steve Kosinsky stepped into her cubicle waving a sheaf of papers. "Yes?"

"Here's what you asked for."

He looked over his shoulder then sat in the chair beside her desk. "Want to tell me what's going on?" he said in a low voice.

Maggie held out her hand. "May I see what you got?"

Kosinsky handed her the papers. Prescott Biddle's report was on top. She skimmed it, seeing that he'd spent two years at a Tennessee bible college before transferring to Harvard. From there he'd done two years of divinity study at an evangelical seminary and then attended M.I.T.'s Sloan School. Afterward, he'd worked at several different money management firms until starting Genesis Advisors. He made large donations to ultra-conservative causes and served on several corporate boards and on the national board of a church called the New Jerusalem Fellowship.

Kosinsky had marked New Jerusalem Fellowship and Genesis Advisors with a yellow highlighter, and now he put his finger on the name of the church. "I looked them up. It's like a nut-ball super-fundamentalist cult. They don't dance or drink. They deny evolution, hate gays and believe the universe was made in six days." He pointed to the highlighted Genesis Advisors. "Everybody but Turner worked at Biddle's firm. Everybody but Smythe is involved with that church."

Maggie nodded. She was continuing to read Biddle's report, thinking his wealth and political donations made him close to untouchable. He had no indictments, a single speeding ticket and one arrest twenty-four years earlier at an anti-abortion rally.

Next, she scanned Wofford's report. He was from Nebraska and had attended a bible college then earned an accounting degree from Nebraska State. He'd worked for an Omaha insurance company for twenty-eight years, becoming its president. He served on the national board of the New Jerusalem Fellowship. If anything, Wofford's record was even cleaner than Biddle's.

Owen Smythe had attended M.I.T. and University of Chicago Business School. He'd worked for several asset managers before coming to Genesis Advisors. He had a few speeding tickets and a drunk and disorderly during college.

Rev. Turner was from Maryland, with his divinity degree from Bob Jones University. He'd served several different evangelical-sounding churches before joining the New Jerusalem Fellowship. He'd been pastor of the Lambertville, New Jersey church for the past fourteen years.

Elizabeth Dowager came from Wisconsin and had attended a Lutheran bible college for two years then worked as a secretary for the pastor of a Pentecostal church in Milwaukee. Kosinsky had added her husband's sheet, and it said he'd worked as a municipal employee at Milwaukee's water works. Nothing appeared remarkable until Maggie saw that Betty Dowager had been indicted for stealing two hundred fifty thousand dollars from her church.

Accompanying newspaper articles and court records reported that the theft had occurred after the Pentecostal church ended merger negotiations with the New Jerusalem Fellowship. It came out in the trial that Ms. Dowager had donated the stolen the money to the New Jerusalem Fellowship, thinking she was following God's will by helping to force the merger. Convicted of embezzlement, her jail term had been commuted due to appeals from her former pastor and officials in the New Jerusalem Fellowship.

By the time Maggie finished, her heart was pounding. It was right here, she thought. She raised her eyes, but Kosinsky's chair was empty. She'd been so intent on reading that she hadn't noticed him leave. She went back to the reports and started again from the top. A few moments later, a fresh coffee cup appeared on the corner of her desk. She glanced up as Kosinsky flopped back down.

She smiled, but his time his expression held no amusement. "What the hell's going on?"

"I told you. I've got a hunch."

"Your hunches normally work like ESP?"

"What are you talking about?" Maggie asked, feeling a vein begin to pulse at her temple.

"While you were reading, I did another search on the New Jerusalem Fellowship. Found some stuff on these wackos I thought you'd want to see. I was waiting for my job to print out when I happened to scan the law enforcement net. Amazing what came over."

He held out a missing person's report filed by Fred Wofford's wife and another report describing the apparent murder/suicide of Rev. Turner and his wife. Maggie feigned shock as she read.

"Check the time," Kosinsky said. The bottom of the report showed the date and time of filing. "That's about thirty-five minutes after I did my search. Plus that guy, Smythe. He's dead, too. Pretty big coincidence, all these dead guys, huh?"

Maggie nodded but did not meet his stare.

Kosinsky sat back in his chair. "You better tell me what's going on."

Maggie looked directly into his eyes. "You don't want to know."

Kosinsky shook his head. "Not a good answer."

She saw several other pieces of paper rolled in his fist. She reached out and tugged them free. "If my theory proves out, I'll tell you everything." She flattened out the pages and read about the New Jerusalem Fellowship, how it was based on a belief in the approaching End of Days, involving the cataclysmic battle of Armageddon and the Second Coming. When she finished she rubbed her eyes with the heels of her hands.

"Talk to me," Kosinsky demanded.

"It's inconclusive."

Kosinsky studied her for a long moment. "Bullshit." He reached into the rear pocket of his trousers and brought out several additional pages. He threw them face down on her desk. She continued to hold his stare, but she thought she knew what they were.

"Let me try," Kosinsky said. He held up a finger. "Two days ago, somebody stole eight hundred and fifty million dollars from a client account at Genesis Advisors." He held up a second finger. "A recently hired portfolio manager was implicated in the theft." He held up a third finger. "The client, a prominent Egyptian peace activist, was found murdered." He held up a fourth finger. "The same portfolio manager was implicated." He held up his thumb. "The New Jerusalem Fellowship believes in this Armageddon and Second Coming stuff, which makes them the opposite of peaceniks when it comes to the Mideast."

He paused, glanced at his extended fingers then held up the first finger of his second hand. "The CIA says those stolen missiles probably cost something short of a billion dollars once you add in the cost of a few pounds of depleted nuclear fuel." He held up a seventh finger. "Oh yeah, almost forgot . . . the CIA said the Wahaddi Brotherhood, who supposedly paid for all that stuff, doesn't have any money." He looked at his seven upheld fingers and raised his eyebrows, as if amazed that he had made so many points. "Nice bit of detective work," he said. "For a desk jockey."

Maggie shrugged. "Told you it was kind of a crazy idea." She couldn't meet his eyes. Kosinsky reached out and flipped the pages he'd thrown on her desk. He slapped them with his palm. "Brings up the question, detective, of why you didn't ask for anything on the one guy who seems to be implicated in all this stuff." He let the silence hang, finally asking, "Well?"

"Well what?" Maggie asked.

"Is he guilty or innocent?"

She glanced down at the bulletin calling for Brent's apprehension and arrest. "Innocent," she croaked.

Kosinsky's expression softened. "I did a background check on my own," he said. He started to read, "Yale, played football, two years all-Ivy, Stanford Business School, worked for some fund manager in Boston, blew the whistle on some bad guys, then went to work with Biddle. Sounds like a super-successful guy with unusually strong ethics. Not a nut or a criminal. He comes from Morristown, New Jersey—coincidentally, so do you. He seems to be approximately your age." He looked up, his eyes narrowing. "Any chance this is the phantom boyfriend?"

Maggie held his gaze. "He was. We broke up a while ago."

Kosinsky sighed. "You know where he is?"

She nodded.

"You're betting everything on this guy. What if he's guilty?"

Maggie felt her uncertainty vanish. "He's being framed," she said in a firm voice.

Kosinsky reached for the stack of papers, put them in his lap and looked them over. "I think I see where you're going with this. It's not going to make you popular." He gave her a skeptical look. "Fundamentalist Christians helping Muslim terrorists?"

"It's consistent with their Armageddon philosophy."

Kosinsky shrugged.

"It's consistent with the amount of money involved and with the CIA's claim that they'd frozen the Wahaddi Brotherhood's accounts."

"Maybe."

"It's consistent with targeting an Arab peace activist, and it's consistent with framing someone else for the theft and murder."

Kosinsky sat forward and put his chin on his hands. "The Christian Coalition is gonna want you burned at the stake."

Maggie said nothing.

"I should turn you in," Kosinsky muttered. "I should have turned you in ten minutes ago."

"That's your call." She handed him a copy of the memo she'd sent to Jenkins two days earlier. "I tried to push this upstairs, but I've heard nothing."

Kosinsky read it and shook his head. "Nobody's gonna pursue this Biddle guy until the bombs go off."

"Probably true."

"If I keep my mouth shut I'm risking my career for a guy I don't know and a woman who won't date me."

"That sounds about right."

He gave her a humorless smile. "Damned if I'm not a self-destructive fool."

FIFTY-ONE

MORRISTOWN, JULY 1

BRENT DROPPED THE last item in the canvas bag he'd found in Maggie's closet. It was a meager collection, but it contained everything he'd been able to find that looked potentially useful—a flashlight, crowbar, wire cutters and several rusty screwdrivers. He had no plan for sneaking past Biddle's security guards, and minimal expectations for what he could accomplish even if he succeeded. But if Maggie's theory was right and Biddle's allies were anything like the people who killed Harry and took the down the Trade Centers, he had to try.

He put the bag on the kitchen table, then pulled up his shirt and checked the pistol stuffed in his waistband, ensuring yet again that the safety was on. He smiled bitterly, thinking his precautions would at least prevent him from shooting off his own balls. He'd leave that task to someone else.

He took a last look around. It was late afternoon, when weekend traffic would be building on the main roads and the best time to make his move. His hair was scruffy, and he now had the better part of a beard, so he no longer looked like his pictures. His first stop would be a nearby shopping center where he hoped to switch the Volvo's New York plates with a pair snatched off a New Jersey car. That should allow him to make it to Long Island.

Last night, making love to Maggie and then holding her in his arms had changed everything. He understood the risks of what he was about to attempt, but also that he had no other choice. Ever since he'd awakened this morning, he'd had the renewed sense of time running out, the last grains of sand dropping through the neck of the hourglass. Maggie had called twice to tell him she was working on things and not to lose hope, but he'd heard the increasing hollowness in her voice. Her superiors would never agree to go after Biddle, and that meant it was up to him.

The morning papers reported that Biddle had cut short his vacation and returned to the United States, and that meant he was within reach. Brent had visited Biddle's estate, so he had at least minimal knowledge of the layout. Also, in spite of the psychiatrist's report that called him "very competitive, resourceful, highly intelligent, unusually devoted to principle but perhaps with insufficient impulse control," he thought no one would expect a lone fugitive to attack. His goal was utterly simplistic–grab Biddle and force a confession. It was a desperate move but the only chance he had.

He had the Volvo keys in his pocket and his hand on the doorknob when a sound came from the driveway. He froze. A car door opened and thumped closed. Sun flooded through the closed curtains of Maggie's little kitchen, and he watched a man's silhouette move past the side windows toward the back door.

He tiptoed out of the room, his heart hammering. If it was the police, he had no chance. But what if it was someone Biddle had sent to kill him? He slid the pistol from his waistband.

The latch turned, and the door rattled against the lock. A knock followed. Brent tensed and waited for a boot to kick in the door, but after a few seconds he heard a loud whisper, "Goddammit, open the door!"

His uncle! Brent felt a wild blast of relief. He rushed into the kitchen, jerked open the door and saw the familiar scowl. "Are you alone?"

"No, I brought the FBI," Fred Lucas shot back as he stepped quickly inside. He went to the side window, pulled the curtain aside and glanced at the neighbor's house. "The damn FBI will be here if people saw me creeping around the back door," he snapped.

His uncle's cantankerousness was a balm, and for a second Brent actually smiled. "What are you doing here?"

His uncle had a big paper shopping bag in one hand, and he hoisted it onto the kitchen table. "Maggie told me to keep an eye on you. She said you're about to do something stupid." He spotted the canvas bag beside the door then tipped it and examined the contents. "Looks like she's got your number."

"I'm getting out of here," Brent said.

Fred Lucas leaned back against the door. "To do what?" His uncle shook his head. "These guys already tagged you for stealing the money and set you up for murder. Whoever they are, they ain't stupid. You try something by yourself, they're gonna plaster your ass on a wall."

"There's no other option," Brent said, reaching around Fred for the doorknob.

His uncle didn't move. "What do I do with the spade?"

Brent blinked. "The what?"

"You heard me—the giant kid. DeLeyon f-ing Jones."

Brent stepped back at hearing the name. "He's my Little Brother. Why?"

"Well, he ain't little, and he's got his black ass sitting in my buddy's car right now." His uncle hooked his thumb at the driveway. "He's my lookout." He smirked. "You know they've had these assholes sitting outside my house—well I know you know cause you had Maggie bring me that note."

"It was her idea."

"Figures."

"Back this up a little," Brent said. "How did DeLeyon get into your buddy's car?"

"Why don't you ask me first how the hell he got to Morristown?"

"Okay, how?"

"He took a bus."

"From New York?"

"No, from Poland."

Brent waved a hand in surrender. "Okay, he took a bus. How'd he find you?"

"Went to the fire station and asked. They called me up from there. He came cause he wants to save your miserable ass. He's apparently one of about three people in the entire United States who give a crap."

Brent shook his head. "He's a sixteen-year-old kid. You've got to send him home."

"Pardon me, but Baby Huey's eight feet tall. I can't make him go anywhere."

"Well, get him out of here. He can't have anything to do with me."

"Well, smart guy, that was my first thought, but since he's come down here to hunt you up and since he knows Maggie's name, this was gonna be his next stop. You think an old white man might draw some questions creeping around a young woman's back door, what about your buddy DeLeyon?"

"Where's your car?"

Fred shook his head. "My buddy's car. I'm not as dumb as the later generation of my family. I got followed to the fire station."

"You went out the back and took someone else's car?"

"Bingo. Hopefully my tails are still watching the fire station."

Brent sighed. "Well, you can't just leave him out there."

Fred scowled as he turned and went out the back door. "Finally a right answer! Anybody in your shoes better take all the help they can get!"

Thirty seconds later, DeLeyon shambled into the kitchen ahead of Fred. He wore a baggy basketball jersey, cut off shorts that reached mid-calf and a huge pair of Nike Air Huaraches. He hung his head in a self-conscious slouch and put out his hand for the ghetto handshake he'd taught Brent when they first met.

In spite of his anger, Brent grabbed DeLeyon's bent fingers, followed by a quick bang of fists one on top of the other. "What the hell are you doing?"

DeLeyon didn't meet his eyes. He shrugged his immense shoulders. "Hey, you know, man," he muttered.

"Your grandma know you're here?" Brent demanded.

"I gonna call her tonight."

"What about school?"

DeLeyon raised his eyes and smiled. "Almost out for the year. I still got straight A's. Don't matter if I ain't there a couple days."

Brent looked away. As angry as he was, he was touched. "DeLeyon," he said after a long silence. "I'm in some really big trouble."

"You didn't do it," the boy said. "I know you."

"Yeah, but being around me is a bad idea. It could ruin your chances for college."

"I let you go down without lifting my finger, I don't deserve no college. You taught me that."

Brent shook his head. "You actually listened?"

"Seem like I did."

"Look, DeLeyon," Brent said, "Your belief in me means everything, but I have to do this myself."

DeLeyon screwed up his lips and shook his head. "You ain't guilty, but they think you guilty and they ain't gonna give you no chance to prove nothing different. A black man know more 'bout this than you. Don't be trying to send me home and telling me you gonna do it all by yourself, cause you ain't."

Brent looked over at Fred who'd already helped himself to a beer from the refrigerator and plopped in one of the kitchen chairs.

Fred shrugged. "I didn't go to some fancy-ass college, but one thing's pretty clear—you got no business turning down help. I'm with the kid."

"Look," Brent said, feeling his temper rise. "You haven't got a clue what I'm dealing with here."

"I'm sure you got a great plan to take care of it all by yourself."

"You can't help."

Fred's attempt at good humor dropped away. "Aren't you even gonna wait for Maggie?" He returned Brent's scowl.

"What the hell are you talking about?" Brent demanded.

"A little bit ago, her cousin from the deli rings my doorbell and hands me some bread with another note." Fred got up from his chair, fished in his pocket then held out a folded piece of paper inside a plastic baggie. "It says to keep you here, that she's got help coming. She'll be here soon."

Brent felt a surge of hope, mixed with suspicion. "What do you mean she's got help coming? Why hasn't she called to tell me that herself?"

Fred shrugged. "I donno." He pointed to the bag he'd put on the kitchen table when he first walked in. "But she gave me a shopping list."

FIFTY-TWO

MORRISTOWN, JULY 1

MAGGIE RACED WESTWARD out of Newark, chafing at the traffic but wondering at the same time why she was in such a hurry. After all, wasn't she about to risk her career, maybe even her freedom, on a wild speculation? She glanced in her rearview mirror and picked out Kosinsky's truck, and her anxiety notched higher. She wasn't the only one rolling the dice. She'd tried to talk him out of coming, but probably not hard enough.

Everything had started to snowball around midday when Ann Jenkins came into her cubicle. She had the memo rolled in her fist and looked exhausted, like she'd had maybe two or three hours sleep in the past several days. "DeVito, if it was my call, I'd go after Biddle yesterday, but I can't convince any of these other bastards to back us. I'm really sorry."

Maggie bit her cheeks. "They're making a huge mistake," she said. "I've done even more work on this and I can—"

Jenkins waved a hand for silence. "I gave it my best shot. Bottom line—nothing's happened since 9/11, and they all think I'm paranoid. I tried, but I lost. It's finished, and I'm too goddamn tired and pissed off to discuss it any further." She tossed Maggie's memo on her desk, turned and left.

A moment later, Kosinsky came into her cubicle. "I overheard."

Maggie stared at the wall and shook her head. A single tear broke loose and trickled down her cheek.

"You gave it your best shot," he said in a gentle voice.

She wiped the tear away with an angry swipe. "I'm right!" she said in a choked voice.

"Let's think about it. Maybe there's some way to run this by other people."

Maggie turned and looked at him, her eyes narrow slits. "You don't get it! Brent's not going to wait!"

Kosinsky's face wrinkled in disbelief. "He'd go after the

terrorists alone?"

"He'll go after Biddle, which may be the same thing." She wiped her other eye.

"You could always arrest him."

She nodded.

"But if you do arrest him, it does nothing to stop the bad guys."

"Yeah." Maggie put her elbows on the desk and covered her face with her hands. "Got any ideas?"

There was a long silence, and she finally took her hands away. Kosinsky was looking at her with a wry expression. "We'll have to blame it on the boyfriend. We'll say we were in hot pursuit. There's really no other way."

Now, as she finally exited the freeway at Morristown, Maggie's thoughts switched to Fred Lucas. He was a poor choice for something like this—a loveable guy but a loose cannon. Still, when she'd talked it over with Kosinsky, they'd agreed they needed help, and the skills of a retired fireman were ideal.

She held her breath as she turned onto her street, afraid Brent might have departed even before Fred arrived. She'd seen it in his eyes that morning, and later she'd heard it in his voice when she'd called, his anger and desperation as he told her he wouldn't wait any longer. His tone had suggested other things as well, but she couldn't dwell on them until they got through the next twenty-four hours.

She let out a moan of relief when she reached her house and saw a rusted Chevrolet Cavalier with a dented bumper in the drive. Hopefully, that meant Fred had followed her orders and ditched his old Voyager minivan. She parked behind the Cavalier, took a long tube of rolled up paper from the seat beside her, then waited for Kosinsky to pull in.

"Did the old guy do what you told him?" he asked, as he climbed out.

"I think so," she said. "But don't call him old to his face. Fred's prickly."

They walked around to the back, but as soon as Maggie opened the door, she froze. A hulking African American kid stood behind Fred and Brent. "Who the hell are you?" she demanded.

"Meet DeLeyon," Fred said, as if it was no big deal. Maggie glared at him as she stepped into the kitchen then held the door for Kosinsky.

Once all five of them were inside and Maggie had closed the door, the small kitchen seemed crowded to the bursting point. Brent looked toward the door. "Who else is coming?" he demanded.

"I'm it," Kosinsky said.

"This is Steve Kosinsky," Maggie explained. "He's a lieutenant in the New York State Police."

Brent eyes flicked back and forth between them. "I assume his presence here isn't official."

Kosinsky gave a wry smile. "No."

"Why are you doing this?"

"Your girlfriend is very persuasive."

After a brief hesitation Brent shook his head. "It's too big a risk."

Kosinsky tipped his head toward Maggie. "I agree with her that it's better than you doing it by yourself."

Maggie stepped in and turned to Fred. "So, who's DeLeyon?" she asked.

"He's Brent's Little Brother."

Maggie swung her gaze. "You're DeLeyon Jones, the high school kid?"

"Yeah," he said.

She knew about him, that he was sixteen, smart as hell. He was slouching, but she guessed he was at least six-seven. She took in the long, bony face, intelligent eyes, lips that lifted at the corners with unexpected humor. "You get on the wrong train?" she demanded.

"Damn," DeLeyon said. "That sound like a cop question."

"Well, I'm a cop," Maggie said, her voice taking on a measure of heat.

"Easy now," Fred interjected. "DeLeyon came looking for me cause he wants to help Brent. I figured it was better to bring him here than leave him."

"He needs to get a train back to New York," Maggie said.

"You best put me in cuffs," DeLeyon said. "Cause I ain't going less you do."

"I think he could help," Fred said.

"Great!" Maggie slapped the counter. "Let's add endangering a minor to everything else they can throw at us." Even as she said it, she knew Fred was right.

"That mean I stay?" DeLeyon asked.

"No!" Brent interjected. "Sorry."

Maggie glanced at him, noting the pallor of his cheeks. She grabbed handfuls of his T-shirt just under his chin. "Everybody here made choices," she said, giving him a shake. "You can be grateful, but you're not responsible."

He looked into her eyes and finally gave a nod. Then he looked around slowly at each of them in turn. "Thank you."

Maggie let go of his shirt, went over to the kitchen table and started to pull the rubber bands off her paper tube. "Okay," she announced, her voice crisp. "The official answer is that neither Project Seahawk nor the FBI is going to pursue Prescott Biddle. However, Steve and I did more homework, and we're convinced that he's the guy." She stopped and looked at Brent. "More important, we're convinced of the terrorism connection."

"Well, let's go kick his ass!" Fred interjected.

Maggie spun and gave him a hard look. "We're not going to kick anyone's ass. We're going to do this very carefully. Biddle's got his own security detail, and we're pretty sure the terrorists are on his property, as well."

She watched Fred's face as the information sunk in, then she unrolled the satellite photographs she'd requested from the NSA.

FIFTY-THREE

NEWARK, NJ, JULY 1

ANN JENKINS WORKED through another pack of M&M's and sipped stale, lukewarm coffee as she reviewed the duty reports. Tonight's batch was mercifully thin because with half her staff reassigned and the others stretched to the breaking point, they had no time to file paperwork. She knew she ought to be grateful for small blessings, but she scowled. From a port security point of view, the situation sucked.

The politicos in Washington were sticking with their plan to bring POTUS to New York, and she was holding to her insistence that Project Seahawk needed to be at Condition Red. A leper would have been more popular than she was right now. Her own people were pissed off and overworked, the politicians were afraid rumors of her Condition Red would leak out and ruin the fantasy that the national security situation was under control, and the bean counters in Washington were grumbling about all the overtime her people were clocking.

Earlier that day, the Under Secretary for Border and Transportation Security had called to remind her that she was only an Acting Director while her boss recovered from his open-heart surgery. The implication was clear–if she wanted to be a real Director someday, she better damn well stand her people down. Well, screw that! She ate the last M&M, crumpled the pack and tossed it in the waste can.

She drummed her fingers against the desk, the only sound a dull thump. She glanced at her ravaged nails, but there was nothing left to chew. What she really wanted was a damn cigarette. No, she reminded herself, she was quitting.

She shook her head, fruitlessly trying to shake off the desire, as she turned again to the duty reports. She finished her review, stuffed them back in their file, then signed and time stamped the cover page. Next, she started in on the requisition summary that showed the information requests that went to the FBI, NSA,

Armed Forces Intelligence or CIA from any Project Seahawk personnel. She reviewed them to make sure everyone was playing ball and sharing information properly, also to make sure people weren't accessing unneeded or inappropriate material.

She jiggled her foot in a staccato beat. God, she wanted a cigarette, a strong one, preferably unfiltered, a Camel or Lucky Strike. She was so busy contemplating getting up and going outside to stand in the smokers' area where she could at least sniff the second-hand smoke, that she almost missed Maggie DeVito's name.

She had been feeling bad all day about her inability to bring any follow-up to DeVito's memo, which had been a sharp piece of deductive reasoning. Moreover, it demonstrated initiative and a creative intellect sorely lacking in too many law-enforcement people. DeVito had been frustrated and disappointed at the turndown, but she hadn't whined or carried on. Jenkins liked the way her prettiness hid a tough character.

But why the hell was DeVito requisitioning satellite photos? She had a staff position, not a line job, which meant she wasn't supposed to be working her own investigations. Jenkins placed a call to the satellite imaging section of the NSA and asked a technician to look up the photographs DeVito had requested. "What are they of?" Jenkins asked.

"Looks like a waterfront estate on Long Island," the man replied.

Jenkins scratched her head, again conscious of the lack of fingernails. "I need to know more. Who owns it?"

"Call you back," the man said.

Ten minutes later, the man got back to her. "Belongs to a guy named Prescott Biddle," he said.

Jenkins's pulse quickened. She quickly looked through the rest of the report and saw that DeVito had ordered a number of images. "What were the other images?"

"Same shot, but for different dates and times."

"What did they show?"

The man promised to check and get back.

Jenkins stood and paced her office. What the hell was DeVito doing? She went back to her desk, typed in a search program and designated DeVito's computer. She called up a list of the searches she had run starting today and going back a week. Nothing looked interesting.

She ran another check, this one general, designed to look at all the Project Seahawk computers, and she put in Prescott Biddle's name. Immediately, she got a hit. A New York State Police lieutenant named Kosinsky had run a check on Biddle. Kosinsky was big and good-looking, the type who looked like he was bred to be a state cop. She hadn't paid him much attention until now, but suddenly she wondered at the connection between Maggie and Kosinsky. An over-search of Kosinsky's computer showed that he'd done concurrent searches on Fred Wofford, Owen Smythe, Betty Dowager and a Rev. Howard Turner. Later, he'd done a search on Brent Lucas.

She felt a prickle at the back of her neck. Lucas' name had appeared in DeVito's memo and been all over the law enforcement net. She remembered that Lucas worked for Biddle and was a suspect in several murders. She brought up Kosinsky's searches and saw that Smythe was one of the murder victims and, along with Wofford and Dowager, he had worked at Biddle's firm.

A symbol blinked beside Turner's name, meaning that more recent information was available. She updated the search, and then her breath caught in her throat. In the past forty-eight hours Turner and his wife had been found dead in what was termed a murder/suicide. Moreover, Wofford's wife had reported her husband missing. What the hell was going on? Was Brent Lucas on a murder rampage, or did this information somehow help prove DeVito's hypothesis? She resumed pacing, lost in thought, absently winding her red hair around her fingers until her phone finally rang.

It was the guy from the NSA. He said one group of satellite photos were close-focus shots of each building on Biddle's estate, also his boat. Another group were images going back thirty days, all of Biddle's yacht and the two small cottages located in one corner of his property. DeVito had also requested infrareds of the same location but NSA needed prior notice for close-focus infrareds. They had, however, taken one shot that afternoon.

"Anything interesting?" Jenkins asked, trying to mask her anxiety.

The man told her that the earlier pictures seemed to show nothing at all, but several from the past week showed figures.

"What time were they taken?" Jenkins asked.

He said they were taken shortly after sunrise and just before sunset. The infrared shot showed what seemed to be three figures—possibly two inside the cottage and one outside in the trees.

She thanked the man for his quick response and ordered her own copies. She hung up then printed copies of Kosinsky's searches and read each of them more closely. She saw that Fred Wofford was the president of Biddle's company and along with Biddle was on the national board of the New Jerusalem Fellowship. Betty Dowager was an executive assistant at the same company, and Owen Smythe had been a portfolio manager there. Kosinsky's search on the New Jerusalem Fellowship described a church dedicated to the most radical and fundamental form of Protestantism with a focus on the approaching End of Days.

She thought again about DeVito's memo, seeing how the dots seemed to connect, and suddenly she absolutely needed that cigarette. She rushed out of her office, went through security and took the elevator to the lobby. She spotted the glow of a cigarette outside the revolving doors, the smoker an African American woman who worked for the Border Patrol. "Can I bum one?" she asked as she came barreling out.

The woman threw her a resentful glance, but after a hesitation reached into her purse and brought out a pack of Marlboro Light 100's. Jenkins snatched one then pulled out the gold-plated Zippo she always carried whether she was smoking or not. She lit the cigarette, took a long, greedy drag then exhaled. "Thanks," she said as the smoke streamed from her mouth.

"No problem," the woman said, though her eyes suggested the opposite.

Jenkins turned and stared out at the dark Newark streets as she smoked. The nicotine hit her system and calmed her, while underneath she could feel her brain starting to crank. She winced at the thought of once again bringing Prescott Biddle's name to her superiors, but then she quashed her fear.

The skeptics would ignore everything—the money, the satellite photos, the multitude of bodies and the interrelationships among the people. Coincidence, they'd say of the New Jerusalem Fellowship and Genesis Advisors connections. They'd insist the figures in the satellite photos were gardeners or houseguests. But Jenkins no longer gave a damn. Her instincts were rock solid.

She recalled a *60 Minutes* segment she'd seen a year earlier, where the leader of a radical Christian group calmly explained that his goal was to create strife in the Mideast in order to hasten the coming of Armageddon.

A person would have to be insane to want that, Jenkins thought, but Biddle's church embraced that craziness. She thought about the Turner murder/suicide. What if it hadn't been a psychotic tragedy but a bizarre sacrifice intended to protect a secret? A secret involving eight hundred and fifty million dollars? Protect it from whom? Possibly DeVito? If this line of thinking was right, how did Brent Lucas and Owen Smythe figure in? Could they be dupes or scapegoats intended to divert attention from the real reason for the theft?

She shook her head, still wanting to poke holes in DeVito's logic because politically, it was poison. Then suddenly everything clicked, and the whole thing hit her: POTUS! The President's visit was tomorrow!

Jenkins had a good half-inch of unsmoked cigarette, but she flicked it away and started back into the building.

"If you gonna bum one, at least smoke the damn thing," the woman snapped.

Jenkins ignored her. She had far bigger things on her mind. She was thinking that tonight, immediately, regardless of consequence, she had to pull together a group to find out if there were terrorists on Prescott Biddle's estate.

And then in the next second she finally understood why DeVito and Kosinsky had said nothing about the satellite photos.

"Holy Shit!" she exclaimed, and she broke into a sprint and headed toward the elevator doors.

FIFTY-FOUR

LONG ISLAND, JULY 1

FRED LUCAS SAT in the passenger seat of Kosinsky's truck and scowled at the thousands of headlights on the Long Island Expressway. Nine-thirty at night, yet traffic crawled in both directions.

"Long Island," he groused as Kosinsky pulled off the expressway and stopped at the pumps of a self-serve gas station. "I'd rather live in Afghanistan."

Kosinsky shrugged. "I've lived here all my life," he said. "You get used to it."

"You're nuts."

Kosinsky gave a wry smile. "I've had that thought a few times tonight."

Fred grunted in agreement. He hated what was about to happen, but then he thought how some Arab shitbirds had killed Harry. Now, tonight, they were going up against the same kind of people. He didn't think he'd want to keep on living if something happened to Brent.

He opened his door and climbed out of the pickup. An empty five-gallon can sat in the truck bed. He took it out, unscrewed the top, then waited while Kosinsky ran his credit card through the pump.

"Regular or high test?" Kosinsky shouted over the freeway noise.

Fred looked up and smiled. "Like it matters," he yelled. He had a fireman's bias that most cops were full of crap, but this was a guy he could get along with, even one he could like.

He squeezed the handle and heard gas stream into the can. Thirty years putting fires out made it impossible to do this with an easy conscience. Still, he'd been over it in his mind and knew this was probably the only way. Besides, it was for Brent—and Harry. Suck it up, you old bastard, he told himself.

FIFTY-FIVE

NEWARK, NJ, JULY 1

AGENT JENKINS SLAMMED down her phone, grabbed a tissue and wiped her oily forehead at the hairline. She felt in need of a shower, her stomach a seething mess. For the past thirty minutes she'd been calling DeVito's house phone and cell phones, ditto for Kosinsky's. There were many possible explanations for why neither of them answered. They might be bowling, out to dinner or at movies. They might not be together, only she knew they were.

"Shit," she whispered, as she finally made her decision. She dialed a Washington number then put her right hand under her nose, sniffing the residual nicotine on her fingers. God, what she'd give to light up right now.

After two rings, the night duty officer answered. She identified herself and said she needed to be patched through to whichever Executive Assistant Director was on duty. As he was no doubt instructed to do–because EADs did not like being disturbed in the evening–the duty officer asked several times whether a lower level person couldn't suffice. After his fifth attempt to sidetrack the call, he put her through.

Jenkins heard the tremor in her voice, but at least she knew this particular EAD to be forceful and decisive. She told him without preamble about the missiles, the stolen money, the lengthening chain of murders that appeared loosely associated with Prescott Biddle, the satellite photos and her conclusion that a raid on Biddle's estate was required to prevent an assassination attempt on POTUS the following day.

To his credit the EAD did not mention chain-of-command issues or ask her why she wasn't calling her titular boss in the U.S. Attorney's Office. "Agent Jenkins, do you have any idea of the shit storm this will create?"

"Yessir," she said.

There was a long silence before the EAD spoke again. "I'm

sure you've considered the impact on your career if this proves unsubstantiated?"

Her pause lasted only a second. She was rolling all the dice on her intuition, but in the past thirty minutes, she'd also learned that Maggie DeVito and Brent Lucas had gone to the same high school and graduated the same year, both at the top of their class. DeVito was in a liaison job, yet her investigation was so precisely targeted that she had to have some outside direction. She intuited that DeVito had enlisted Kosinsky to help cover her tracks. All of which implied that DeVito was in contact with Brent Lucas.

"Yessir," she told the EAD.

"I had to ask." There was another silence. Finally, the EAD said, "Permission granted to conduct a raid with all due haste."

"Thank you, sir." In FBI parlance, "all due haste" meant the raid would be preceded by an exhaustive planning session, only tonight there was no time. "Um, there's another piece of information. I believe two Project Seahawk agents may already be attempting an interdiction."

"On their own?" the EAD squawked.

"Yessir. I'll provide details later. Right now, I don't think they're important."

"Jesus H. Christ!" the EAD groaned. "I'll mobilize the New York office and have all available agents at your disposal. I'll also have Nassau County S.W.A.T. standing by for instructions. Get moving, Jenkins."

"Yessir."

Jenkins hung up and grabbed her copies of the NSA photos. She pulled her bulletproof vest from the hanger behind her office door then ran down two flights to the Border Patrol area. She found the woman she'd bummed the cigarette from earlier and tossed a five-dollar bill on her desk. "I need a few more. It's an emergency."

The woman looked up from her computer. She glanced at the money, shrugged, then pulled the pack out of her desk drawer and held it out. Jenkins snatched six cigarettes and stuffed one behind each ear and four in the breast pocket of her jacket. "Thanks," she mumbled, then rushed toward the elevator.

Moments later with her blue light flashing and a lit cigarette clamped in her teeth, she roared through the deserted Newark streets. She phoned the Manhattan FBI office, and the night Duty Officer told her five agents would be waiting for her in a navy blue van outside Federal Plaza. She told the DO to requisition night vision goggles and an M16 with a laser aiming device and extra magazines for each agent and for her, as well. She also asked for communications gear, flash-bangs and smoke grenades.

Next, she phoned the Nassau County Police and identified herself to the night sergeant. He in turn patched her straight through to the Chief, whose angry tone told her he'd been awaiting the call. "First off, I want to go on record as telling you this may be the craziest goddamn idea for a raid I've ever heard. You got that?"

The Chief's voice was rough with age, and Jenkins pictured a careful survivor, probably a man looking to retire in a year or so without major stains on his reputation. She ground her teeth, knowing she needed his cooperation. "Thank you for expressing you thoughts, Chief," she managed.

The next thing surprised her. "I just had to say it," he said. "SWAT's been alerted. I'll have twenty-five officers for you, armed and ready in less than an hour. Our helo's already been given coordinates, but the weather's turning to crap. I just hope to hell you know what you're doing."

That makes two of us, Jenkins thought. "I assume you have fire department maps of the property?"

"My SWAT team trains every damn week. They've got maps of every major building and every piece of ground in this county."

"What about the town police?"

"Oyster Bay Cove?" the Chief scoffed. "They won't get near this. Anything happens that makes us look bad, they're gonna be in the newspapers and on TV saying they fought this tooth and nail. They're gonna say we're the dumbest bunch of bastards ever born. You better expect it."

"I hear you," Jenkins said. If she was wrong on thi, the Director would personally flay her with a rusty knife, so she couldn't sweat the small stuff.

Fortunately, the night traffic was light in the Lincoln

Tunnel, and the navy blue van was parked outside Federal Plaza as promised, the five agents standing on the sidewalk. They obviously knew the purpose of the raid because they wore combat gear and unhappy expressions. Jenkins parked, locked her car and introduced herself to the four men and one woman.

"I hope you know what you're doing," one of the men said.

Jenkins walked up to him, pulled herself up as tall as possible so she could look him straight in the eyes. "That makes two of us."

FIFTY-SIX

LONG ISLAND, JULY 1

PRESCOTT BIDDLE HAD just begun to tease Anneliës's left nipple with his tongue when his cell phone began to ring. He ignored it. It stopped but then went off again almost immediately. This time he rolled across the hotel's king-sized bed, checked the caller ID and saw that it was an "unknown number."

"Don't answer," Anneliës whispered, putting her arms around him as she tried to take the phone from his hand.

The ringing stopped, then started a third time. Only now the readout showed the call coming from his cottage, and he hit the answer button.

"Mr. Biddle." Abu Sayeed's voice was calm, almost languorous.

"You shouldn't be using this phone!" Biddle snapped.

"You didn't answer when I used my cell," Abu Sayeed said. "And I need something."

Biddle felt his pulse begin to hammer. "You have everything you need already."

"Not quite."

Biddle knew Anneliës could overhear because he felt her body stiffen. "What are you talking about?"

"We need you."

"That's ridiculous."

"I'm not going to argue with you, Mr. Biddle. Suffice it to say that we have something that belongs to you."

Biddle heard the sound of a door opening in the background, then a scream of pain followed by a woman's voice calling his name. The door slammed. "That was your wife, Mr. Biddle," Abu Sayeed said as he came back on the line. "I think she is quite anxious that you return quickly."

Biddle's heart bucked helplessly, caught in a vice grip of guilt. He began to hyperventilate. Weeks earlier he'd considered sending Faith to another of the alcohol treatment clinics that always failed to help, but he'd put it off. Why, he now wondered? In some shameful recess had he harbored a secret hope that the terrorists would remove the problem of his marriage? "You have no right!" he sputtered.

"Hurry back, Mr. Biddle," Abu Sayeed said, then hung up.

Biddle sat on the side of the bed and looked back at Anneliës. She lay with the sheet bunched at her hips, her perfect breasts rising and falling with her respirations. She reached out for him, but he moved farther away, hit with a sudden flash of intuition. "This is why you insisted we come here," he said. "How long have you known?"

Anneliës held his stare, but he could see caution and anxiety flickering in her eyes. "There is no way I could have prevented it," she said.

"You could have warned me!"

She said nothing.

"I have to go," he said after a moment, then turned away from her and began to pull on his clothes.

"No!" Anneliës cried.

Biddle ignored her. This was the last thing he wanted, but he had no choice.

Neither one spoke as they dressed. Biddle found it odd when she followed him from the room and into the elevator, but his thoughts and emotions were too jumbled. He was about to say something when she climbed into the driver's seat of the Land Rover, but his attention was diverted by the weather. A wall of low black clouds eclipsed the moon. Distant thunder rumbled in the heavens, and the wind cut and swirled in savage gusts.

It was only a summer storm, he told himself, as Anneliës began to drive, but he sensed an approaching maelstrom that was anything but normal. Was this God speaking? A band of rain lashed the windshield then stopped. Wind buffeted the heavy car, rocking it on its axles. Biddle closed his eyes and tried to picture himself as a Christian warrior striding across a vanquished earth, but he saw only the image of a normal man.

They were a half-mile from his estate when Anneliës braked savagely to a halt. The headlights glistened on the wet pavement, and leaves skittered past in the wind. The sight reminded him more of autumn and death than summer. Anneliës hammered the steering wheel with her fist. "You can't do this!"

"You don't have to come."

She gave him a bloodless smile. "You don't understand any of it!"

Biddle looked at her with dawning awareness. "What's to understand?"

"I know what Abu Sayeed is capable of!"

He kept staring at her in stunned silence. Finally, she continued. "Sayeed hired me. He paid me to gain your confidence, and I was willing to do it. I just had no idea that I would fall in love with you!"

Biddle felt numb. One part of him wanted to believe what she was telling him, but the analytical part cried out that she was lying, that she'd been lying from the very start. "The Lord wants me to confront the infidels."

Anneliës sat with her head bowed, hands locked on the wheel, appearing to wrestle with some decision. Finally she turned to him, her eyes filled with tiny points of red light. "Abu Sayeed is not going to follow your plan!"

"He has to!" Biddle cried.

"He's going to fire his missiles into Manhattan, then use you as a hostage to escape!"

Biddle put his palms over his ears, as if by shutting out her words he could make them false.

"You're his enemy!" Anneliës shouted.

"God will make Abu Sayeed fulfill His purpose!" he roared. His mind could not—would not—contemplate another possibility.

"Well, Abu Sayeed's God may have a different plan!"

His wild rush of anger took him by surprise. He slapped her hard enough to draw blood at the edge of her lip. She made no sound but turned her eyes away, and he felt something draw back into her, almost like heat leaving a room.

"Never take the name of the Lord in vain or talk about other gods as His equal," he said in a tight voice. He paused and waited for a response.

She kept her eyes on the road. "Idiot!" she snapped.

Biddle watched her and tried to analyze the enormity of what had just taken place. She had suddenly become a different person, someone hard and cold. Only it couldn't be. God would not let him lose her, not now, not when he was so close to returning Jesus to earth!

FIFTY-SEVEN

LONG ISLAND, JULY 2

BRENT PACED THE narrow space between Maggie's Toyota and Kosinsky's truck and tried to wrestle his emotions under control. Impatience and anxiety raged against his guilt that others were taking so much risk.

"Hey," Maggie said, sounding exasperated, "will you please pay attention. We have time to review this only once."

They were parked behind a McDonald's, beside the enclosure for the trash container. Maggie had her door open, her feet on the pavement. Fred Lucas and Kosinsky stood to either side, while DeLeyon sat in the passenger seat. Maggie held the aerial photograph spread across her lap and used a small flashlight as a pointer.

Brent relented and came over to watch as she traced Biddle's driveway. "Remember, there are three private security guards on duty, one right inside the gate." She indicated the small octagonal hut that Brent had pointed out earlier. "Another up here beside the main house." She pointed to an identical small building on one side of what looked like a six-or eight-car garage. She indicated a third structure down along the water, between the dock and the house. "And there's number three," she said. "I called the security company and verified that there are three guards on duty at all times, and that they're long-time employees."

"Which means they're probably ignorant of what's going on," Kosinsky added.

Maggie nodded. "We have to hope that's the case. It's Biddle's best bet for a tight alibi. If the guards are innocent, they won't be expecting an attack, so we just have to keep them busy. Even if there's shooting away from the house, they probably won't try to be heroes. They'll hunker down and call the police. That leaves the terrorists." She turned toward DeLeyon. "Okay, what's your job?"

"I'm lost," DeLeyon answered. "I stop right here," he said, pointing to the driveway entrance. "I ring the bell on the front gate and yell that I be needing some help. I ask to use the phone."

"Just keep him distracted," Maggie said.

Brent felt another stab of guilt. "Be damn careful," he snapped. "You're an African American kid in a rich white neighborhood late at night. You don't know how some rent-a-cop might react."

DeLeyon raised his hand up in front of his face, and his eyes widened in mock horror. "Oh, Lawdy, look at me! I am African American! I never notice that before!"

"It's not funny," Brent growled.

Maggie reached out and gave Brent's hand a quick squeeze. "He's just trying to lighten things up," she said gently.

Brent shrugged but said nothing.

"Okay, when DeLeyon distracts the guard, we go over the wall," Maggie continued. She looked up at Fred. "When we do, you're going to split off and get yourself into position near the house."

Brent took a quick glance at his uncle and thought that for once in his life, he looked serious. Fred nodded and cast a dour glance into the back of Kosinsky's truck at the cardboard liquor carton. The two half-gallon bottles in the carton had been full of Boodles Gin until a few minutes earlier but now held gasoline. Wet rags protruded from the top of each.

"You may not need to use them," Maggie cautioned. "The three of us will head for the cottage in the back."

"Who takes Biddle down?" Brent demanded, unable to get past the idea that Biddle might escape.

"There'll be no place he can run," Maggie said.

"I know how you feel about Biddle," Kosinsky said. "But the missiles and terrorists have to be our first objective."

Brent started to fire back a reply, but then he caught himself and nodded. Kosinsky was right.

"Give me the signal," Fred said. "I'll hit the garage."

Brent pointed at the guard station that was right beside the garage. "It's too risky. What if the guard starts shooting?"

"It's there, or it's no place. I need to make sure people can get out."

Maggie indicated what looked like a porch or perhaps a sunroom extending off the opposite end of the house. "What about here?"

Fred scowled, but he studied the picture for a few more seconds. Finally, he shrugged. "I guess that's okay," he mumbled.

"Good," Maggie said. "Steve, Brent and I go in along this side of the property." She traced a line down the property's border that would keep them well clear of Biddle's guards.

"We need to spread out before we go through those trees," Kosinsky said, indicating the trees that screened the cottage. He reached for the infrared close-up taken earlier that day. It showed a sharp green glow in the trees, two duller glows beneath the cottage roof. "There are three of these guys, one posted outside." He pointed to the brightest glow. "He'll almost certainly have night vision." He glanced up at Maggie and Brent. "Until we get the fires going, he'll be able to see us like it's daylight."

Maggie nodded. "I'll come in here." She pointed to a spot that put her furthest toward the center of the property. She pointed to the middle of the stand of trees. "Steve comes in here." She pointed to a spot along the property line. "Brent, you're here."

"No," Brent said. He pointed to the spot she intended to take, the one that was most exposed and therefore most dangerous. "This is mine."

"You haven't had the training," Kosinsky offered.

"Too bad," Brent said. He pointed to the map, moving from the middle of the property outward. "I'm here," he said. "Maggie here, and Steve, you're right here on the property line."

There was an uneasy silence, but Maggie finally nodded then glanced toward an oversized squirt gun that lay on the ground. It was nearly as big as a rifle, a brand that advertised its ability to squirt fifty feet. "Still working?" she asked Brent.

Brent picked it up, pumped up the pressure and shot a long stream into the darkness. He'd come up with the idea when they'd passed a Wal-Mart. Initially, it had seemed insane, but the more he'd thought about it, the more sense it made. By now, the gasoline had been inside the squirt gun for nearly thirty minutes and the plastic pieces were still holding up. It was only a matter of time before they started to soften, but if they had lasted this long, it was more than enough. They'd purchased five of the squirt guns along with a set of walkie-talkies and an extra-long stepladder.

"One more thing we have to talk about," Kosinsky said. "If the bad guys hole up in the cottage, we call in reinforcements and we call the security company and order them to stand their people down. But if they come out shooting—which they may—what are you gonna do?" He was looking directly at Brent, but then he swung his head toward Maggie. "A terrorist that's worth half a shit will kill you in a heartbeat, so what are you gonna do?"

He turned back toward Brent. "You say 'drop the gun,' he'll kill you, so you don't say anything. You shoot him. I'm talking about killing a guy in cold blood before he has a chance to shoot you or me or Maggie. Can you do that?"

Brent tried to hold Kosinsky's stare. He'd never aimed a gun at another human being, much less pulled the trigger, but he thought about Harry. "Yes," he said, his voice firm.

Kosinsky turned to Maggie. "This goes against every bit of law enforcement training you've ever had. Can you do it?"

"I think so."

"Don't think. Be sure."

Maggie took a deep breath, exhaled. "I'm sure."

"When the guy goes down, shoot him again, close up, in the head. You can't afford a wounded guy crawling around."

Brent cleared his throat. "What about you, Steve? Are you sure?"

Kosinsky gave him a humorless smile. "I did six years in the Special Forces before I became a cop. I don't like it, but I'm very sure."

Maggie picked up one of her walkie-talkies, turned it on and nodded for Fred and DeLeyon to do the same. "Okay, Fred, any shots fired, you toss your Molotovs and run. Once you're safe, call the security company and tell them to keep their people at the house. Under no circumstances are they to wander around the property. DeLeyon, you get your ass straight into Oyster Bay. Report a fire and shots fired at the Biddle estate. Afterward, call the FBI and the Nassau County Police. Got it?"

Fred and DeLeyon nodded.

"Okay," Maggie continued. "Situation number two—no shots fired and I give you two clicks," she said, pushing the Talk button on the walkie-talkie twice as she said it. "That means no terrorists, so no Molotovs, no phone calls and no cops." She waited for more nods. "Okay, last situation—no shots but three clicks. It means we've got trouble. Throw the cocktails and call for help. Any questions?"

"Let's assume we find no terrorists," Brent said. "We go get Biddle, right?"

"Yeah," Maggie said. "But get it through your head—the guy's got company." She pulled another sheet of paper from beneath the satellite photo. It was the interior and exterior schematic of a large boat. "This is a Hatteras like Biddle's," she said. "There's probably a fifty percent chance the missiles are onboard, so everyone ought to be familiar with the layout."

Brent gave the diagrams a quick glance and thought back to a few times when the seas were too rough for fishing and he and Harry had helped friends do maintenance work on larger yachts. He hated the prospect of chasing people through the tight passages and blind passageways of a boat's interior.

Suddenly the lights began to go out inside the McDonald's. He checked his watch. Ten past midnight. He didn't have the patience for any more planning. "Let's get this show on the road," he said.

FIFTY-EIGHT
LONG ISLAND, JULY 2

BIDDLE SQUEEZED HIS hands into fists as the gates of his estate swung open. Abu Sayeed had taken Faith hostage! The thought sickened him, buffeted him with guilt and rage. This was his fault! Even worse, the change he'd felt when he slapped Anneliës was still there, and that, too, sapped his confidence.

The car started to move again, and Biddle tried to re-focus. As they came around the first curve, he saw the octagonal guard hut and felt a surge of reassurance at the sight of his personal security. His guards knew nothing about the Arabs, of course, yet having them on the property evened things considerably.

A low-wattage light burned inside the guardhouse, and on closer inspection he could see that the building was empty. He squinted into the surrounding darkness. The man was probably nearby smoking a cigarette or taking a leak, but nonetheless he didn't like it. He expected Anneliës to stop, lower her window and wait for the guard, but she kept going.

"Stop the car!" Biddle demanded.

Anneliës didn't look at him. When Biddle reached for her arm, she jerked it out of his grasp. "This is what you wanted!" she hissed. She hit the accelerator, and they picked up speed. The lights along the driveway began to rocket past.

"I'm giving you an order!" Biddle shouted, but he didn't dare touch her again. They were hurtling toward the fork that would take them left toward the cottages. Even there Anneliës did not slow. The Range Rover yawed as she jerked the wheel, and the tires slid off the pavement and across the grass.

"What in God's name?"

She wrested the car back onto the blacktop. Biddle was at a loss. Anneliës loved him! She wanted to spend her life making him happy! Also, wasn't Abu Sayeed putting his whole mission at risk? Biddle had given him a chance to kill the President of the United States! No terrorist would jeopardize such an opportunity!

Anneliës wouldn't even glance at him. Her face was grim and hatchet-like in the glow of the dashboard lights, the face of someone he had never met.

He reached out and put his hand on her arm again, gently this time. "Please talk to me."

They raced past the barn and tennis courts, then the headlights slashed through the thick grove of pines that separated the cottages from the broad lawns of the estate. Anneliës braked hard, the anti-lock brakes shuddered, and they came to a halt on the wet pavement of the small courtyard. Very deliberately, she took his hand and removed it from her arm. "Here we are," she said with deadly calm.

Biddle looked out at the dark cottage, its shape suddenly squat and sinister. Wind whipped the trees. The courtyard felt foreboding, no longer a place under his domain. Not even a splinter of light escaped the cottage windows, but he felt the lurking presence of evil. It seemed so black and overwhelming that it might have been a dream, a hallucination induced by guilt and anxiety, or by the weather that seemed sent by God, Himself, as a warning.

Anneliës turned off the engine and climbed out into the gale. Biddle continued to sit, realizing that God had brought things to this impasse and stunned by how vulnerable he felt suddenly. After a moment he stepped out of the car. His mind was a jumble, but he registered the coldness of Anneliës's expression.

"Raise your hands," a heavily accented voice said from somewhere in the darkness.

Biddle stiffened. He knew the voice—the short terrorist, the one named Mohammed—but he did as the man ordered.

Anneliës stood a few feet away but did not raise her hands. "He is unarmed," she said in a businesslike tone.

Mohammed stepped out of the trees, wearing a pair of black night vision goggles and holding a small machine gun. He spoke softly into a small microphone at his collar, and a second later Biddle heard the cottage door open.

He turned to see the dark-skinned Arab, the one who appeared more African than Arab, studying him with his delicate, almost feminine eyes. The man's face was scabbed and bandaged as if he'd been in a fight. He swung the door all the way open and waved Biddle inside. Biddle's fear dissipated slightly as he moved toward the cottage, his mind seizing on the idea that he would be dealing with Abu Sayeed, a man far more civilized than his lackeys.

The moment he went through the door he noted the staleness in the air. It was the odor of dirty clothes, old food and something else, an acrid stink that seemed a combination of anxiety and expectation. As soon as he smelled it, he found it contagious, and his fear rose back up in his gut. He cast his eyes around the room until they found Abu Sayeed, sitting peacefully in a chair beside the fireplace.

"Mr. Biddle," the Saudi said with a casual wave of his long fingers. "How nice of you to grace us with your company."

"Yes," Biddle said, his throat so dry that his voice squeaked.

Abu Sayeed uttered an easy laugh. "I must admit you surprised me." He gave Anneliës an unreadable glance. "I had started to think you would not come."

Mohammed said something to Abu Sayeed in what sounded like Arabic, a question. When Abu Sayeed nodded, the man went back outside, closing the door behind him.

Now trapped in this tight space, Biddle felt his confidence ebbing. "I demand that you let my wife go immediately," he said, but heard the hollowness in his words.

Abu Sayeed shrugged. "Regrettably, we will not be able to do that."

Biddle shot another glance at Anneliës. "I thought we were partners."

Abu Sayeed uttered a gentle laugh. "Please, Mr. Biddle."

Biddle closed his eyes and took a breath to steady himself. "What do you intend to do with us?"

Abu Sayeed put his fingertips together and appeared to study their shape. He glanced at Anneliës. "It all comes down to endgames, does it not?"

"What are you talking about?"

Abu Sayeed frowned, seeming saddened by Biddle's lack of understanding. He continued to stare at his fingertips. "You thought the silly Arabs would blow themselves up, while you would go on to your great victory."

A wave of vertigo washed through Biddle, as though a bottomless chasm had opened at his feet. Of course Abu Sayeed should have followed the plan! He believed with all his heart that God had ordained it . . . but could he be mistaken?

He looked around the room, at the muted TV turned to an old movie, the plate of half-eaten dates beside the sink, a bowl of hummus on the table, the overflowing garbage can with an empty bag of Ruffles potato chips sitting on top. Suddenly, with a sense of abandonment so complete that it nearly buckled his knees, he realized he was alone. How had he miscalculated? Why was God forsaking him?

When he looked back at Abu Sayeed, his feigned pleasantry had dropped away and his dark eyes were brimming with malevolence. "You have been too condescending to see past your nose, Mr. Biddle. For such an intelligent man, your stupidity shocks me."

He glanced toward the bedroom and snapped his fingers. The dark-skinned terrorist opened the door to show Biddle the sight of his wife bound and gagged on the bed. Faith's head snapped up, eyes white with terror. Taped into a chair beside the bed sat Fred Wofford, his head hanging and his white shirt stained with blood. Biddle started to say something, but the man closed the door again, then stood beside it with his arms folded across his chest.

Biddle's heart thundered in his chest. His stomach roiled. He turned to Abu Sayeed ready to plead, barter, give him anything he wanted. "Please," he said.

Abu Sayeed was smiling as if the whole thing was a wonderful joke. "When I saw this wife of yours up close, I feared our insurance policy would be of little value."

"Let her go," Biddle moaned.

"She is a filthy creature, foul-mouthed and reeking of alcohol and tobacco. She does not honor you. I would not cross the street to save such a wife."

"She lost God," Biddle said. "She's been wandering ever since."

Abu Sayeed picked a piece of dirt from a fingernail. "A

shame." He glanced back toward the dark-skinned terrorist. "Kill her," he said.

Biddle couldn't seem to get enough oxygen in his lungs. Dear Father, he prayed silently, protect me in this hour of my need. His eyes darted to the front door.

Anneliës leaned against the wall beside it, her face a mask. If he could just get her between Abu Sayeed and himself, she would find a way to help him. He was sure of it.

He broke for the door, thinking he could jerk it open, run outside, through the hedge and toward the lights on his lawn. He had read somewhere that lights would blind night vision equipment.

The second he moved, Anneliës came away from the wall, but instead of helping, she stepped directly in his path.

He tried to dodge around her, but her foot lashed out, catching him in the side of the leg. Pain wracked him as his knee buckled. He hit the floor hard and lay stunned with Anneliës's feet just inches away. After a second she turned and went back to the wall. Biddle raised his head, but her expression was like stone.

Abu Sayeed laughed gently. "Mr. Biddle, did you never guess that she was in my employ? You never suspected?"

Biddle could feel his anger and hurt painted on his face. That instant if he had had a gun, he would have forsaken his great mission and killed Abu Sayeed. He would have killed all of them. Only, he had nothing. He had come utterly unprepared. How could he have been so arrogant? *Father*, he started to pray yet again, *protect me in this hour of my—*

He didn't finish. Outside the cottage a roar erupted, sounding like a big gust of wind, only louder. Anneliës jerked the door open, and Biddle saw the reflection of towering flames dancing wildly in the courtyard. His heart rejoiced. Praise the Lord! He delivereth me!

FIFTY-NINE

OYSTER BAY, JULY 2

BRENT TENSED AS the wind whipped his hair and a fresh peal of thunder ripped the sky. The rain would resume any second. He was in position, but the backlit face on his watch showed he was several minutes early. He lay flat in a shallow depression beneath some thick azaleas, his clothing soaked by the wet ground, his nose filled with the scent of fresh mulch. He was pretty sure the bushes would screen him even from someone wearing night vision goggles.

He checked his watch again. Three minutes. The pistol in his waistband jammed the cut on his stomach. He had a shell in the chamber, and he knew what he had to do–aim, click off the safety, hold his breath, squeeze the trigger. The prospect of shooting someone made him physically ill, but it wouldn't stop him.

His squirt gun lay beside him, reeking of gasoline. He gave it another shake to make certain the fuel hadn't leaked, then crossed his fingers that the internal workings hadn't melted. The test gun had still worked after forty-five minutes. Amazingly, it had only been twenty minutes since they'd left the McDonald's parking lot, maybe ten or twelve since they'd filled the other squirt guns and started across the wall.

He took a deep breath and listened. He'd made it to the middle of the estate without hearing a sound except the wind keening in the trees and the rumble of the approaching storm. Biddle's mansion was a little over a hundred yards to his right, and he wondered if Biddle was sitting in his den right now, sipping a brandy. He was even starting to wonder whether Maggie was wrong and the cottages were empty when he saw the headlights.

The vehicle came fast, its engine racing, its beams knifing through the ground mist. At the fork in the drive, it swerved toward the cottages, and Brent pressed down into the wood chips. The car momentarily slid off the blacktop as if the driver was panicked. Was it Biddle's security or someone coming to warn the terrorists? The car disappeared behind the trees, and a second later he heard its brakes chatter as it squealed to a halt. Its doors opened and then thumped shut.

Brent checked his watch. Ninety seconds. Ahead in the darkness a voice rose momentarily above the wind. The speaker was invisible, the words indistinct, but Brent thought he caught a heavy accent.

His heart thumped as he recalled the face of the man who'd tried to kill him in the garage. Seconds ticked by. He concentrated, listening for every sound. Momentarily he thought he heard footsteps nearby. He gazed into the darkness but saw nothing and heard only the wind and the hiss of rustling leaves. His watch gradually showed forty-five seconds, thirty seconds. Finally, it was time.

He inched out from the azaleas, stood, aimed his super-soaker high into the boughs of the nearest pines. He hosed the branches until he could smell gas dripping all around, then he waited, looking in Kosinsky's direction. After another second, there was a glimmer of light, and very quickly three or four pines along the edge of Biddle's property burst into flame.

A second later several more trees, these much closer, also went up, and now he lit his match and tossed it. The instant whoosh of the igniting gas took him by surprise, and in only seconds the heat knocked him back a step. He stood there, momentarily silhouetted against the night, but then he crouched and began to move toward Maggie and Kosinsky.

At least six trees were burning. The wind whipped the flames, and limbs began to pop as the sap and pine needles caught. Glowing sparks raced off the trees and blew over the lawns, and the roar of the flames overrode even the sound of the wind. He finally saw movement out of the corner of his eye, veered toward it and found Maggie squatting at the base of a thick oak.

He knelt beside her, shouting to be heard over the fire. "Where's Kosinsky?"

She shook her head just as three quick shots cracked over the sound of the storm. Brent looked toward the sound but saw only the wind-lashed flames twenty or thirty yards away. Without thinking he freed his pistol and began crawling. Behind him Maggie shouted into the walkie-talkie, "We have shots fired! Fred, throw the bombs and get out right now. DeLeyon, get your ass into town. Copy?"

Brent was already too far away to hear any response, but a second later when he glanced back he spotted a new glimmer of flames in the direction of the main house. He was snaking along the side of the azalea bed, trying to stay low. He hoped he wasn't too visible but he didn't slow down. Kosinsky had risked his life for him.

Up ahead a dark shape lay on the grass. He froze as light from the burning pines wavered across the still form. Overhead, thunder boomed. Finally, he inched forward, watching for movement while his mind raced. Was it a terrorist? He remembered Kosinsky's warning, but even if the guy moved, he couldn't shoot until he knew for sure.

He was only a couple of feet away before he recognized Kosinsky, lying on his back with his hand clamped tight over his left shoulder. Brent could see blood glistening in the firelight. "Steve," he whispered, "it's me. I'll get help."

"Careful," Kosinsky groaned. "The guy came up so fast. He's got a silencer. I got off a couple of shots, but I think I missed." He fought a wave of pain and closed his eyes. After a deep breath he opened them again. "This guy's a pro."

Brent looked out at darkness behind them and the conflagration in front. Which way had the guy gone? Kosinsky seemed to read his mind. He pointed a bloody finger toward the cottage. "Over there."

The pine trees were burning on their own now, the wind sucking flames along the branches, spreading them to the main trunks. An asteroid shower of burning pine needles rained through the air. Beyond the pines, the night was a pool of black ink.

Brent heard a sound behind him. He spun away from the fire and aimed blindly, realizing belatedly that he'd lost his night vision.

"It's me!" Maggie called as she appeared out of the dark. "Hold tight, Steve," she said. She pulled a small flashlight from her pocket, cupped the beam and shined it on his wounded arm, then on his chest where three holes had shredded the fabric around his heart, exposing the bulletproof vest beneath. She clicked off the light and grabbed her walkie-talkie. "DeLeyon, you copy? We need an ambulance. Kosinsky's hit. Repeat. Kosinsky's hit. Do you copy?"

Fred's voice came to her, filled with static from the approaching storm. "I copy," he said. "I'm calling 911 on my cell phone, and I'll be there in a second. Where are you?"

Brent snatched the walkie-talkie out of Maggie's hand. "Fred, stay the hell away from here!"

"Forget it. I've got years of first aid. Are you near Kosinsky's original position?"

Brent gritted his teeth. "Yes," he said. "Be careful."

A second later Fred came back, sounding breathless, as though he was running and trying to talk at the same time. "The guard up at the house is dead."

Maggie grabbed the walkie-talkie. "Repeat?"

"Dead," Fred huffed. "I saw him in the firelight after I tossed my bombs, slumped over in his little guardhouse."

Brent gave his head a shake. Think! What was happening? Was somebody else attacking? Police? FBI? No way—there would be lights, sirens, and helicopters. No, it had to be the terrorists, but why would they kill Biddle's guards?

"We can't worry about it," Maggie said, as if she'd read his mind. "Let's cover the driveway in case they try to get away."

"Get going!" Kosinsky said. "I'll be okay."

Footsteps thumped behind them. Brent turned as Fred limped into sight. "I could see you bastards all the way across the lawn," he whispered. "You stand out real good against the fire. Just thought you'd like to know."

"Take care of Steve," Brent said. "I'll cover the driveway." He started running back the way he'd come, but almost immediately he sensed someone behind him. "Stay with Kosinsky!" he said, trying to wave Maggie back.

"No!" she said. "I'm coming with you. Get it through your head!"

He started to run again. In spite of the circumstances, a brief hope flickered. Maggie was with him. There was nothing he wanted more.

SIXTY

OYSTER BAY, NY, JULY 2

ABU SAYEED WAS already flattened against the cottage wall when the second stand of trees ignited. He inched to the door and looked out in time to see a third group of trees go up in flames. Naif ran past him, across the courtyard, but even before he had taken up a covering position beside the garage, three shots sounded in the trees. They were loud, from a heavy gauge pistol, not Mohammed's silenced Heckler & Koch.

Abu Sayeed looked up at the approaching blackness in the western sky and deep within it the lurid flicker of lightning. He raced mentally through his options, then pulled plastic cuffs from his pocket and tossed them to Anneliës. "Get him on the boat," he said, his voice clipped but unhurried.

He noted the defeat in Biddle's face as Anneliës knelt and jerked his wrists behind his back. A second later Mohammed appeared, backing out of the trees. He was breathing heavily, his shirt soaked through with rain and sweat. He squatted near the door. "I saw one man," he said quickly. "I killed him."

"How many others?"

Mohammed shook his head in confusion. "There are no sirens and no lights. It is most strange."

"And the security people?"

Mohammed nodded. "Dead."

Abu Sayeed nodded. There was no time for understanding, only for action. "To the boat!" he snapped. Mohammed turned and ran toward the opening in the hedge. Next, Abu Sayeed jerked his head, and Anneliës dragged Biddle to his feet.

"Let Faith go," Biddle pleaded as Anneliës shoved him outside. Biddle stumbled across the courtyard like a doomed man, offering no resistance.

Abu Sayeed walked into the bedroom. He unsheathed his Russian combat knife and cut the tape that bound Wofford to the chair. He pulled Wofford roughly to his feet. "Wait there," he commanded, shoving him out of the room.

He turned toward the woman, who raised her head and looked at him, her eyes wide with panic. He raised his submachine gun and fired. A spray of blood hit the pillow and wall as her head exploded.

He went back into the sitting room to find Wofford cowering beside the front door, a horrified look on his bruised face. Abu Sayeed barely glanced at him as he opened the flap of a leather satchel that lay on the dining table. He set the timer for ninety seconds, then went to where three backpacks leaned against the wall. He slipped one on his back, slung his machine gun over his neck and slung the other two packs along one arm. He moved to Wofford, gripped him by the back of the neck, his arm weighed down by the packs, and shoved him out the door.

With Wofford as his shield, he hurried across the courtyard to where Naif squatted in the shadows.

"Forty-five seconds," he hissed, as he dropped the two packs. "Go."

Naif nodded and slipped on his pack, took the other in his hand then raced for the opening in the hedge. Abu Sayeed peered toward the burning trees, trying to pick out silhouettes. It made no sense. There should be teams of attackers. Biddle certainly hadn't arranged this, but then who?

He started backing toward the boat, tightening his grip on Wofford's neck. As he neared the hedge and Mohammed brought the yacht's diesel engines rumbling to life, he thanked Allah for giving him the foresight to put the missiles back on board.

He paused in the shadows of the hedge. Naif whistled behind him, signaling that the shoreline was clear. Beside the cottage, Abu Sayeed heard a woman's voice shouting, "Freeze! Police!"

He raised his gun over Wofford's shoulder, caught a momentary glimpse of a silhouette and fired a silenced burst. The woman's handgun barked several times, the shots hitting a few feet to his right. He needed only seconds. He fired a longer burst to keep his attackers pinned.

A moment later, the charge went off. The cottage windows blew out and the roof buckled, spraying a deadly shower of broken shingles. To Abu Sayeed's surprise, Wofford exploded out of his grasp and began running toward the ruined cottage even as shards of flying slate flew all around.

In the courtyard, where she'd been partially sheltered by the Range Rover, a woman was on her hands and knees, trying to stand. Abu Sayeed made a quick calculation then pulled the trigger. He watched Wofford pitch face down on the paving blocks. Then he dashed forward, put his foot on the woman's back and flattened her to the ground.

The air had become a slurry of rain and wet dust, but he could see she no longer had a weapon. Her shirt was tattered from the explosion, revealing a bulletproof vest. He placed the machine gun against her head then squinted toward the trees, looking for more attackers. He saw nothing and heard only a single voice calling, "Maggie! Maggie!"

He jerked the woman to her feet and put her in a throat lock. She cried out in pain, swaying limp as a rag doll, but he dragged her back to the opening in the hedge using her body as a shield. In the darkness, the voice drew closer, calling, "Maggie!"

Abu Sayeed glanced to the side, across Biddle's acres of well-lit lawn. Flames poured from one corner of the big house, but otherwise nothing moved. "Maggie!" the voice cried out from the courtyard. Abu Sayeed loosed a burst of machine gun fire in the direction of the sound, then grabbing the pack he had dropped, he dragged the woman across the open space to the dock. Her legs were unsteady, so that she was nearly deadweight. He considered shooting her but then heard Naif's footsteps behind him.

"Help me get her onto the boat," he called. They each took one of the woman's arms and hauled her up the gangplank. Abu Sayeed threw her into the salon and tossed the extra backpack on a chair. He ordered Anneliës to find a set of cuffs for the woman in one of pouches, then he ran out to help Naif untie the lines. As they heaved off, Mohammed reversed the engines and swung the big boat away from the dock, pointing the bow into the teeth of the squall coming from the west.

Abu Sayeed squatted against the transom and watched the shore. After a second he saw movement, a single silhouette running down the dock, framed every fifteen feet or so in the piling lights. They were picking up speed as he tried to aim, timing his shot to the yacht's roll. He pulled the trigger as the man came into view again, then watched him spin and fall.

Abu Sayeed stood and ran through the aft salon, then climbed to the upper deck and the bridge. He left Mohammed at the helm, went to the radar and set the resolution to a hundred yards, then two-fifty, then five hundred yards, looking for the blip of a big boat, a Coast Guard cutter perhaps, something with armament that could blow the Hatteras out of the water. Only, he saw nothing, just the usual yachts, fishing boats and sailboats on their moorings.

His enemies had attacked, yet they had left the back door open. Why? He tried to think. Allah, clear my mind, he prayed as he went below to the salon. Anneliës had the woman cuffed, and he jerked her into a sitting position and struck her hard across the cheekbones. "Who do you work for?" he demanded. "FBI? CIA? Police?"

The woman blinked away tears of pain and glared back in silence. He saw fear in her eyes but also will and resolve and knew he had too little time to break her down. Where was the helicopter that ought to be overhead right now? Where was the Navy, the Coast Guard? There seemed only one plausible explanation—that in any military operation even with meticulous planning, things went wrong. Tonight, something had gone wrong for his enemies. Apparently, the Americans had prepared a trap, yet thanks to Allah, someone had moved early. No doubt at this very moment, Coast Guard boats and helicopters were on their way to Biddle's estate and a mob of government agents were gathering outside the gate.

His understanding of "what" gave him no comfort because the question of "how" still loomed. He was certain Biddle wasn't the leak. It couldn't be Biddle's wife because the skinny beast had been utterly shocked when they burst into her home and dragged her away from her martini and cigarettes. It might have been Wofford, the man he'd killed.

He looked down at the woman. "How did you learn of us?" he demanded.

"It was easy," she said.

Abu Sayeed struck her harder this time then knelt on her

back and ripped off her black T-shirt to expose the bulletproof vest beneath. The stenciled initials "FBI" confirmed what he'd already guessed. He left her and went back to the stern where he stood in the open and tried to gauge the weather. The wind continued to strengthen, and the bay now boiled with whitecaps. When he looked ahead, he could see that the storm was almost on them, blackening the sky and cutting off any sight of Long Island Sound.

A shudder ran through him. He hated the ocean, and this dense, suffocating weather caused an almost unbearable claustrophobia. Even so, he knew that Allah had sent this storm to confuse his enemies.

He went back into the salon and jerked the woman to her feet. He pushed her up the steps to the bridge, wondering again how to make her talk in the shortest time. He slapped her again, hard, knocking her to her knees, then threw her against the bulwark while he re-checked the navigation instruments. There was still nothing unusual on the radar, no large boat bearing toward them.

The woman appeared semi-conscious. He grabbed the back of her vest and dragged her from the bridge onto the flybridge. No helicopters hovering low, no searchlights on the water. The temperature was dropping, the wind-blown rain cold and stinging. In only seconds they would plunge into the swirling fog, becoming invisible, one more anonymous blip on radar.

His heart lightened for a moment because his enemies were confused, and he was about to elude them. Allah's blessings could be as massive as an earthquake, or subtle as fog over a harbor. Either way, they were great. "Allah Akbar," Abu Sayeed whispered, giving thanks for his delivery.

Finally, he looked down at the woman. She blinked as the rain started to revive her, and he reached down and turned her head toward the two crates that sat under canvas tarps. "There," he said, reaching with one hand to yank back one of the tarps and reveal a large metal crate. "Is this what you hoped to prevent us from using?" He smiled. "You are too late, but if you want to live, you will tell me what I want to know."

The woman's lip was split along the side of her mouth, and when she tried to talk, her teeth were stained with blood.

"Brent's going to kill you," she said.

With a cry of rage, Abu Sayeed struck her with his fist, knocking her to the deck where she lay unmoving. He returned to the bridge. "Anneliës!" he shouted down into the salon. "Take this piece of excrement below!"

SIXTY-ONE
OYSTER BAY, NY, JULY 2

BRENT HEARD A rapid pop-pop-pop-pop, followed by a rain of heavy slaps and thumps on the dock, the pilings and the water, before one caught him in the arm. As if a horse had kicked him, it spun him around and off his feet.

When he sat up again, his right arm was numb, with a tingling like a limb that had gone to sleep. He felt above the elbow, his fingers finding warm blood and then the indentation where a chunk of muscle as big around as his thumb had been blown out. When he flexed his elbow, the pain began.

He climbed to his feet, fighting off the sudden nausea, and squinted at the dark shape of the yacht already becoming indistinct in the storm. A single thought drove him–Maggie! From the opening in the hedge, he'd seen them dragging her up the gangplank. His first instinct was to call the police or FBI, but to what point? Even if they believed him, the storm already covered Long Island Sound. Boats or helicopters would never arrive in time.

He cast a desperate look toward the floating section of dock to his right. There were several skiffs and jet skis but also a decent-sized Boston Whaler. He ran around to its berth, fighting the pain in his arm and holding out a wild hope that the keys were in the ignition. They weren't.

He remembered the small octagonal building on the shore beside the dock–it had to be where Biddle kept the boat keys. His arm pulsed red waves of agony as he ran to the building, circled to the door and stopped.

One of Biddle's security guards lay sprawled inside, face-up, a bullet hole in his forehead. The sight redoubled his fears for Maggie, and he forced his eyes to a pegboard where several keys hung on floating key chains. He grabbed one labeled "Whaler" and raced back along the dock. On the way, he stooped over to snatch the super-soaker he dropped when he'd been hit.

A second later, behind the Whaler's wheel, he looked over controls that were roughly the same as in Harry's boat. He shoved the key in the ignition, found the tilt button and lowered the engines into the water, pulled out the choke and engaged the starter. The engines didn't catch. He cursed. Nothing ever worked in boats! He tried again, but then he remembered the gas lines. He stumbled into the stern, found them and squeezed the two balls that fed gas to the engines.

When he turned the key again, the engines caught. He let them run hot for several seconds as he untied the lines, then he pushed in the choke, backed away from the dock and roared into the darkness. His eyes watered in the wind, and the black wall of the storm lay straight ahead in the west. With the throttle jammed all the way forward, he prayed he had enough gas in the tanks.

He sped along with whitecaps pounding the hull but just enough ambient light from the shoreline to avoid moored boats. Away from shore the air grew misty and cold, the rain slashed, and he began to shiver. He had no plan and wondered what the hell was he going to do when he caught the yacht, assuming he could find it in the fog? He strained his eyes into the thickening storm, knowing that in only a few hundred yards, he'd be running absolutely blind.

He looked down at the control panel, searching for the radio, but found only some screw holes and an empty space. "Shit!" he screamed. It had been pulled out, no doubt for repairs. Two boxy instruments sat atop the console, and he tore off the plastic covers. It was nearly impossible with the slamming waves, but he managed to find the switches. A moment later, he had radar and also a GPS showing his direction and location. The radar indicated a thick cluster of moored boats directly ahead, and he swung well clear of them but kept his heading toward the Sound.

He hit the fog with the engines wide open. He was going insanely fast for the conditions, but if he went slower, he'd never find Maggie. After several tries he located the button that extended or decreased the radar's viewing area, and he widened it until he spotted an image heading west out of Oyster Bay. It was the nearest thing moving on the water, and he assumed it had to be the yacht. A few minutes later, as he reached the mouth of the bay, he guessed he was about five hundred yards behind.

Given the power of the twin outboards, he'd hoped to catch the yacht quickly, but as he turned into the Sound, three-and four-foot swells were rolling hard from the northwest, causing the boat to pitch wildly. Unable to brace himself with his wounded arm, he backed off the throttle. He stared at the radar screen, monitoring the yacht's heading as the gap refused to narrow.

What were the terrorists planning? Were the missiles on board? In his guts he knew that they were, that somehow this was all part of their plan. Maggie had guessed it would be an assassination attempt on the President, but that no longer seemed possible. Now, with the Coast Guard and FBI alerted, Biddle's boat would be an easy target in New York Harbor. But then he thought—maybe the terrorists were simply planning to launch their dirty weapons in the dark then try to escape. Maybe that's why they'd taken Maggie hostage.

That realization made his heart sink anew. The increasing likelihood of interdiction by the FBI or Coast Guard meant hostages would have zero probability of survival. That in turn meant Maggie's only hope of rescue depended on him. Once she was safe, he'd do his best to stop the terrorists, but she came first. He'd need surprise and perfect timing, and if he blew any part of it, both of them would end up dead. He raised his wounded arm and flexed the joint. The bleeding had slowed, but it had stiffened, making movement even more painful. He couldn't let it matter.

After a time, the radar showed the yacht changing course, turning southwest. It was still about five hundred yards out, but now with the new heading, the wind was off his stern, so he was able to increase speed. Over the next twenty minutes, he narrowed the gap and was only about two hundred yards back when the yacht changed course again and began moving almost directly south. The GPS showed the Sound beginning to narrow as the land squeezed closer from both shores. The seas had subsided slightly, but hard rain still pelted. His teeth chattered uncontrollably.

Minutes later, even though the yacht was only a hundred

yards ahead, he realized he had a new problem. The cold had debilitated him. His wounded arm now hung almost immobile at his side, and the fingers on his other hand were nearly too stiff to move. If he was going to try to leap on the yacht's stern, he risked falling helplessly into the water.

He shook his head, refusing to focus on failure. He was staring at the radar screen, watching what was now a second radar blip converging with the first, when the rain ceased abruptly. He tore his eyes off the screen and looked overhead. Almost immediately, the absence of driving rain allowed warmth to begin flooding back into his limbs. It took several seconds to comprehend that he was passing beneath what had to be the Throgs Neck Bridge. Low clouds obscured the structure, but from overhead came the unmistakable thump of car tires crossing expansion joints.

Seconds later, he roared back into the cold rain, but the shelter of the bridge had bought him a little extra time. Now his fingers would move again and the uncontrollable shivering had diminished.

He looked back at the radar and struggled to pick the yacht out of the two convergent blips. One of the blips was moving directly toward the shore, so he decided the yacht had to be the other one. From here, his lead narrowed quickly. He drew to within fifty yards, then forty, thirty. He stared at the screen but snatched quick glances at the fog, trying to perceive a shape, something solid against the shifting whiteness. He continued to close the gap, backing off the throttles as he suddenly noticed that he was in the smooth wake of the other boat. He looked down at the water, thinking it seemed oddly calm, given the churning screws of the yacht's engines. He inched closer and closer until a shape materialized. Panic hit him then. It was no yacht, but a tug pushing a barge!

SIXTY-TWO

OYSTER BAY, NY, JULY 2

ANN JENKINS CHEWED her cuticles bloody as she peered out the window of the Coast Guard chopper and thought how the past forty-five minutes had probably turned her career to toast. About that long ago she'd been standing in the parking lot behind the Oyster Bay Cove Police Department going over the satellite photos with her team of FBI agents and Nassau County Police S.W.A.T. officers.

She'd been expecting a radio call any second from the Nassau County Police helo announcing that they were on station offshore of Biddle's dock, positioned to prevent an escape by boat and otherwise provide general backup and assistance. The call had come all right, only the Nassau County PD said the weather was deteriorating too rapidly for their chopper to fly. Sorry, but she'd need to call the Coast Guard.

Just then the black kid showed up, almost hysterical, babbling about a fire at Biddle's estate, shots fired and a wounded cop. That was also when she'd learned that the Oyster Bay Fire Department had been notified first and was already rolling. She'd blown off the planning and raced everyone out to Biddle's estate where they spent fifteen precious minutes arguing with the fire chief and EMT's about who would go in first. Finding the dead security man behind the guardhouse won the argument for her, but they'd gone into Biddle's property a full hour before the Coast Guard chopper's scheduled arrival.

Then, of course, there was the situation they'd found: Kosinsky wounded and being tended by a retired fireman, Maggie DeVito missing along with Brent Lucas, three dead security guards, no sign of the terrorists, a blown-up cottage with some bloody human remains and another body in the courtyard. Also, Prescott Biddle and his wife were missing, along with Biddle's yacht.

The chopper finally circled in, just as the weather was

completely shutting down, but Jenkins had ordered them to land anyway so she could jump aboard. Now she stared out fogged-up windows that showed only the reflection of their flying lights against the dense clouds, while trying to hold down the contents of her stomach in the buffeting.

Initially, thinking the terrorists might have run for the open ocean, they'd made an easterly sweep out of Oyster Bay, where they found three ships. They'd gone in low over each one, and the co-pilot had adjusted the radar to give them a good idea of length and size. There'd been two towed barges and a small commercial boat, but nothing remotely the shape of a hundred-foot yacht.

From there they circled west, and in the past few minutes, they'd checked out several more blips—all barges—between Oyster Bay and the Throgs Neck Bridge. They were following a fresh blip and gaining altitude to go over the bridge, when she noticed the co-pilot stiffen and sit forward.

She tapped his shoulder. "Got anything?" she shouted over the roar of the rotors.

He shrugged, pointing to the screen. "A second ago, I thought I saw something along the western shore, but it disappeared." They came over the bridge and closed on the first target, and as the pilot sharpened the resolution, Jenkins saw the signal split into two parts.

The co-pilot shook his head. "That's weird," he shouted. "Looks like a small boat, maybe twenty-five feet, almost on top of a tug."

Jenkins tried to ignore her heaving stomach and think. What if the terrorists were on a smaller boat than she'd thought? What if were they trying to take over a tug? It was a possibility. On the other hand, where were DeVito and Lucas? Were they dead, or taken hostage, or were they also out in the fog trying to find the terrorists?

As she watched the screen, the smaller blip fell back and came to a stop, letting the barge pull ahead. Suddenly, Jenkins had an idea, and she tapped on the co-pilot's shoulder again. "What about that other blip you saw?" she shouted.

He pointed to a spot behind them, close to the shoreline.

"Let's check it out," she called.

As they headed in that direction and the co-pilot adjusted the radar, the blip appeared once again.

"Is it moving?" she shouted.

The co-pilot stared at the screen a moment, then nodded. "Very slowly."

What if the terrorists were sneaking instead of running? Fog made that the superior strategy.

Suddenly, the co-pilot shouted, "Whitestone Bridge." They began an abrupt climb and swung in a tight circle as they reacquired their target, then dropped so quickly that Jenkins though her stomach would tear loose. The pilot positioned them almost directly behind the blip while the co-pilot adjusted the radar and studied the image. After a second, he said something to the pilot. Suddenly, the flying lights went out, and the helicopter began to descend, getting nearer and nearer the boat.

Jenkins pressed her face to the window, but she could see only thick clouds. The helicopter dropped a few more feet. Her stomach lurched; her hands were slick with sweat.

Finally, the pilot shook his head. "I was hoping for a visual, but I don't dare go lower."

They rose again and moved out over the water to hover. Below them the blip continued to creep, almost touching the shoreline.

SIXTY-THREE

EAST RIVER, JULY 2

ABU SAYEED STOOD at Mohammed's shoulder and stared into the fog. It swelled and heaved like a living thing, swirling, as full of confusion as a labyrinth. Its misty folds destroyed his equilibrium, so every few minutes he closed his eyes until the whirling stopped.

A moment earlier the helicopter had passed close overhead, its hollow whup, whup, whup changing tone and volume as it hovered in different places. Abu Sayeed had known immediately that it was the sound of someone hunting them, and he'd ordered Mohammed to steer even closer to shore. They risked running aground or hitting old piers or pilings, but it couldn't be helped. The yacht was moving very slowly, only five knots. With luck, and with Allah's help, they would be invisible on radar.

Aft of them on the flybridge, Naif had started breaking the missiles out of their crates. Six of the missiles were tipped with the depleted nuclear fuel. Two were unconverted anti-aircraft weapons. Abu Sayeed had ordered him to prepare one of the unconverted missiles, just in case.

Another bridge lay just ahead. Abu Sayeed could see on the GPS that it was called the Whitestone. As they approached it, the weather worsened again. The wind notched up, gusting across the bow, forcing the cold rain almost sideways. He glanced back at Naif, who struggled with the tarp, doing his best to keep the missiles dry. He took the wheel and pointed Mohammed outside to help. A moment later he turned to see Mohammed and Naif bent together over one of the crates.

The sound of the helicopter disappeared completely as they crept beneath the Whitestone Bridge, but it came back again as they motored around a point of land and into the mouth of a small creek. Abu Sayeed took them across to the creek's far shore then steered back out into the East River, always hugging the land.

Manhattan was not far ahead now, and the knowledge sparked his flagging confidence. The fog and rain were Allah's gifts. Even now, Anneliës would be down below calling the limo driver and telling him where to meet them. Once they fired the missiles, they would cross to the New Jersey shore, tie up beside a condominium and have the limo take them to Teterboro. There, again thanks to Anneliës, Biddle's pilots would have the Gulfstream fueled for a flight to Istanbul. In mid-flight they would change course to Syria, then travel by car and boat and camel and lose themselves in the swirling confusion of the desert wastes. They would be out of range of retribution by the time the Americans had even begun to plan a counterstrike.

His thoughts were interrupted by the sound of the helicopter circling back, the blades sounding so close that Abu Sayeed was amazed he couldn't reach up and touch the landing gear. As it passed directly over their heads, the downdraft from the rotors hammered the boat and carved patterns on the water.

He fought the temptation to ram the throttles forward, then glanced back at Naif and Mohammed and saw them crouched low on the flybridge. They were aiming their machine guns upward, but thankfully they were holding their fire. Whoever was up there wasn't certain they'd found the right target. Otherwise they would have attacked already.

The most important thing was to be calm, to do nothing, so he continued on, motoring at five knots. After what seemed like an eternity, the helicopter moved off, but it held position, hovering over the water to their left, maybe several hundred yards distant. Abu Sayeed saw that the wind was slackening again, the fog growing thicker.

On the flybridge, Mohammed heard the helicopter coming lower and closer, until he could feel the rotor wash pressing him down against the deck. His brain flashed back to Afghanistan, when countless times he'd tried to crush his body into the very rocks themselves to escape detection by the Americans. The fog, the fact that he could feel the presence of this terrible machine yet not see it, magnified his powerlessness and made his heart flame with rage. He hated this strange country! He hated being on water! And he hated staring up into these impenetrable clouds as he struggled to see his enemies. Come down and fight, he wanted to scream! But the Americans never would. They would use their technology. By Allah, he hated their technology!

As the helicopter finally circled away, Mohammed felt something give way in his mind. He glared at the sky, all sense of Abu Sayeed's orders forgotten, his thoughts nothing but a frothing sea of hatred and fear.

Beside him, Naif seemed unaffected. He was already back at work, preparing the missiles they would soon fire into the city. Mohammed stared at him for a few seconds, his eyes dull, his brain comprehending only the unseen helicopter hovering somewhere nearby and his need for vengeance.

Without conscious thoughtm his hands closed around the launcher with an unconverted Strella already loaded. He flicked the system on and got a radar fix and then a heat-seek fix. Naif must have looked up at him then because he screamed, "No, you fool!" but too late. Mohammed pressed the trigger and felt an instantaneous rush of joy as the missile roared from its launch tube and disappeared in the clouds.

SIXTY-FOUR

EAST RIVER, JULY 2

BRENT STARED INTO the fog where the stern of the tug had been visible only seconds before and slammed his good hand against the steering wheel. How was this possible? Had he been chasing an oil barge the entire time? No way, but then where was Biddle's boat?

He looked at the screen, silently begging the second blip to materialize again, but it was gone. He remembered going under the bridge how he had looked away from the screen for a few seconds, but still, how had a yacht disappeared? He remembered that it had been heading toward shore. Had it docked or made some kind of rendezvous?

He started to turn toward the same shore when a sudden roar surrounded him. Powerful winds buffeted him from all sides. It took several seconds to understand that a helicopter had come up from behind and was almost directly overhead. He'd heard the rotors earlier, but he'd been too focused on Maggie to pay attention. Now, he knew it had to be the police.

He cursed. No way he could let himself be captured, not with Maggie on the yacht! He threw a wild look at the GPS and saw the Whitestone Bridge ahead. He edged the throttles forward, knowing the bridge would force the helicopter away.

Just short of the bridge, it veered and climbed sharply, heading toward the shore where the blip had disappeared. It hovered there, but after another moment it rose to clear the bridge. He cut the throttles and let the Whaler drift, the current moving him beneath the bridge and then into the clear as the helicopter came in low again, somewhere along the shore. This time it held position for over a minute, but finally it swung out ahead of him and hovered over the center of the river.

He continued to drift. Were they marking him, alerting Coast Guard to his position? No, he decided. They weren't after him. They'd spent too much time over there where the blip had disappeared. They must be hunting for the yacht!

The helicopter was pacing the current, playing what seemed to be a waiting game. Brent didn't know what they were waiting for, but he knew he had to act. He was starting to push the throttles forward when a blinding flash came from his right. It disappeared in the clouds, but he glimpsed it once more, running fast and low. Then came a great bang. A second later in a flicker of flames, something big dropped into the river.

SIXTY-FIVE

EAST RIVER, JULY 2

JENKINS FELT THE shock and heard the rending of metal as the helicopter began to drop. "Hold on!" the pilot screamed.

The impact sent Jenkins' head crashing into something. She must have blacked out because she came to seconds later with a terrible pain in her skull and the co-pilot slapping her face.

"Come on, move!" the man was saying. "We're sinking." He pulled her over to the side door. Water swirled around her ankles. The pilot was already there, but something was wrong. He was bleeding from the head and looked barely conscious.

"I'm going to push you out," the co-pilot shouted. "You inflate your vest, and when I push him out, you get his. Can you do that?"

She barely had time to nod before he pulled a door lever, and more water rushed into the chopper. The co-pilot threw Maggie out onto the river, and she fumbled with her life vest, found the ring and pulled. A second later, the pilot was in the water, too, face down. She kicked over, reached his ring and inflated. By that time the co-pilot was out as well and kicking toward them. Jenkins didn't even have time to watch as the helicopter disappeared.

Jesus, she thought, what the hell had happened? It had all been so fast, there'd been no time to radio their position. Nobody knew they were down. They needed to get out of the river and locate a phone. But how? The current was fast and powerful, and they were being swept with the tide. She couldn't see a thing. She didn't know which shore was closer, whether there were bulwarks or whether she could climb out.

"Hey!" a voice shouted from somewhere in the fog. "Can anybody hear me?"

"Over here!" the co-pilot shouted.

Jenkins felt a ray of hope as she heard an engine throttle up and then back. "Hey!" the voice came again, a little closer.

"Keep coming!" the co-pilot shouted.

"Talk to me!"

"Here," Jenkins shouted.

They kept calling back and forth, and a boat emerged out of the fog, nearly running over them. The person at the wheel reached an arm over the side. "Come on, someone grab on," he said.

"Take him," the co-pilot shouted, pushing the pilot forward.

"I can't get him. I only have one good arm."

The man was reaching down, and Jenkins grabbed his wrist and let him help pull her aboard. She turned around and they both grabbed the pilot's life jacket and hauled him up and over the gunwale. Finally they pulled the co-pilot on board.

The pilot lay gasping on the bottom of the boat while the co-pilot tended him. Jenkins looked at their rescuer, noting the face she'd seen on the law enforcement net and the bloody arm.

"You're Brent Lucas," she said.

He said nothing.

"What are you doing out here?"

"Looking for Biddle's boat."

There was something in his tone that made her guess. "Is DeVito on board?"

He nodded.

"Know what else is on that boat?" she said.

He shook his head as he peered ahead into the fog. "I'll worry about that after I get Maggie."

"Where's your radio?"

He pointed at the hole in the control panel. "Missing."

She was going to say something else, but he grabbed the controls. "Hold on!" he shouted then pushed the throttle forward and steered toward the right shore.

Jenkins grabbed desperately for the back of a seat as she barely kept her balance. "Stop!"

Lucas ignored her. The boat picked up speed. Jenkins could see only baffles of fog, but the sound of the engine began to echo off the nearby river wall, telling her they were way too close.

"Stop the boat!" Jenkins commanded. "I'm putting you under arrest!"

Lucas shook his head.

Jenkins took her pistol from her holster and put it to the Brent's back. "Hands in the air! Now!"

Lucas ignored her. He was busy adjusting the radar resolution. "There!" he cried, pointing to the image that suddenly jumped out from the clutter of the shoreline. "Just ahead!"

Jenkins shook her head, knowing she wasn't going to try and take him down physically, not here. "Shit!" she snapped.

Lucas glanced back. "You steer. Get me close enough to jump on."

"You're crazy!"

Lucas actually smiled as he turned back to the radar screen. "Runs in the family," he said.

SIXTY-SIX

EAST RIVER, JULY 2

MAGGIE OPENED HER eyes, tried to blink away the pain and dizziness and get a sense of where she was. She was lying on her side, on a large bed, her hands cuffed behind her back, her knees drawn up in a fetal position. She'd been dragged down some stairs, but she couldn't say how long ago. Ten minutes? An hour? She'd been slipping in and out of consciousness for a while, but she had to find her bearings and make a plan.

A man lay facing her on the other side of the mattress. His eyes were open but glazed over, his mouth slack with either hopelessness or defeat. He was thin with sandy hair, middle fifties she guessed. Like her, his hands were bound behind his back. He had to be Prescott Biddle.

At the other end of the room, a woman paced the floor, talking on a cell phone, moving in and out of Maggie's line of sight. She was surprisingly beautiful, blonde, mid-thirties, but her mouth was curled in a tight scowl.

Suddenly, Biddle stirred. "Anneliës," he said plaintively. He rolled over, threw his legs over the side of the mattress and struggled into a sitting position. "For God's sake, let us go!"

The woman closed her phone and spun. "Shut up!" she cried with icy fury, then she stepped over and hit him across the mouth with the back of her hand.

Biddle's head snapped sideways at the blow. "You told me not to come," he persisted. "You knew! You've always known! How could you do this to me?"

"I'm warning you," the woman whispered in cold fury. "I will kill you if you say more!"

"Why? You're afraid I'll tell Sayeed? Well, I will!"

The woman grabbed Biddle by the shirt and jerked him off the bed and onto the floor. She slammed her foot on his chest and stood over him, her back turned to Maggie.

Maggie struggled desperately to remain conscious. Through

a fog of pain she watched the woman pull a long folding knife out of her blue jeans, flick it open with a snap of the wrist and place the point at Biddle's throat. The woman's back was still turned as Maggie shifted across the bed.

"Not one fucking word!" the woman was saying to Biddle. The boat hit some rougher water, and she straightened and groped for the bedside table to steady herself. Maggie shifted farther and pivoted so her feet pointed off the side of the bed. The yacht shifted again, causing the woman to brace her knife hand against the ceiling. With a furious effort, Maggie rolled onto her back, balancing painfully on her bound wrists, her vision blurred. She brought her knees to her chin then exploded with every bit of strength she possessed, firing both heels at the woman's kidney.

Even as she struck she knew she would miss. The boat's roll caused the woman to turn slightly, so that the full force of Maggie's kick missed the vital kidney and instead exploded against her spine. A dull crack sounded as Maggie's heels hit full force.

No! she thought. Struggling not to black out, she cocked her legs again, expecting the woman to jump to her feet and attack with the knife. She was about to die, but she would go out fighting.

She waited like that, teetering at the edge of blackness. Finally, she looked around. Had it been five seconds? Thirty seconds? A minute? Where was the woman? She heard a horrified cry, "Mein Gott!" and the sound of something dragging.

Maggie shifted her shoulders to the edge of the mattress. First she saw Biddle lying on his side, then she shifted again and saw the woman. She was lying where she had fallen beyond the foot of the bed, propped on her elbows, staring in horror at her legs where they lay splayed like discarded toys. "Help me," Biddle mumbled, as the woman flashed Maggie a look of hatred mixed with fear. Maggie glanced at the floor between them and saw the knife.

SIXTY-SEVEN

EAST RIVER, JULY 2

BRENT DROPPED TO his hands and knees and groped about the stern beneath the fuel lines until his fingers touched the super-soaker. He threw the sling over his head then moved toward the bow. The FBI woman had the wheel. As he moved past her, he shouted, "You have any matches?"

She looked at the oversized child's toy hanging around his shoulders. Whatever her thoughts, she held them back. She reached into her pocket and withdrew a gold lighter. "It should still work." As he took it, she looked at his bloody arm and shook her head.

Brent climbed into the bow, holding the forward rail with his good hand and peering into the fog. The water directly ahead was flattened, a sign they were very close. Suddenly, there was sound, a rumble of exhaust as the yacht hit a swell. It seemed near enough to touch, and a second later the stern materialized out of the mist.

They closed the last few yards, and Brent recalled the yacht's schematic, how the stern had a platform right at the water line. When he jumped, he'd only need to clear a low safety rail.

He glanced back at the FBI agent and nodded to signal that he was ready. Then he crouched, timing the rise and fall to the pitch of the swells. Finally, he leaped. He cleared the rail but felt his stomach wound tear as he pitched forward into the bulkhead. He hit hard, going momentarily light-headed.

After a few seconds he struggled to his feet. He glanced back, but the Whaler was already lost in the fog. He groped with his left hand and brought the pistol out of his trouser pocket. He tried to hold it in his right hand, but gave up because his arm shook too badly.

On both sides of the hull, stairways curved to the main deck, while in the center a watertight door led into the crews' quarters and engine room. He was certain the terrorists and their hostages would be either above or forward, so he crept up the starboard stairs until he could scan the deserted deck area. The salon was directly ahead, the sliding glass doors open, the interior pitch black.

He closed his eyes and pictured the salon and dining area immediately forward, then the stairs leading down to the staterooms or up to the bridge, then forward of that, the galley and lower cockpit. Maggie was there somewhere, but she would be guarded, and he was outnumbered. Attempting to sneak in would leave his back exposed. Surprise and confusion could help even the odds, but only a little. He wracked his brain to remember things about the large boats he and Harry had helped work on. A single possibility came to mind. It involved terrible risk, but he had no other choice.

He backed down the stairs and went through the watertight door in the aft bulkhead. Inside, dim floor lights lit the passageway. He crept forward and checked the crew's sitting room and sleeping rooms to make certain they were empty. At the end of the passage, he opened a second watertight door, and the roar of diesel engines spilled out.

He located a light switch, flipped it on and saw the two massive engines, a spotless floor and rows of switches with red and green lights along the walls. Left of the door he found what he needed, a valve marked with a brass plate reading "Halon Cut-Off." The fire extinguishment system was meant to be on at all times, except for when the system was repaired or recharged. He twisted the valve closed.

He moved forward, past the tanks that held the diesel fuel, hesitating as he thought again about Maggie and his slim odds. A voice came to him over the shriek of the engines, as though Harry were right there shouting in his ear. *She'd do the same thing in your shoes. She'd never let those bastards anywhere near Manhattan.*

A workbench stood along one wall with several large piles of oily rags on a lower shelf. He gathered the rags and put them in the forward portside corner, then he pulled out the plug on the super-soaker and emptied the remaining gas. Drawing the pistol, he fired two shots into each of the fuel tanks. Immediately, diesel began to leak onto the metal floor. Finally, he took out the woman's Zippo and tried to make it light. He struck it once, twice, three times, blew hard on the striker and finally got a tiny guttering flame, but it was enough. He held it near the rags, and the gas-soaked pile erupted. As soon as it did, he sprinted back down the passage and out the watertight door.

He raced up the stairs to the main deck, ignoring the pain in his stomach and arm, then hurried into the darkened salon. A bar curved out from the wall to his left, just as in Maggie's diagram, and he ducked behind the partition, knowing he had only seconds before an alarm brought one or more of the terrorists. If things happened according to his plan, the rag fire would begin to burn the fiberglass, and once the temperature became sufficiently high, the diesel would ignite. He had some time—by his estimate maybe ten minutes—until the diesel caught and the whole lower section of the boat was engulfed in flame. That was his window to get Maggie out of there alive.

SIXTY-EIGHT

EAST RIVER, JULY 2

ABU SAYEED COULDN'T decide whether to shoot Mohammed or hug him. Downing the helicopter might have been the worst thing they could have done, but in another way it had been brilliant. There had been little noise and no explosion because the missile had not flown far enough from the launcher to arm itself, but clearly it had destroyed the helicopter's engine. Had the crew had time to radio? He doubted it. From the sound of the rotors just before Mohammed fired, they'd been too low over the water to do anything.

Nonetheless, he had continued his slow pace, running as close to shore as he dared, keeping Naif and Mohammed on the flybridge to listen for more helicopters. He stared at the GPS and glanced continuously at the radar, set now at a thousand yards to detect the presence of large ships that might be attempting to block the river, then cutting it back to a hundred yards to navigate directly ahead. So far, nothing. Allah was protecting them.

A moment earlier when he'd reduced the radar's range, something had appeared to be very close on their stern, but when he looked again it was gone or mixed up in the shore clutter. He knew that for several minutes after Mohammed fired the missile, he had paid little attention to the screen, but he also knew he was growing tired. Stress affected everyone, and sooner or later imagined enemies began to appear in the darkness. Calm, he cautioned himself.

It was time to change tactics. They had been creeping for a long time. With the helicopter destroyed, their enemy was momentarily blinded. Now was the time to charge ahead, past Rikers Island, under the Triboro and then down the east side of Manhattan. They would fire the weapons as they went. Damage would be slight, just some random explosions and few people killed. But by tomorrow, New York would be a city of refugees with whole sections rendered uninhabitable for years. Imagine the effect when his enemies had to abandon a huge swath of their most important city!

Abu Sayeed gripped the throttles, ready to feed power to the engines when a warning light on the control panel indicated a fire in the engine room. He raced onto the flybridge and shouted for Mohammed.

SIXTY-NINE

EAST RIVER, JULY 2

BRENT CAUGHT THE movement, no more than a shadowy flicker in his peripheral vision. Someone was on the rear deck. Where had they come from? With a sick feeling, he realized there had to be a ladder he'd overlooked, and at least one of the terrorists was now behind him. In another moment yellow smoke began pouring out the aft section of the yacht, which meant the man had opened the watertight door.

He needed to get to the engine room because everything depended on the fire crippling the yacht. But what about the other terrorists? Would they follow the first man? Based on Maggie's satellite pictures, he'd assumed there were three, but what about Biddle? Was he a prisoner or an ally? There was no time to worry.

He crept out of the salon and strained his eyes in the darkness. The rear deck appeared empty, so he hurried down the stairs. Blinding smoke belched from the watertight door, but if the terrorist had done his homework and knew where the halon cut-off valve was located, he would still be able to find it and turn it back on.

Brent took a deep breath, squatted low, and went in. As he reached the engine room door, he spotted a shape in the smoke, a man fumbling along the port bulkhead for the halon valve. Brent's lungs burned as he aimed his pistol. Shoot! He commanded his finger to pull the trigger, but it wouldn't obey.

The man bent down to take a choking breath, and in that same motion he turned toward the door. His eyes went wide in surprise as he saw Brent. A machine gun of some type was slung over his shoulder and hung at his chest, and faster than Brent would have thought possible, it was in the man's hands.

Brent pulled the trigger three times, the bullets knocking the man back into the smoke. He took a reflexive breath, feeling the smoke sear his lungs. He started to cough, then backed into the passageway where the air was better and took several deep breaths. Finally, he crept forward again, toward the heat of the spreading fire. The man lay unmoving. Brent bent over him and jerked the machine gun free.

He moved back down the passage with the machine gun aimed at the open watertight door. Outside, as he sucked greedy lungfuls of clean air, the engines suddenly stopped, their mechanical racket and vibration going utterly still. Brent moved to the bulkhead, and from somewhere forward, he heard a voice. He inched up the stairs until he spotted the ladder he'd missed earlier, then he waited. Very soon a pair of feet appeared on the upper rungs. A man started to descend, facing outward, his gun sweeping the area.

Brent backed down the steps, through the watertight door and into the crew's sitting room where he hid behind the door. A second later the man came into the passage. "Mohammed?" he called.

Brent heard him take a deep breath then start toward the engine room. He waited until the man walked by, then he stepped into the passageway, put the machine gun's metal stock to his wounded shoulder and ignored the wrenching pain. "Freeze," he cried. "Hands in the air!"

The terrorist raised his hands to shoulder height and turned very slowly, first only his head, a second later his shoulders. A machine gun similar to Brent's hung from a sling around his neck. His expression showed neither surprise nor alarm. In spite of the thick yellow smoke, Brent recognized his assailant from the parking garage. "Where is she?" he demanded. "The woman."

The terrorist said nothing. "Where is she?" Brent said again.

The terrorist shook his head imperceptibly. Brent had been sighting down the barrel of the machine gun, but he raised his head slightly. "You're going to tell me, you sonofabitch," he said, just as the terrorist moved.

The man was extraordinarily quick. Because he didn't reach for the machine gun, Brent hesitated, and the knife seemed to appear from nowhere, just an instantaneous flash in the smoke. At the last possible instant Brent threw himself sideways and pulled the trigger. The knife hit, clipping his ear where his throat had been a half-second earlier. The terrorist's machine gun was already in his hands, but Brent's burst tore into his legs.

Brent rushed forward, ignoring the warmth of fresh blood on the side of his face. He grabbed the man's gun and jerked the sling free of his shoulders. The man was conscious although from the amount of blood, Brent's shots had clearly caught an artery.

"Where is she?" Brent demanded.

The terrorist looked up at him and shook his head.

"Tell me!" Brent shouted. He put his foot on the man's mangled thigh and pressed.

The terrorist arched his back in agony, and air hissed through his teeth, but he said nothing.

Brent straightened up and looked down. The man was bleeding to death, but one of his hands was busy with something on the inside of his belt. Suddenly, Brent saw the blade of a second knife. He aimed at the man's chest, but the terrorist's hand never paused. "Game's over," he said, then pulled the trigger.

SEVENTY

EAST RIVER, JULY 2

WHEN THE BOAT'S power systems went dead, Abu Sayeed froze in the silence and listened. The wind and rain had slackened. He could hear the faint slap of waves against the hull. Seconds ticked past as he waited for some sign from Naif. Nothing happened for nearly a minute, but then came a muffled coughing sound, the bark of a silenced machine gun. A moment later, a second burst. When Naif still did not call out, Abu Sayeed assumed the worst. Where had his enemies come from? How had they gotten on board? When? How many?

With no time for hesitation or regret, he moved to the flybridge. The boat was on fire, its engines dead. They were rudderless and drifting with the current. He would never reach Manhattan, but he would wound America all the same. One-by-one he would launch the Strellas. After he'd sunk his poisoned harpoons deep in his enemy's hide, he would try and escape with his hostages.

As he knelt beside the weapons crates, his mind raced with his contingency plan. He'd use each of the hostages, Anneliës as well, to trade for time or whatever he needed. Every warrior had to die—he had no regrets if it came to that. The Americans might eventually destroy him, but first he would strike a great blow for Allah.

He picked up the launcher, activated the system and waited for the tone to indicate the passive infrared homing was operational. It needed only a few seconds to come on line, but the missile wouldn't fire without the tone. It had a range of nearly three and a half miles. He planned to fire in the direction of LaGuardia Airport.

The tone was beeping faster, building toward a solid whine that would indicate the homing device was active, when something moved in his peripheral vision. He swung his head, saw a partial silhouette and the barrel of a gun at the top of the stern ladder. He put the launcher down and reached for his Heckler & Koch, but a burst caught him twice in the abdomen and knocked him backward.

He felt rage and surprise, and his guts were on fire. He fired wildly toward the top of the steps. He backed into the cockpit, lifted his shirt and saw two small holes. There was little blood, but he sensed the damage. He fired again through the open door, then ignored the searing pain as he darted down the steps toward the lower deck. His only thought now–the hostages.

SEVENTY-ONE

EAST RIVER, JULY 2

MAGGIE STRUGGLED TO focus. The knife was everything. The other woman was clawing at the carpet, trying to pivot around her dead legs in order to reach it. Biddle, too, had rolled on his side and was backing toward it. Maggie knew her life depended on getting there first, but she was terribly tired. The cabin lights had gone out then other lights had come on, but these were dim, soothing as night-lights. She wanted to close her eyes and sleep.

With all her effort she swung her legs off the bed and tried to stand. Her knees buckled. She went down hard, her shoulder striking a dresser. The pain gave her a few seconds of clarity.

She realized the room was filling with smoke, also that Biddle was about the grab the knife. She kicked him in the back, rolling him away and onto his stomach, then she turned on her side and slid backward, groping blindly. The plastic cuffs had cut her circulation, and her fingers felt almost lifeless. She grasped the knife and tried to slide the blade inside the loop that bound her left wrist, only to lose her grip. Biddle was kicking at her, but she ignored him and kept struggling. The other woman was clearly injured, but she too was moving closer, her hands outstretched. On her fourth try, Maggie managed to work the blade into the loop and began to saw.

The smoke was growing thicker. Her lungs burned. Biddle's foot lashed out and caught her painfully in the thigh, but she didn't stop. Finally, the left loop began to loosen. She sawed harder, and at last her hand came free.

The woman was trying to grab her legs as Maggie struggled to her feet, fighting dizziness and confusion, in some part of her brain knowing she had a concussion. She wondered if the boat was sinking. She had to escape, but first she needed air. Portholes were set into the hull on both sides of the stateroom, above the built-in dressers. She clambered onto one of the dressers and began frantically unscrewing the brass wing nuts around a porthole.

"Cut me loose!" Biddle rasped. "Please!"

Maggie ignored him and kept working. She was on the verge of blacking out when she managed to swing the porthole open. She shoved her face into the opening and pulled clean air into her lungs. Her head had barely starting to clear when the stateroom door opened and closed again.

She looked around to see the man who had beaten her. He was leaning against the door clutching his abdomen. A machine gun dangled from one hand. As she watched, he fell to one knee, then struggled to his feet. A dark stain was spreading across his torso.

He squinted at the woman on the floor as if he couldn't understand why she was down there, then he staggered past her and sat heavily on the edge of the bed. His eyes moved to Biddle. "Get up!" he groaned.

Suddenly, Biddle seemed to come alive. "You betrayed me!" he shouted then began to cough.

"This was never for your God," the other man wheezed. "It was always for mine."

"Well, where is your God now?" Biddle demanded.

"Here," the man said, as he shoved his machine gun into Biddle's face. "Get up!"

Biddle's brief resistance seemed to flag, as the terrorist grabbed hold of him and dragged him slowly to his knees. The terrorist sat back on the bed and took a deep breath, seeming momentarily overcome with pain, but then he swung his eyes up to Maggie.

SEVENTY-TWO

EAST RIVER, JULY 2

BRENT STOOD AT the top of the stairs and strained his eyes into the twisting yellow smoke. It gouted upward, scalding his lungs. The fiberglass was burning unchecked now, the fire already eating through the bulkhead separating the engine room from the staterooms.

The rest of the yacht was empty, which meant Maggie was down below in the smoke, along with at least one terrorist. Brent was sure he'd wounded the guy, but maybe not so badly that the guy wasn't down there waiting in ambush? It didn't matter. At some level far below reason, he knew Maggie was alive, which meant he was going after her.

Over the roar of the flames and the sucking air he heard the yacht groan, the sound coming from somewhere deep in her bowels, as if the fire was literally tearing her apart. He shuddered, knowing that once the diesel started to burn, no one below decks would have a chance.

It brought his lifelong nightmare charging back. He saw burning walls. He saw his father and Harry, both trapped by impenetrable flames, both knowing they were about to die horrible, excruciating deaths.

Unaccountably, the next thing he heard was the sound of laughter and then Harry's voice. *No one lives forever, little bro.* In spite of his terror at dying the same death, Harry's words made him smile. His whole damn family had been insane, he thought, beautifully irretrievably nuts.

With that, he took the deepest breath possible, getting too much smoke and too little good air, and he stumbled down the stairs, immediately blind, unable to see even his hand on the railing. The railing became too hot to grip even before he found the bottom step. His lungs were wild with the need for a fresh breath, and his eyes were on fire. The smoke was thick as wood, completely disorienting, but he moved instinctively away from the heat.

He moved by touch along a short passage, finding several open doors but then a closed door at the end. Voices came from the other side. He could hold his breath no longer, and he expelled the acrid air. His reflexive gulp of smoke made him double over with coughing.

Knowing that he had no other choice, he threw open the door and stumbled inside, slamming the door behind him, his choked lungs heaving. His eyes were partly blind with tears, but he made out a blonde woman on the floor. He recognized Biddle's thin shoulders and blond hair where he knelt in one corner. And the man he'd shot sitting on the bed. That man was pointing a gun at a fourth person, a woman, who was kneeling beside an open porthole—Maggie! He saw it but could do nothing, as coughing drove him straight to his knees.

The coughing also saved his life because the man on the bed swung his gun, firing an awkward one-handed burst that would have cut him in half. Brent fired instinctively, just as he was wracked with more coughing and gagging.

As his lungs slowly recovered, he tensed, expecting bullets to tear into him, but they never came. Finally, he raised his head and saw the terrorist sprawled across the bed, unmoving. He used his last dregs of consciousness to crawl toward the porthole. At that point, he recognized the woman on the floor, but his mind was too numb to register shock. She made a feeble grab for his gun, but he shoved her away. The air near the wall was slightly better, but when he tried to take a deeper breath he doubled up again with coughing.

"Come on!" Maggie's voice came to him.

It took everything he had to grab the edge of the dresser and drag himself up, but after a second, he felt Maggie's hands on his head as she forced him to the porthole.

For several moments they clung there, gripping the edge, greedily sucking the clear air. Along with oxygen came the fresh realization that they were out of time. Any second the diesel would start to burn, and there would be no escape. He turned and saw the blood in Maggie's hair and on her face. The way she clung to the porthole told him she had nothing left.

"Wait here," he mumbled. He was close to passing out, but

he took one more clean breath and climbed off the dresser. He pulled the dead terrorist onto the floor then jerked the spread from the bed, dragged it into the head and put it under the shower. He prayed the pressure tank still worked as he turned the spigots and got an answering sputter of water. With the spread soaked and heavy he staggered back into the stateroom.

With a last lungful of good air, he lifted Maggie over his shoulder in a fireman's carry, then started to pull the blanket over them.

"Take me with you!" Biddle said in a choked whisper. "Please!" He was still on his knees in the corner.

Even if he wanted to help, Brent knew there was no time. Maggie's weight was nearly unbearable, and already his knees threatened to buckle. He stumbled to the door, his only thought getting her away from the fire.

"Lucas!" Biddle cried, his voice rising to a high pitch.

Brent raised the corner of the spread just enough to glance back. Biddle's hands were free, and he was trying to pull the machine gun sling over the dead terrorist's head. The woman—Simone or whoever she really was—had her arms wrapped around Biddle's legs.

Brent jerked open the door and plunged blindly down the passage, following the wall with his left hand, desperate to regain the stairs. Ahead, the orange glow of flames glimmered, and steam already rose off the thin fabric, which felt hot enough to ignite.

Don't let the stairs be burning, he prayed. When he finally gripped the banister in his left hand, it nearly blistered his flesh. He ignored the pain and stumbled upward, feeling the steps shudder, saying to himself, someone in this family has to make it out. His foot hit the top step. He somehow found the strength to keep going, up the next set of stairs to the bridge and then out the door into the open air of the flybridge, where he fell to his knees.

From below decks over the roaring of the flames, a sudden scream rose and fell away. He'd never know what happened, but he knew no one could have made it up the stairs behind them.

He rolled Maggie gently from his shoulder, and they rested side by side on their hands and knees, pulling the night air into their seared lungs. After a moment, he raised his head and looked around. The fog had lifted slightly, and he could see the Whaler about fifty yards off the stern. He got to his knees and waved and saw the Whaler start forward. With the fire spreading, they couldn't risk going down the stairs and through the salon to the aft deck. It meant going down the aft ladder to reach the stern where the Whaler could pick them up.

"Come on!" he said as he pulled Maggie to her feet and led her to the stern. Her eyes kept closing as if she was unable to stay awake. "I'm going down first, then you come. I'll catch you if you fall." He shouted the words as if volume would help keep her awake. "Can you do it?"

She nodded, and he started down the ladder. The descent seemed to take forever, the pain in his arm making it nearly impossible to grip the rungs. Maggie followed, each movement precarious. Brent knew he could never hold her if she fell.

As he reached the bottom, he heard a sound and turned, thinking the woman FBI agent or one of the helicopter pilots had come to help. Instead, he saw Biddle stagger from the burning salon–at least he thought it was Biddle. His face was soot black, one side distorted by raw blistered skin. He was weaving, smoking like a piece of overdone meat, but he held the machine gun in his hands. He opened his mouth, and some garbled words came out.

Brent glanced up. Maggie was still on the ladder, halfway down, struggling to stay conscious. Biddle swung the gun in Brent's direction. "Messiah bringer," he croaked this time, his voice no longer human. He was probably ten feet away, too far to charge with any hope of success. Brent felt the hard shape of the railing at his back. He could throw himself over the side and live, but he stayed rooted in place. He wasn't leaving Maggie.

He gathered what was left of his strength and prepared to launch himself at Biddle. He knew what it meant. Harry's voice came to him. *Been there, done that*.

He bent his knees to charge when the first shots came. Blessedly, he felt nothing. It was a good way to die, he thought.

After what seemed like forever, his muscles began to relax, and he turned his head to see the red-haired woman in a shooter's crouch at the stop of the port staircase. Biddle had disappeared, blown backward into the flaming salon by her gunshots. The agent came over, moved Brent aside and helped Maggie. Together they hobbled down the stern steps to the Whaler.

The yacht was drifting sideways on the current. Up ahead a line of flashing lights charged toward them. It came from what looked like an entire fleet of boats.

Brent could see Coast Guard boats and police boats and helicopters in the air. There would be doctors for Maggie. Most of all there would be firemen on fireboats, Brent thought. God, how he wanted to see the firemen.

SEVENTY-THREE

EAST RIVER, JULY 2

AN HOUR LATER, Brent sat in the back of an ambulance with an oxygen mask pressed to his face. Every few seconds another question came, and he would pull the mask away to give a hoarse reply. All around a myriad of lights flashed—on ambulances, fire engines, S.W.A.T., and FBI vehicles. Nearby, at an old industrial pier, Biddle's yacht still belched smoke into the clearing sky, and every few moments a jet would roar past on its descent into LaGuardia.

The ambulance attendants wanted to take Brent directly to the hospital, but the red-haired FBI agent he'd pulled from the river insisted on questioning him first. Now, he was giving her his story for the second time.

An ambulance had already taken Maggie away—Brent had insisted on that before he'd say a word. The attendants said she appeared to have a concussion, hopefully nothing more. Brent had also learned that Steve Kosinsky's wound was apparently serious but not life-threatening. He would be back at work in a month or two.

Now, as hard as he tried to answer the agent's questions, he had to admit that much of what had happened remained a blur. The two moments that existed with clarity were personal and mattered to him alone. They had come when he'd stood at the top of the stairs, staring down into the smoke, and when he had prepared to charge Biddle's machine gun. Both times he'd known he was going to die. As much as he'd wanted to live, there had been no regrets, and he'd realized suddenly how it had been for Harry and his father and Fred . . . and even for his mother. It was his choice, and for all of his family it had always been just that, a choice.

EPILOGUE

MORRISTOWN, NJ, SEPTEMBER 6

BRENT WAS BENT over, hands on his knees, sweat pouring from his scalp and down the sides of his face as the sun pounded his back and scorched the baked grass. Spread before him, some kneeling, others squatting, two even prone on the ground, a squad of thirty-six young men sucked the burning late afternoon air into oxygen-starved lungs. Brent had run the wind sprints right along with them, and now he waited several seconds before he finally relented and blew his whistle to end practice.

Today was the last of the pre-season two-a-days, and Morris County Prep's varsity football team was going to have a pretty good season if physical conditioning had anything to do with it. Brent had come close to breaking half the members of his squad over the past few weeks, but he could already see a tremendous difference. His boys were going to be able to hit and keep on hitting right through the final seconds of the game.

His boys, the thought made him smile. As he watched them trudge off the practice field toward the locker room, he heard a familiar voice behind him. "How are your pansies today?"

He turned to see Fred in a ragged pair of khaki shorts and the Morris County Prep T-shirt Brent had given him. "They're going to beat up all the other pansies," Brent replied.

"Some pansies have to be the toughest," his uncle said. "Might as well be yours."

Brent smiled. Fred had been scandalized when Brent accepted the job. "A private school?" he'd screamed when Brent told him. "You want me to go down to the firehouse and tell the guys you're coaching at a private school?"

In spite of his apparent horror, Fred hadn't missed a day of practice, often bringing jugs of cold water and even giving whispered words of encouragement when a kid was down from exhaustion and didn't want to get up.

Brent couldn't have cared less that it was a private school. He only cared that he'd be teaching math and had a head coaching job and that the whole package seemed tailor-made. From the day the news hit the papers that Prescott Biddle had helped terrorists plot the assassination of the President, the money had flowed out of Genesis Advisors like oil from a ruptured tanker. The remaining partners had been delighted to buy Brent out of his contract in return for a promise that he wouldn't sue them.

Now, even after paying taxes on his severance, there had been enough to buy Fred a small house with a well-landscaped yard in Fort Meyers, Florida, and a bungalow for himself in Morristown. Fred had initially told Brent he was a fool and refused to have anything to do with the house, but Brent knew that sometime around mid-November, when his garden had died for the winter, Fred would relent and start driving south.

Maggie was back at the Morristown Police Department. She'd had enough deskwork, she said. She liked people too much and loved working cases. She was determined to remain a cop until she stopped working, whenever that would be. Maybe she'd be a cop forever, which was fine with him.

Last night he'd taken her to dinner to give her the ring and finally pop the question. They were never going to live on a fifteen-acre estate in Far Hills or Mendham, but so what? He had what he needed. He'd had it the whole time, just hadn't been able to see it.

In classic Maggie style, she hadn't said yes, at least not right away. "Couple things come to mind," she'd said after she'd taken a sip of wine.

"Like?"

"It sure took you long enough."

Brent nodded. "We've discussed that."

In the weeks after the raid on Biddle's estate, they'd talked night after night about their lives and their futures, and he'd slowly convinced her that something had changed for him. He'd made a choice, finally realizing that choices themselves were more important than outcomes and that choices came from either strength or weakness. He knew his father and Harry had made strong choices. His mother had made a weak one. It helped him stop believing some kind of incurable defect permeated his bloodline.

"I ought to think about this a long time and make you sweat," Maggie added.

"You could," he agreed.

Now Brent glanced over at his uncle as the two of them ambled toward the locker room, and after a second he put his arm around Fred's shoulders. "By the way," he said, "I got engaged last night."

Fred Lucas looked off in the distance and nodded. "Anybody I know?"

"Maybe."

"Bout time you did something intelligent."

Brent nodded. Over the past few months he'd been waking up quite often in the middle of the night and thinking about everything that had happened. He'd read everything he could on the Wahaddi Brotherhood and the New Jerusalem Fellowship. He knew he needed to understand men like Abu Sayeed and Prescott Biddle, how they and their followers could so easily forsake their common humanity to embrace violence, all in the name of their selfish and self-serving sense of God.

Some people, like Harry, his father and Fred, chose to honor and defend their fellow man, but these days so many others were choosing narrowly defined groups that rejected anyone who didn't agree with their strict tenets. Brent had few illusions. He knew it would keep happenin—some people making the decent, compassionate choice, others acting out of appalling ignorance, superstition or venality. It was enough to frighten a man into permanent bachelorhood, but in spite of that, he was choosing hope. He was getting married. Who could tell if he was right? He shook his head and tightened his grip on Fred's shoulder. He had to keep hoping.

To order copies of *Armageddon Conspiracy* as well as other titles from Harbor House, visit our Web site:

www.harborhousebooks.com

JOHN THOMPSON spent twenty-five years as an investment banker in New York before retiring to write full-time. He lives with his wife and daughter and divides his time between Charleston, South Carolina, and a mountain home in Hawley, Pennsylvania. He is actively involved in his local community, serving as chairman of the Charleston (S.C.) Education Network and on the Executive Committee of the Medical University of South Carolina Foundation and the National Advisory Board of Donors Choose. *Armageddon Conspiracy* is his first published novel.